noo

DATE DUE

OCT 0 3

DEC 16 02			
FEB 6 04			
APR 14 04			
2/24/05			
JUL 27			
GAYLORD			PRINTED IN U.S.A.

TRAILBACK

Also by Robert Vaughan
in Large Print:

Ralph Compton's The Alamosa Trail
Ralph Compton's The Boseman Trail

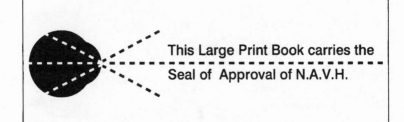

This Large Print Book carries the
Seal of Approval of N.A.V.H.

TRAILBACK

Robert Vaughan

Thorndike Press • Waterville, Maine

Published in 2003 by arrangement with Kensington Books, an imprint of Kensington Publishing Corp.

Thorndike Press® Large Print Western.

The tree indicium is a trademark of Thorndike Press.

The text of this Large Print edition is unabridged.
Other aspects of the book may vary from the original edition.

Set in 16 pt. Plantin.

Printed in the United States on permanent paper.

Library of Congress Cataloging-in-Publication Data

Vaughan, Robert, 1937–
    Trailback / Robert Vaughan.
        p. cm.
    ISBN 0-7862-5529-3 (lg. print : hc : alk. paper)
    1. Hereford cattle — Fiction. 2. Ranch life — Fiction.
3. Cooks — Fiction. 4. Texas — Fiction. 5. Large type
books. I. Title
PS3572.A93T73 2003
813'.54—dc21   2003053032

This book is for my friend and agent,
Robbie Robison.

As the Founder/CEO of NAVH, the only national health agency solely devoted to those who, although not totally blind, have an eye disease which could lead to serious visual impairment, I am pleased to recognize Thorndike Press* as one of the leading publishers in the large print field.

Founded in 1954 in San Francisco to prepare large print textbooks for partially seeing children, NAVH became the pioneer and standard setting agency in the preparation of large type.

Today, those publishers who meet our standards carry the prestigious "Seal of Approval" indicating high quality large print. We are delighted that Thorndike Press is one of the publishers whose titles meet these standards. We are also pleased to recognize the significant contribution Thorndike Press is making in this important and growing field.

Lorraine H. Marchi, L.H.D.
Founder/CEO
NAVH

* Thorndike Press encompasses the following imprints: Thorndike, Wheeler, Walker and Large Print Press.

ONE

Southwest Texas, 1870:

Puxico was just ahead, small and fly-blown, rising from the dust in a little collection of weathered buildings that lined each side of the single street. Cole Collier, who was thirty-five but looked fifteen years older, stopped about a quarter of a mile away and stood in the stirrups to get the blood circulating again. He looked around at the sagebrush and shimmering heat waves rising from the prairie that surrounded the little town.

A rabbit popped up in front of him, ran for several feet along the trail, then darted under a low-lying, dusty, mesquite tree. The thick musk of cattle drifted to Cole's nostrils, carried on a breeze that felt as if it had been blown from a blast furnace.

He reached around to massage the cheeks of his butt, then sat back in his saddle and urged his horse forward with the barest suggestion of a squeeze from his knees. As he rode down the street, the hoofbeats sounded hollow on the sun-baked surface, and little puffs of dust drifted up to hang suspended behind him as if reluctant to return to the hot, hard ground.

There was no railroad serving Puxico, and no sign of the outside world greeted him. It was a self-contained little community, inbred and festering.

Cole examined the rip-sawed, clapboard buildings. There were a few houses, a tannery, a leather-goods store, a livery stable with a smithy's shop to one side, and a general store that had its name, Donavan's, displayed on the high false front. Next door to the general store was a smaller building with painted red letters spelling out the words: Red Star Saloon.

From the blacksmith shop came the ring of steel on steel as the smithy pounded his hammer against a red-hot horseshoe, re-shaping it to his needs. A sign, hanging from an arm that protruded from the front of the leather-goods store, squeaked as it moved back and forth in answer to a hot breath of wind.

Cole rode up to the hitching rail in front of the saloon, dismounted, and patted his tan-colored duster a few times, sending up puffs of gray dust that settled again on the cloth like a fly swarm. Looping the reins around the hitching rail, he stepped up onto the porch, pushed the door open, and went inside.

The shadowed interior of the saloon gave the illusion of coolness, though it was illusion only. There was no sun, but the air was hot, still, and redolent of the sour smells of beer and whiskey and the stench of sweaty, unwashed bodies.

Cole walked over to the bar and put a nickel down.

"Beer," he said.

When the beer was served, he thanked the bartender with a slight nod, then turned and slowly surveyed the interior of the saloon. It was typical of many he had seen. Wide, rough-hewn boards formed the plank floor, and against the wall behind the long, brown-stained bar was a shelf of whiskey bottles, their number doubled by the mirror they stood against. Half a dozen tables, occupied by a dozen or more men, filled the room, and tobacco smoke hovered under the ceiling in a noxious cloud.

During the past five years these kinds of surroundings had become Cole Collier's heritage. He was defined by the saloons, cow towns, stables, dusty streets, and open prairies he had encountered in his wanderings. He was here, in a tiny Texas town that he had never visited before, for no other reason than that the town had risen on the horizon before him.

Cole was once asked why he moved around so much.

"I am hiding from the Devil," he answered. "If he can't find me, he can't collect his due."

Cole's response was only partially in jest. A graduate of Westminster College, Cole was a circuit-riding preacher before hostilities broke out between the North and South. He gave up his ministry to join the Confederacy. By participating in the bloody savagery that ensued, Cole believed that he had sold his soul to Satan.

Like many other restless and soul-scarred warriors of the bloody Civil War, Cole could not return to his old life. He considered himself unfit for civilized society, and to even think of resuming the ministry seemed blasphemous. There was nothing left for him but to fall in with outlaws, and that is exactly what he did.

At first, Cole stole only from the Yankee army, justifying his action by saying that, while the Confederacy may have surrendered, he hadn't. But he quickly expanded his operation and began robbing stage-coaches, banks, and trains. On a few occasions he even rustled cattle.

The outlaw trail often led to violent confrontations, and Cole, who had developed quite a talent with the pistol during the war, honed his skills even further. He had never killed any of his robbery victims, but he had killed men who were trying to kill him, including a few whose only transgression was to be a member of the posse that was chasing him. However, he had not killed as many as his growing reputation intimated.

"You got anything to eat?" Cole asked after he took his first drink of beer.

"Beans, bacon," the saloon barkeep answered.

"Good enough," Cole replied. He nodded toward an empty table. "I'll be over there."

"Excuse me, Mister," the barkeep said.

Cole stopped. "Yes?"

"Would your name be Collier? Cold Blood Collier?"

"I don't like that name," Cole replied.

The bartender smiled, broadly. "It is you, ain't it? I *knew* it. I seen you up at San Angelo last year when you went up against Deekus O'Riley. Man oh man, I ain't never

11

seen nothin' like that before or since. O'Riley was drawin' his gun as he called you out, but you beat 'im to the draw anyway. And when you shot him, you hit him dead center."

"If you've got a pepper to go with those beans, I'd appreciate it," Cole said, making no further response to the barkeep's homage.

As the bartender left to see to his order, Cole moved over to the table to await his food. When he did so, one of the other saloon patrons left, walking slowly until he was outside. Once outside, he ran down the street to the tannery where three men were working, curing hides. The biggest of the three, and the only one with a beard, looked up.

"Here, Les, what's put that burr under your saddle? Why you runnin'?"

"He's here, Abner. He's here in Puxico."

"Who's here?"

"Cold Blood Collier. He's down at the Red Star, just as big as life, he is."

Abner had been scraping hide with a knife, and now he reached up to pull at his chin, leaving blood and little pieces of flesh hanging from his beard.

"How do you know it's him?"

"How do I know it's him? 'Cause, the barkeep recognized him, that's how I know," Les answered. "He called him out on it, and Collier didn't deny it."

"Is he still down at the Red Star?"

"He was when I left, and I figure he still is, seein' as he's eatin' some beans."

There were two other men working at the tannery as well, brothers to each other, and cousins to Les and Abner. They quit what they were doing and came over to listen to the conversation.

"As you recall, the law didn't call it murder," one of the cousins said. "They said it was a fair fight."

"Weren't no fair fight and you know it, Marvin. Ain't no way that you could call only one man goin' up agin' somebody like Cold Blood Collier a fair fight."

"Maybe so, but you mind Jimmy, don't you? He figured he was fastern' anyone there is. He thought he could beat Collier. He had to learn the hard way."

"Yeah, well, don't none of that matter now, does it?" Les asked. "The thing is Jimmy's dead and Cold Blood Collier is alive." Les paused long enough to take a chew of tobacco. "But, I don't figure he's goin' to be alive much longer."

"How do you figure that?"

" 'Cause they's four of us, and only one of him."

"Look here, Jimmy was brother to you an' Abner, not to me'n Sam," Marvin said.

"Alright, maybe Jimmy was only your cousin, but he was still blood," Les said. "And in our family, blood counts the same whether it's brother or cousin."

"He's right, Marvin," Sam said. "Blood's blood."

"Thanks, Sam. I know'd you boys would come around. Now, the way I see it, is we go down to the saloon right now and . . ."

"Call him out?" Marvin interrupted, his eyes wide with fright. "Ain't no way I'm going to call him out, be they four of us or not."

"Marvin's right, Les," Sam said. "The only way to deal with someone like Collier is for all four of us to go down there and start shootin'."

Les shook his head. "No, the law'd never let us get away with that. There's a better way." He smiled. "Only one of us has to call him out."

"Yeah? Who's that going to be?" Marvin asked.

"Me," Les answered.

"Now, hold on there, Les," Abner said. "You seen what happened to Jimmy when he tried to go it alone. I don't aim to be losin' me another brother."

"I said I'll call him out by myself," Les said. He flashed a conspiratorial smile. "I didn't say nothin' 'bout fightin' him by myself."

Cole was halfway through his beans when a big man, wearing a beard, came into the saloon. Cole probably wouldn't have noticed him at all except for the unusual sight of a gun belt strapped over a tanner's apron.

The big man went to the near end of the bar and ordered a beer. Shortly thereafter, another man came in, also with a tanner's apron. He, too, was wearing a gun belt, strapped over the apron. Since both were tanners, and probably working together, Cole thought it odd that this person went to the opposite end of the bar from the big, bearded man.

Another man came in shortly after the second tanner.

"Damn, Marvin, what'd you fellas do, close the tannery for the afternoon?" the barkeep asked the third man who came in. Marvin grunted, then found an empty table at the back of the saloon.

Cole Collier was a man who lived on the edge, surviving on instinct and the ability to perceive danger long before it was apparent to anyone else. To ninety-nine of a hundred men, the fact that three tanners came in close together, all three armed and taking up positions far apart from each other, would mean nothing. But in Cole, it activated a little signal of alarm. Slowly, and without being seen, Cole slid his pistol out of his holster, then held it on his lap, under the table.

A fourth man came into the saloon. This was the same man Cole had seen leave a few minutes earlier. This man walked right to the center of the bar, then turned to face Cole.

"Would you be the fella they call Cold Blood Collier?" he asked.

This was it, Cole thought. This was the payoff.

"The name is Cole Collier."

"Well, Mr. Cold Blood Collier, my name is Les Sardis, and I'm callin' you out," the man at the bar said.

With that announcement there was a sudden repositioning of all the other patrons in the saloon as everyone moved to get out of the line of fire, should shooting begin. Cole noticed, however, that none of the three men who came in just before Les Sardis had moved. In fact, they seemed totally uninterested in the conversation that was going on between Cole Collier and his adversary, which in itself, was a dead giveaway.

"Are you calling me out for any particular reason?"

"Yeah, there's a reason. His name was Jimmy Sardis. Do you remember him?"

Jimmy Sardis had drawn on him two months ago. There was no reason for the fight that Cole could discern, other than the young man's wish to make a name for himself.

"I remember him."

"You killed him."

"That's right," Cole answered, without elaboration.

"Jimmy was my brother."

"Too bad you weren't there when it happened," Cole said. "Maybe you could've talked some sense into him."

"Yeah, well, here's the thing, Collier. Jimmy was good. Damn good. I don't think you could've taken him in a fair fight. I don't know how you did it, but, somehow, you cheated."

"Let me tell you something, Sardis," Cole said, "and I hope you listen to it, learn by it, and walk away from here, right now, before this goes any further. In a life and death fight, there is no such thing as

17

fair, and there is no such thing as cheating. A man does what he has to do."

"Is that right?"

Quietly, Cole cocked the pistol he was holding under the table. "Do you understand what I just said? In something like this, you do what you have to do."

A huge smile spread across Les's face. "I'm just real glad to hear you say that," he said, pulling his gun, even as he spoke.

As Les started his draw, Cole squeezed the trigger. His gun blazed from under the table and Les's smile changed to an expression of shock as he felt the bullet tear into his stomach.

Even as blood was pooling in the hands Les clasped over his wound, Cole was turning his pistol toward the man the bartender had called Marvin. Marvin was already halfway out of his chair. His gun had cleared his holster, but he had not yet brought it to bear. Cole's second shot caught Marvin in the throat and drove him back against the wall.

Almost at the same time he was shooting Marvin, Cole was turning over the table to use it and the adjacent pot-bellied, iron stove as cover. While he was diving to the floor the two men in the tanners' aprons, who were standing at opposite ends of the bar, fired at him. One of those bullets hit the stove, ringing loudly and sending up an aromatic puff of coal dust. The other bullet burned into Cole's left side, feeling exactly as if someone had held a red-hot poker against his flesh.

Rolling over to his right side, Cole fired at the big, bearded man, choosing him because he had proven to be the more accurate of the two remaining assailants. Cole saw a black hole appear in the bearded man's forehead, and knew that he was dead before he even hit the floor. The remaining shooter fired a second time, again missing but getting close enough to Cole that Cole could feel hot shards of lead from the bullet as it was shredded by impact with the stove. Cole's final shot crashed into the shooter's heart, soaking the already blood-stained tanner's apron with a sudden gush of blood.

The bearded man had gotten one shot off; the other man who had been wearing a tanner's apron fired twice. Neither Sardis, who started the whole thing, nor Marvin, who had been sitting at the table in the back, had managed a shot. Cole pulled the trigger four times, each bullet finding its mark. The acrid smoke resulting from seven discharges was now curling into a dark gray cloud to push away the tobacco smoke gathered just beneath the ceiling of the saloon.

After the final crash of gunfire there was a long moment of absolute silence, broken only by a measured *tick-tock, tick-tock* from the swinging pendulum of the Regulator Clock that hung on the back wall by the scarred piano.

"Holy shit," someone said quietly. A few of the others laughed nervously.

Cole remained on the floor behind the overturned table and the stove.

"Mr. Collier?" someone called. "Mr. Collier, you still alive?"

Cole didn't answer.

"Abner's dead," someone said.

"So's his brother, Les."

"What about Sam and Marvin?"

"I don't know. Sam's at the far end of the bar and Marvin's at the back. Ain't no way I'm goin' over to check them 'til I know whether Collier is dead or alive."

"Go ahead," Cole said from behind the table. "Check them out." Two or three men started across the saloon floor, but Cole stopped them. "It only takes one of you," he said.

All the men moved back to the periphery except one. He crossed the saloon to check on the Gleason brothers.

"Sam's dead," the one who checked called from the far end of the bar. He walked to the back of the saloon where Marvin lay face down where he fell. "Marvin's dead, too."

With a grunt and a groan, Cole pulled himself up from the floor and settled into the chair. He was holding his hand over the wound in his side.

"They're all dead?" Cole asked.

"Ever' one of 'em."

Cole looked at the four bodies, lying in various places around the room.

"As for sinners, they shall be consumed out of earth, and the ungodly shall come to an end," Cole said, holding his hand up in front of him.

"Mister, I ain't never seen nothin' like that," the barkeep said in awe. "You took on four of them."

"Bring me a bottle of whiskey and a clean towel," Cole ordered through gritted teeth.

"Yes, sir, you got it," the barkeep said. "It's on the house, too. You got'ny idea what you just did for business? Folks'll be comin' from all over to see where Cold Blood Collier took on the Sardis and the Gleason brothers."

The barkeep hurried to the bar, got a bottle of whiskey and a clean towel, then brought the items back to Cole. Cole poured whiskey onto his wound, then tore off a piece of the towel and poured whiskey on it as well. He stuck the whiskey-soaked towel into the bullet hole, grimacing as he did so.

"You ought to let a doc see that," one of the men said.

Cole looked up. "Is there a doctor in this town?"

"No, but there's one about fifty miles from here. We could send for him."

"Never mind," Cole said. "I'll take care of it myself."

Taking the bottle with him, Cole got up from the chair, and, still holding his hand over his side, staggered toward the door. Just before he left, he looked back at those who were watching him so intently.

"I'm leaving now. If anyone sticks his head through this door before I've left town, I'll kill him."

Almost involuntarily it seemed, everyone in the saloon drew back. Cole looked at them, nodded once, then left.

TWO

There were more than five thousand people sitting in bleachers on both sides of the field, watching a football game between two undefeated teams. Thus far in the season, both Princeton and Yale had compiled records of nine wins to no losses.

The game had been hard fought and evenly matched. On their previous possession, Yale had tried a field goal which sailed wide of the goalposts. Now it was Princeton's ball.

Clinton Bird, who was captain of the Princeton eleven, stared into the tired and strained faces of his players as they huddled to decide upon the next play. All were wearing uniforms of black canvas, tightly wrapped to provide some padding against the ferocity of play. The black was trimmed in orange. On the front of the black shirt, was a large, orange, block letter P. Black eyes, cut cheeks, and swollen lips were some indication of the roughness of the game.

Bird looked at one of his players, a man named Todd James Williams. "Todd, you are our biggest and strongest player," Bird said. "I want you to anchor the center of the line. The rest of you fellas form a wedge on him. Our only hope is to try and force through their line and get us close enough to kick a field goal."

"How much time do we have remaining?" one of the players asked.

"I don't know," Bird answered. "But it can't be more than a minute or two."

"Then let's go! Time is running out on us," Todd said.

"Todd, put the ball in play on the count of three," Moffat said.

Leaving the huddle, the players moved up to the line to face the Bulldogs of Yale. The Yale players were similarly dressed, though their uniforms were blue with white trim, and had a large, white, block letter Y on the front of their shirts.

"Williams," one of the Yale players taunted. "What do you think of football now? It's a little harder than racing your yacht, isn't it?"

The taunt referred to the fact that Todd Williams, who was the son of one of the wealthiest men in the country, had skippered his yacht, *Prometheus*, against the *Mischief* in a bid to represent the United States in the America's Cup. It had been a close race, but *Mischief* won, then went on to win the America's Cup, as well.

"I'm going to put you on your ass, Williams. Yes, sir, down you go, boy, down you go."

Todd looked up to see who was making the taunt. It was Morgan Spenser, the biggest man on the Yale team. Todd and Spenser had been going after each other all day and, like the score in the game, the two big men were about even with each other. The taunting, Todd knew, was actually a part of the game psychology. Todd had met Spenser off the field, and the meeting was quite cordial.

Todd bent over and looked between his legs. On the count of three, he flipped the ball back to Bird, and the two teams came together.

Todd looked up, just in time to see Spenser coming toward him. The two big men hit each other with the impact of colliding bulls. This time, Todd had the position of leverage, and he had the satisfaction of knocking Spenser down. Unfortunately, that wasn't enough. Bird was tackled short of the goal. Then, to prevent Princeton from scoring, the Yale players piled on top, keeping Bird pinned to the ground as precious time continued to tick off the clock.

"Come on, men!" Todd shouted. "We must clear them out!"

Led by Todd, the Princeton players began pulling the Yale players off their ball carrier until finally, Bird was able to scramble to his feet. Then they hurried back to huddle for one more play but, even as they were returning to the line, the referee fired a pistol into the air, indicating that the game was over. The titanic struggle had ended in a scoreless tie.

It was relatively quiet in the Princeton dressing room, the players silent in gloom and disappointment over not winning the game. Bird was going around to each of his players, complimenting them for their effort. He came over to stand in front of Todd, who was sitting on a bench tending to an abrasion on the back of his hand.

"Does it hurt much?" Bird asked.

"Not too much," Todd replied. "It wouldn't hurt at all if we had won."

"Listen, we won nine games this year and lost none. It was a good season," Bird said. He put his hand on Todd's shoulder. "And much of it is because of you. You were our Rock of Gibraltar, the way you anchored the line, tackling opposing runners, and protecting our runners. I'm glad you decided to join the team."

"It was an interesting experiment, and I enjoyed it immensely," Todd said. "But I think it would be very hard on a man to play a football game every day."

Bird chuckled. "I love the game," he said. "But I don't think I could play it every day either."

Trailback Ranch, Monday, May 4th, 1885:

Roselyn Vavak was a pretty girl. She was twenty-one years old, tall and slender, though certainly rounded enough that no one would doubt her sex, even from a distance. Auburn haired and brown eyed, her skin was fair and her cheekbones were high. Rising at dawn, Roselyn left the house while her mother and father were still sleeping, then went to the barn to saddle Pepper. She heard a noise behind her and, startled, turned quickly to see someone standing in the shadows, just inside the door.

"Who's there?" she asked, trying hard to

conceal the fright in her voice.

"I didn't mean to frighten you, Miss Vavak," the figure said. The rather small, bandy-legged man who stepped out of the shadows was Kenneth Crites, the ranch cook.

"Oh, Mr. Crites, it's you," Roselyn said, breathing a sigh of relief. "You didn't scare me, exactly. You might have startled me."

"Yes, ma'am, well, being startled can unsettle a person, nearly as much as being frightened can," Crites said. Crites rubbed Pepper behind his ear. "Pepper seems glad to see you again."

"I've missed Pepper, almost as much as I've missed my folks and this place," Roselyn said.

"He's a fine horse, all right."

"Mama told me how you watched out for him while I was gone. I appreciate that, Mr. Crites."

"Wasn't any more than anyone else would do," Crites replied. He held out a little bundle. "I thought you might want this."

"What is it?"

"A couple of biscuit and bacon sandwiches," he said. "And I have a canteen with some coffee here, sweetened and creamed just the way you like."

"You didn't have to do all that."

"I know. But I figured if you were going to go up to your secret spot, you would probably get a little hungry before too long."

"You know about my secret spot?"

"Yes, ma'am. I think everyone who works on the ranch knows about it."

Roselyn laughed. "Can't be that much of a secret then, can it?"

"Sure it can," Crites said. "As long as it's a place where you can go to be alone, have your own private thoughts and all . . . well, that would be secret enough, wouldn't it?"

"I suppose that's right."

"Of course it's right," Crites said. "There's a poem that covers it, I think, if you'd like to hear it."

"Oh, yes, please do say it for me."

Crites cleared his throat, looked around the barn to make certain no one was close enough to overhear him, then began reciting:

The little cares that fretted me
I lost them yesterday
Among the field, above the sea
Among the winds at play,
Among the lowing of the herds,

The rustling of the trees,
Among the singing of the birds,
The humming of the bees.

The foolish fears of what might happen,
I cast them all away,
Among the clover-scented grass,
Among the new-mown hay,
Among the husking of the corn,
Where drowsy poppies nod,
Where ill thoughts die and good are born,
Out in the fields with God.

"Oh, Mr. Crites," Roselyn said, clapping her hands in delight. "Oh, what a lovely poem. That was absolutely beautiful. Did you write it?"

"No, I wish I could claim credit for it. Actually it's an anonymous work. Nobody knows who wrote it."

"Thank you for reciting for me. And, thank you for this, as well," she added, holding up the little package he had given here.

"You're more than welcome," Crites replied.

Roselyn took the bundle and put it in her saddlebag, hooked the canteen of coffee around the pommel, then mounted. She looked down at Crites.

"Mr. Crites, you never cease to amaze me," she said.

"It's good to have you back," Crites said.

"It's good to be back. I can't tell you how much I missed this beautiful place."

"You be careful, Miss Vavak," Crites said. "You've been away awhile. You need to get used to riding again."

Roselyn reached down and patted her horse on the neck. "Pepper won't let me fall," she said.

"Well, I must get back to the kitchen now," Crites said. "I've got a second batch of biscuits in the oven."

"And I know the boys are looking forward to that," Roselyn said, as she turned Pepper away.

Most ranch hands were temporary, employed for roundups and trail drives, then moving on when the work was done. For a cook though, especially a good cook, the position was more permanent. Ken Crites was a very good cook, and had worked on Trailback Ranch since Roselyn was seven years old. Roselyn had no relatives in Texas, other than her mother and father, so Ken, by longevity, as well as by the kindness and personal attention he had shown her all her life, became her de facto uncle.

Urging Pepper into a trot, Roselyn left the corral and headed toward the trail that led up to Sky Meadow.

Ken Crites watched Roselyn ride away. A beautiful young woman now, Roselyn had been a skinny, big-eyed little girl when he arrived at the ranch, fifteen years ago. He had watched her grow up, through the gangly teen-age years, and into young womanhood. As Crites had no family, he had adopted the Vavak family. If it came down to it, he would die for any one of them. Or kill.

Roselyn had discovered, and named, Sky Meadow twelve years ago, when she was eight. Reached by a circuitous and often hidden trail, Sky Meadow was actually a grassy glade on top of Bread Loaf Hill, a high escarpment that guarded the north end of Trailback, protecting it from the icy blasts of winter. Bread Loaf was covered with a mixture of pine and deciduous trees that offered green all year, while also providing a painter's palette of color in the spring when the dogwoods and redbud trees bloomed, and again in the fall when the leaves changed. In addition, the meadow itself was blanketed with wildflowers of every hue and description.

It was so like Ken Crites to have a poem to welcome her return. The poem was quite appropriate for the way Roselyn felt about this place. She often came up here when something was troubling her. The tranquility and beauty of the place had been a haven during those times when she was certain that her parents didn't understand her, and weren't ready to accept the fact that she was growing up. She had also come up here to say goodbye when she left to go to school in San Antonio. Recently returned from that school, Roselyn was up here this morning to re-establish her connection with the land and people of her youth.

From Sky Meadow, she could see the big house, bunkhouse, cook's shack, barn, granary, and other outbuildings. She could also see much of the two hundred thousand acres that made up Trailback Ranch.

Trailback was the largest ranch in El Paso County, and one of the largest in West Texas. Her father managed, but did not own, Trailback. It was owned by Endicott Williams, an absentee owner. Roselyn had learned the term *absentee owner* a long time ago. Absentee owners were not very highly regarded by those ranch owners who lived on and worked their own land. By extension, those who managed the ranches of absentee owners were also looked at askance.

One of the principal complaints local ranch owners had of absentee owners was that since they didn't live here, they often made decisions that adversely affected those who did. And when an absentee owner made such a decision, there was nothing the ranch manager could do to counter it. But Vavak insisted that Endicott Williams wasn't that way. He was an absentee owner who gave his ranch manager full authority and Vavak was absolutely devoted to him.

Roselyn had met the owner only once, when he visited the ranch many years ago. She had met his son then, as well. Roselyn was 10, and Endicott's son, Todd, was 12. Although she had never mentioned it to anyone, Roselyn developed a crush on young Todd, and maintained that infatuation for many years. She used to entertain the fantasy that Todd would come live on the ranch when he was grown. Of course, she didn't know where that would leave her family. There was only the big house and the bunkhouse. There was no house for a ranch foreman, and if Todd did come to Trailback to live, he would naturally take the big house.

Although that was a troublesome part of her fantasy, Roselyn didn't dwell on it. And, as she grew older, the rest of the fantasy left her as well, especially as her opinion of Todd changed. He seemed to be a man with no apparent purpose in life, other than to spend his father's money in pursuit of fun.

Roselyn came to that conclusion as a result of keeping track of Todd through *The New York Times*. Her father subscribed to the newspaper, doing so because he believed that knowing about the world where his employer lived would make him a better ranch manager. The paper was delivered by train every day, though of course, as they didn't get into town every day, the papers were often picked up in batches of nine or ten, or even more, issues at a time.

When that happened, Vavak would very carefully put them in order and read them chronologically, often with a dictionary by his side to help him with the words he couldn't understand.

In the early years Roselyn was amused by her father's fascination with the paper, but she gradually became a reader herself, and appreciated the fact that she was able to read about national, and even world events, far in advance of anyone else in the Sierra Blanca Valley.

But the newspaper also covered New York events, and as young Todd Williams grew older, he began appearing in the newspapers with some frequency. Roselyn often found Todd Williams's name in the columns, telling of his exploits playing the game of football, as the captain of a racing yacht, or as the escort for some young debutante. Roselyn now believed that the best way to describe Endicott Williams's son was as a wastrel.

Roselyn ground-hobbled Pepper, then walked over to sit on a large, flat rock. She had discovered the rock on the first day she came up to Sky Meadow; indeed, it was one of the things she liked best about being up here. The rock had probably been here for a million years or so, and Roselyn would sometimes feel as if, by sitting here, she was actually in communion with everyone who had ever sat here, going all the way back to the beginning of time.

"Yeee haaa!!!"

The yell, though made tinny by distance, floated all the way up to Sky Meadow, and Roselyn couldn't help but laugh as she looked down on the ranch to see the cowboys pouring out of the bunkhouse, heading toward the cook shack where Mr. Crites would already have breakfast ready for them. She knew, without having to actually see, that Harold Shedd had given the yell. He was, easily, the most boisterous of all who worked on the ranch.

Roselyn got up and walked to take her biscuits and bacon from the saddlebag and retrieve the canteen of coffee. Then she returned to sit on the big flat rock to have her breakfast. She took a deep breath of the pine- and flower-scented air, then let it out in a long, satisfied sigh. It was great to be back home.

Princeton University, Friday,
   May 8th, 1885:

Football had been a noble and interesting experiment, one in which Todd was glad he had participated. But, as soon as football season was over, Todd applied himself diligently to his studies and, in the first week of May, was graduated from Princeton with a license to practice veterinary medicine.

When he returned to his room to clear it out, Todd found a letter waiting for him.

Dear Mr. Williams:

Two years ago, I watched from the deck of my yacht as you captained the racing yacht Prometheus *in a brilliant challenge to the* Mischief. *But for 90 seconds, it would have been you and your crew, rather than the* Mischief, *that represented the United States in the Americas Cup. And, as the* Mischief *won, I've no doubt but that you would have won as well.*

I am sure you know of Mr. John Beavor-Webb, the famous designer of racing yachts. I have recently had him design and build the Butterfly, *a yacht that I plan to enter into the trials against the* Puritan, *for purposes of representing our country in the Americas Cup Challenge, to be contested this summer. Would you be interested in acting as skipper of this vessel?*

If so, please contact me at your earliest convenience. Naturally, I will allow you to pick your own crew for this event.

> *Sincerely,*
> *Edward Burgess*

"Yes!" Todd said aloud. He hit his hand in his fist in excitement. He was very familiar with Edward Burgess, the sponsor of many yacht-racing events, and of the designs of John Beavor-Webb. Beavor-

Webb's yachts were known for their speed and beauty, and he felt that with such a yacht, he would have a very good chance of beating the *Puritan*.

"Mr. Burgess," he said to himself. "You've got yourself a yacht captain."

As he was looking for paper and an envelope with which to answer Burgess's letter, there was a knock on the door of his room.

"Go away! I've got better things to do than get drunk with a bunch of rowdy football players!" he shouted good naturedly, remembering their talk of celebrating after graduation by drinking the town dry.

There was a second knock on the door.

"All right, what is it?" Todd demanded, jerking the door open. Standing just outside his door was a rather smallish, middle-aged man with thinning hair and pince-nez spectacles.

"Hello, Todd. I'm glad I was able to catch you before you left," the man said.

"Mr. Virdin! What are you doing here?" Todd asked in surprise.

"I think you had better come home quickly," Virdin said. "Your father is dying."

THREE

New York City, Sunday, May 10th, 1885:

Endicott Williams's four-story mansion sat like an iced and decorated four-layer cake on the northwest corner of 48th Street and Park Avenue. Its sumptuously furnished interior more than met the promise made by the marble façade that projected the owner's wealth to passersby. The 24-room house had an elevator, indoor plumbing, a telephone, and electric lights, being one of the first homes to take advantage of the generating station New York had installed two years earlier.

Todd stood at the foot of his father's bed, looking down at the old man, whose face was now bathed in perspiration. Dr. Colfax was tending to him, but Todd knew there was little that could be done now. His father was dying, and he was thankful that he had managed to make it back home before it was too late.

The elder Williams had been quiet for some time, and Todd thought that perhaps he had slipped into a coma. But he opened his eyes and looked around the room.

"Todd?" he called in a weak voice.

"Yes, Dad, I'm here," Todd answered, stepping up beside him. Todd held his father's hand, and his father squeezed it.

"I have never been able to express my feelings very well. It may seem that I wasn't there for you. But I have always loved you."

"I know you have, Father."

"I'll be leaving you with a lot of responsibility," he said. "I hope you are up to the task."

"I'll try, Father."

"You'll find that running a business isn't like any of the games you play. You must be serious minded."

Todd believed that there was actually a great deal of benefit to be derived from the games he played. From football, one developed courage and learned teamwork. And from his experiences as captain of a racing yacht, he had developed leadership skills. But he knew he couldn't make his father understand and, under the circumstances, he had no intention of trying.

"I will take my responsibilities seriously, Father," he said.

"I have faith that you will," Endicott said.

He was silent for a moment longer, then he said, "I'm dying."

Todd didn't answer, because he didn't know what to answer.

"But don't weep for me, boy. It's not as bad as you might think."

Todd continued to hold his father's hand until it went limp. It was almost as if he could feel the moment life left the body, and he looked over at Dr. Colfax.

Dr. Colfax moved quickly to his patient. He held his finger to Endicott Williams's neck, checking for a pulse, then he leaned down to listen for a heartbeat. Hearing none, he straightened up and looked at Todd, then shook his head quietly.

"Colonel Williams is gone," he said. The military title referred to the fact that Todd's father had commanded a regiment of New York Volunteers during the Civil War.

Todd nodded, then walked over to the window. Raising the shade, he looked down onto the street below. Darkness had fallen, but the street was well lit by electric arc-lamps. A carriage clattered by, its passage illuminated by the glowing lanterns on its dashboard.

Todd's mother had died when Todd was ten years old, and Endicott had never remarried. Although the senior Williams was always a presence in Todd's life, he had taken very little hand in actually raising his son. Shortly after his mother died, his father did take Todd to Texas to visit the ranch, but that was the only gesture he ever made toward the boy. Todd sometimes got the impression that Endicott Williams regarded him as just one more business enterprise to manage. And as such, he hired a series of nannies and nurses to tend to Todd, just as he hired employees in his various commercial ventures. When Todd got older, and less direct supervision was needed, Ernie Virdin, his father's private secretary, replaced the nannies and nurses and acted as liaison between Todd and his father.

"Don't be misled by your father's cut-throat business reputation," Virdin told him once, after Todd had made some comment about his father's ruthlessness. "It is advantageous for him to be thought of in such a way, so he makes no effort to correct it, but it is a misconception. Your father has gone out of his way, many, many times to help others. But he does so quietly, and without fanfare." Todd continued to stare through the window as he remembered.

"Are you all right, Mr. Williams?" Virdin asked. It was the first time Virdin had ever addressed Todd as Mr. Williams. Todd started to correct him, but realized that this was his moment of passage.

"Yes, I'm fine, thank you."

"Will you be going back to school?"

"No, I'm all through there," Todd replied. "I suppose the first thing I must do is make arrangements for the funeral."

"That won't be necessary," Virdin said. "The arrangements are already made. The funeral will take place tomorrow morning."

"So soon?" Todd turned away from the window and saw that Dr. Colfax had pulled the sheet up over his father's face.

"It was your father's wish. He didn't want you to be burdened with the details," Virdin said.

"He didn't want me to be burdened, or he didn't think I could handle it?" Todd asked.

"Your father had every confidence in you, Mr. Williams."

Despite the solemnity of the moment, Todd chuckled. "Perhaps so. He managed every other aspect of his life, it is no surprise that he would arrange his own funeral."

"However, if you would rather make your own arrangements, there is no one to contradict you," Virdin suggested.

"No, no. We'll do it the way my father wanted."

"Very well, sir. At your convenience, I will fill you in on all I know about the current status of your father's business," Virdin offered.

"Thank you," Todd replied. He thought of the changes this would bring about in his life, beginning with the letter he would have to write to Mr. Burgess tomorrow, declining the offer to captain the *Butterfly*. Oddly, he wasn't disappointed. None of that — the football, the yacht racing, or anything else with which he had occupied his time — seemed important now.

What did seem important was that he was now in charge of the Williams business enterprises, and he did have one idea he wanted to try. He had actually planned to approach his father with the idea as soon as he completed school, prepared to put forth his case in the strongest possible way. He knew that the chances of convincing his father to try the plan were, at best, slim, but he intended to try. Now, he had no one to convince but himself.

"Do you have any specific plans in mind

for the business?" Virdin asked.

Todd nodded. "In fact, I do have," he said. "But we'll talk about it later."

"Very good, sir," Virdin replied.

A storm beat against the tall windows of St. Thomas Episcopal Church so that what light did come in was gray and rain-washed. Outside the church, carriages were double-parked on both sides of the street for a block in either direction. The drivers of the carriages had abandoned their vehicles to seek shelter under the church porte-cochère, while the hapless animals, as well as the policemen who were directing traffic, had to endure the rain.

Todd was Endicott Williams's only surviving relative. As a result, the true mourners were few in number. The attendance was swelled, however, by the fact that Endicott Williams had been one of the city's most powerful businessmen.

The priest measured the length of the service by the intensity of the storm, and not until the rain let up, did he finish. Then the doors to the great, Gothic edifice were opened and the coffin was carried down the foot-polished concrete steps to be placed in a glass-sided hearse. The mourners, having fulfilled their obligation

46

by attending the service in the church, did not deem it necessary to hang around for the interment. As a result, a mere handful of people were there when the coffin was lowered into the grave.

It was one week after the funeral before Pierpont Braxton, from the law firm of Braxton, Powers, Jacobs, and Field, came to the Williams home for the reading of the will. The man who had been the family lawyer for many years died three years ago, necessitating a change. Braxton, Powers, Jacobs, and Field had not come into the picture until Todd was away in school, and because of that, the lawyer, and the firm he represented, were strangers to him.

"Your father's estate was quite substantial, Mr. Williams," Braxton said. "You are a wealthy man."

"Yes, I suppose I am," Todd replied.

"I do hope you will continue to allow our firm to represent you, as we represented your father."

"We'll discuss that later," Todd said. He nodded toward the folder Braxton was carrying. "That's the will?"

"It is, sir."

"Would you read it, please?"

"Yes, I'd be glad to," Braxton said.

Opening the document, he cleared his throat, then began to read.

"I, Endicott Williams of New York, New York, a citizen of the United States of America, and having served this nation during the great war of rebellion as a colonel in the New York Volunteers, do make, ordain, and declare this instrument, which is written with my own hand and every page thereof subscribed with my name, to be my last Will and Testament, revoking all others.

"All my debts, of which there are but few, and none of magnitude, are to be punctually and speedily paid, and the legacies hereinafter bequeathed are to be discharged as soon as circumstances will permit, and in the manner directed.

"To my faithful employee and friend, Ernest Virdin, I give and bequeath the sum of fifteen thousand dollars. To Señor Juan Bustamante, manager of Endicott Copper Mine, I give and bequeath the sum of two thousand five hundred dollars. To Mr. Joshua Culpepper, the manager of Amelia Cotton Plantation, I give and bequeath the sum of five thousand dollars. To Ivan Vavak, manager of my ranch, Trailback, I give and bequeath the sum of ten thousand

dollars. To the general fund of St. Thomas Episcopal Church, of which I am a member, I give and bequeath the sum of five thousand dollars.

"To my son, Todd James, I give and bequeath the use, profit, and benefit of the remainder of my whole estate, real and personal, for the term of his natural life, except such parts thereof as are previously disposed of in this document.

"Signed by my hand on this day, October 11th, in the Year Of Our Lord, 1884, in my home in New York, New York."

Braxton finished reading the will, then looked up at Todd and Ernie.

"That concludes the reading of the will," he said. "Do either of you have any questions?"

"No questions," Todd said.

"No questions," Ernie said. "He was indeed, a generous man, to remember me in such a way."

"Mr. Williams, although your father left you property, I would advise you to convert all of the holdings into cash as soon as possible," Braxton said.

"Oh?" Todd said, raising an eyebrow. "And why is that?"

"Well, sir, I imagine that your, uh, way of

49

life, is quite expensive. You will need funds to continue living at the level to which you have become accustomed, and, without the necessary business experience to run your late father's operations, the most logical solution would be to convert all your holdings . . . except for this house of course . . . into cash."

"I see," Todd replied. "And I suppose you have some idea as to how I might go about doing that?"

"In fact, I do, sir. I am happy to say that I have located buyers for the East Star Shipping Lines and Trailback Ranch," Braxton said.

"But if I convert all those assets to cash, won't that money eventually run out?" Todd asked. "It would seem to me that these businesses, skillfully run, would continue to be a source of income."

"Yes, sir, and when you say 'skillfully run,' you have come to the rub, so to speak. As for the businesses continuing to be a source of income, let me acquaint you with some unpleasant facts."

Braxton pulled a paper from a folder, and began reading. "The copper market has been depressed for the last three years, so your copper mining operation is barely holding its own. I do expect copper to come back, however, so you could probably hold on to the mine for another few years before being forced to sell. There has been a two-year drought in Georgia, so for the last two years, your cotton plantation hasn't made a crop sufficient to carry the expenses. East Star Shipping Lines consists of twelve ships. Four of these ships will require major maintenance this year, to the tune of several hundred, perhaps even several thousand, dollars. I'm sure you weren't aware of this but . . ."

"Mr. Braxton," Todd interrupted. "As it so happens, I am not without nautical experience. I captained the *Prometheus* in her challenge to the *Mischief*, and nearly beat her. And as a young man, I sailed as a junior officer on one of my father's ships, so I am well acquainted with the operation. The maintenance you speak of is nothing more than routine scheduled maintenance: replacing rope and cable, scraping the hulls, that sort of thing. Our maintenance program is on a three-year schedule. And, as we have twelve ships, that means that four come due every year."

Braxton cleared his throat. "I see," he said. "Well, then you are better acquainted with the nautical side of your father's business than I. The offer to buy the shipping line is still there, however, should you wish to accept it. But, I do urge you to sell both the cotton plantation in Georgia, and the ranch in Texas."

Again, Braxton referred to one of the papers he was carrying. "Like the cotton plantation, the ranch has lost a considerable amount of money over the last three years. Though, unlike the cotton plantation, it does not have a drought as an excuse. No doubt, the loss is due to poor administration by the on-site ranch manager."

Todd looked at Virdin. "Is that true, Mr. Virdin? Has the ranch lost a lot of money?"

"Only to a point," Virdin replied. "The ranch lost money three years ago because of the great blizzard. Everyone lost money that year. And although the ranch has been profitable for the last two years, it is still running at a deficit as a result of the losses incurred three years ago. But those losses have nearly all been recovered, and barring anything unforeseen, the ranch should return to profitability this year."

"What about the management?" Todd asked.

"Mr. Vavak has proven to be a very good ranch manager," Virdin said. "Mr. Williams had the utmost confidence in him, and experience has shown that his confidence was not misplaced."

Todd turned back to Braxton.

"Having heard that, Mr. Braxton, are you still advising me to sell?"

"Yes, sir, that would be my advice."

"Well, I appreciate it, but I don't plan to sell any of the current holdings," Todd said.

"I see. Well, of course, that is your decision to make," Braxton said. "But I did feel honor bound to tell you of the option of selling."

"And honor bound to locate a buyer?"

"Yes."

"Mr. Virdin, I believe you have something for me," Todd said.

"I do," Virdin replied. He handed Todd an envelope.

Braxton didn't know what was going on, and he looked uncomfortable as Todd removed a sheet of paper from the envelope Virdin had given him.

"Tell me, Mr. Braxton," Todd said, reading from the sheet of paper, "Would the buyer you have found for the plantation, ranch, and ships be Atlantic Partners?"

"Atlantic Partners, yes," Braxton said.

"And this is their offer?" Todd asked, showing Braxton a figure on a piece of paper.

"Yes. I think you will find that the offer is quite generous, under the circumstances."

"You call the offer generous, yet it is but one-half of the appraised value of those holdings."

"Mr. Williams, you must understand that the appraisal you are speaking of was based upon the profit potential under your father's management," Braxton said. "Your father is deceased. Surely, you don't think you can take your father's place? You are much too young, too inexperienced and too . . . ," he let the word hang.

"Too what?" Todd asked.

"Too much the *bon vivant*. Everyone knows, Mr. Williams, that you are more interested in the coming theater season, the next dance, or the next yacht race to give your full attention to running a business of this size. I fear that you will lose so much money that your entire estate will be in jeopardy. I strongly advise you to sell it."

"To Atlantic Partners?"

"To Atlantic Partners, yes."

"I see. But *you* are Atlantic Partners

aren't you, Mr. Braxton? And, I believe, there are no partners as such. There is just you."

"I, uh . . . ," Braxton replied, caught off guard by the fact that Todd knew this. He couldn't come up with an answer.

"Tell me, Mr. Braxton, do you consider this ethical? Am I the only one you were trying to keep the information from? What about your law firm? Do they know that you were trying to commit fraud against one of the firm's clients?"

"I'd hardly call it fraud, sir," Braxton said, indignantly.

"Oh? And, what would you call it?"

"I would call it a sincere effort to help," Braxton said, nervously. "And, no, the rest of the firm does not know. I saw no need in involving the rest of the firm in what was, essentially, a gesture of good will."

"A gesture of good will," Todd repeated.

"Yes," Braxton said. He removed his handkerchief and used it to wipe the sweat from his face.

"Very well, thank you, Mr. Braxton," Todd said. "I'll not be needing your services any longer. From now on, Mr. Virdin will be handling all of my affairs, including those that have been handled by your office."

"That's quite absurd, sir. Mr. Virdin isn't a lawyer."

"No. But he is an honest man. Good day, Mr. Braxton."

"Bon appetit," the waiter said as he put covered plates on the table before Todd and Virdin.

"Thank you," Todd replied.

Todd and Ernie Virdin were having dinner at the Union Club, a private club on Fifth Avenue at 21st Street.

Ernie Virdin laughed. "Did you see the expression on Mr. Braxton's face when you told him that you knew he was Atlantic Partners? He never would have tried such a thing while your father was alive. No doubt he thought he could put one over on you."

"And he could have, had you not found out about him. I appreciate that, very much."

"I'm glad I could help. I've no doubt you could bring charges that would land him in jail."

"Perhaps, but I've no wish to pursue the matter any further," Todd said.

"You mentioned earlier that you had some plans for the operation of the business. Would it be impertinent of me to inquire about those plans?"

Todd smiled. "Not at all," he said. "In fact, I'm about to give you a demonstration of those plans."

"A demonstration? What do you mean?"

Todd pointed toward the silver cover that was over the plates the waiter had just delivered. "Uncover your plate," he said.

Virdin did so.

"Now, if you will notice, there are two cuts of meat on your plate," Todd said.

"So I see," Virdin said. "I fear you have overestimated my appetite."

"Oh, your appetite has nothing to do with it," Todd said. "But your taste does. I want you to taste each cut, and tell me which you like best."

Virdin cut a piece of meat from one of the steaks and chewed it thoughtfully. "This is very good," he said.

"Yes, it is. But now, try that piece."

Virdin cut the second piece of meat, and began to chew it. As he chewed, his face lit up with a smile.

"Oh, I say," he said. "Oh, I say, this is . . . this is *quite* good! It is much better."

"It is, isn't it?"

"Is this beef?"

"Yes, but it is from a breed known as the

Hereford. The other cut was taken from a Longhorn."

"Longhorns. I believe that is what is raised on Trailback, isn't it?"

"It's what we are raising now, yes," Todd said. "It's also what a large percent of all ranchers are raising. But I intend to change that. I'm going to sell off our entire herd of Longhorns, and introduce Herefords."

"To produce meat like this?"

"Yes."

"Oh, what a marvelous idea," Virdin said. "Once word gets out as to how good this meat is, the market will be unlimited. I don't know why it hasn't been done before now."

"Well, for one thing, people are normally resistant to change," Todd said. "And for another, Longhorns are a much sturdier breed of cow than Herefords. Making the change isn't going to be easy."

"How long have you been thinking about this?"

"I started reading about it while I was in school," Todd said. "I was going to approach father with the idea as soon as I graduated, but I never got the opportunity."

"How soon do you plan to do this?"

"Right away," Todd replied. "In fact, as quickly as I can make arrangements for a replacement herd. I intend to move to Texas."

"To Texas? Will that be a permanent move?" Virdin asked in surprise.

"Yes. Unless of course, this entire thing doesn't work out." Todd smiled. "If it fails, then I shall come back with egg on my face."

"It won't fail. You are too determined to let it fail."

"Oh? You don't think I'm the *bon vivant* Braxton suggested?"

"I have known you for a long time. I know you better than just about anyone alive, and I know that you have the strength, intelligence, and determination to do just about anything you put your mind to. If you say you are going to replace a herd of Longhorns with Herefords, then I say to the meatpackers, get ready."

Todd laughed. "Thanks for the vote of confidence."

"And, I hope you know that you can count on me to take care of things here for you."

"Oh, indeed, I do know that, Mr. Virdin," Todd said. "That's why I'm making you a full partner in East Star

Shipping Lines."

Virdin gasped. "I beg your pardon?"

"I want you to run the shipping operation," Todd said. "And, to provide the proper incentive, I'm making you a full partner." He pulled a folded piece of paper from the inside pocket of his jacket and handed it to Virdin. "Here is the paperwork."

"I . . . I don't know what to say," Virdin replied, awestruck by the offer.

"That's easy. Just say you'll do it," Todd said.

"Do it? Yes, of course I will do it."

"And, if you don't mind, I would also like for you to continue to live in the house. I'd hate to close it up. Use it as your own. Just keep my room ready for when I return to visit."

"Yes, yes, of course I will. Mr. Williams, I . . ."

Todd held up his hand to stop Virdin in mid-sentence. "I think that, in lieu of the fact that we are now equal partners, you could start calling me Todd again. Don't you?"

Virdin chuckled, then nodded. "All right, Todd," he said.

Todd picked up his glass of wine and held it toward Virdin in the form of a toast.

"To East Star Shipping Lines," he said.

"East Star Shipping," Virdin replied, touching his glass to Todd's.

"And," Todd added, holding a piece of steak on the end of his fork, "to the Hereford. Long may it reign."

"To the Hereford," Virdin repeated, holding up his own piece of steak. They touched the two pieces of meat as if they were glasses, in a toast.

Wednesday, May 20th, 1885:

A forest green carriage, pulled along by a team of matched, high-stepping grays, turned west off Park Avenue, onto East 42nd Street. The hollow clopping of prancing hooves made a staccato beat on the pavement, still glistening wet from an early morning rain. The driver maneuvered the carriage through the traffic, then brought it to a stop in front of Grand Central Station. Todd Williams stepped down, then turned back to speak to Virdin, who had ridden to the station with him.

"Now, remember," he said, "if you have to communicate with me, don't contact me as Todd Williams. As far as those folks are concerned, I'm a veterinarian named Bill Todd."

"Are you sure you want to do that, Todd?" Virdin asked. "I mean, it seems to me that you would get a lot more cooperation from them if they knew who you really were."

"I've thought about that," Todd replied. "But I want to win them over on the merits of the idea, not because they feel an obligation to the owner."

A redcap approached the carriage.

"Your bags, sir?" the redcap asked.

"There is just the one trunk," Todd said, pointing to it.

Seeing the size of the trunk, the redcap signaled for another redcap to join him, and the two men strained as they moved it from the carriage to a cart.

Todd reached back into the carriage and shook Virdin's hand. "Goodbye, Mr. Virdin," he said.

"Goodbye, Todd. And good luck to you."

FOUR

Saturday, May 23rd, 1885, Trailback Ranch:

It was just after breakfast, and armed with shopping lists from the cook and Mr. and Mrs. Vavak, Harold Shedd hitched up a team to drive into Sierra Blanca. Dewayne Blackwell approached him, giving him a fifty-cent piece.

"I want Red Mule chewing tobacco, you got that?" Dewayne Blackwell insisted. "Red Mule, none of that other nasty stuff. Also, a pair of work gloves. And I should have me some change comin' back. At least a nickel." Dewayne, long-legged and thin, was a few years older than Harold. Dewayne had spent a few years in the Cavalry but was nonspecific when pressed for details. Harold had the distinct impression that Dewayne had deserted the army, though he never pressed him about it.

John Harder also had a request of Harold. He gave Harold a dollar and a quarter. "Get me a bottle of Old Overholt Whiskey," he said. "If you can't get that,

63

get me whatever whiskey you can get for a dollar and a quarter."

John was forty-nine, gray-haired, and with a face that could best be described as weathered. He walked with a limp which was the result of — depending on his most recent telling — either a Yankee minie ball, an outlaw's bullet, or a Comanche arrow. He had ridden with a half-dozen outfits, scouted for the army, wintered in the Rockies, and was rumored to have an Indian wife somewhere.

John and the cook had an understanding. At first, Harold thought the understanding was because they were the oldest of the hands. But he had come around to believing that they may have known each other from somewhere before their association on Trailback. But whatever relationship they may have had in the past, stayed in the past.

Don Walton waited until the others had put in their order before he came to Harold. At sixteen, Don was the youngest cowboy on the ranch. His pa was a cotton farmer near Galveston, so Don was no stranger to hard work, but farming wasn't for him. He left the farm as soon as he was old enough to get out on his own. He was quick to explain, however, that he wasn't running out on any family obligations. He was the youngest of four brothers and two sisters, so there were plenty of homegrown hands to help run the farm.

Looking around to make certain that no one would overhear him, Don said quietly, "Would you get me a sack of horehound candy?"

"Hell, Don, what you talkin' so quiet for? You don't have to be embarrassed. There's not a cowboy on the ranch that don't like horehound."

"I ain't embarrassed," Don replied. "I just don't want anyone else to know I got it, else they'll always be trying to get some off me."

"You got a point there," Harold agreed. "Don't worry, your secret is safe with me . . . for a price," he added.

"I'll give you a couple pieces," Don promised. "As long as you don't tell nobody else I got it."

With the team hitched to the wagon, Harold climbed up into the driver's seat. It was then that Ivan Vavak came out of the big house, holding his hand up as a signal for Harold to wait a moment.

Of average height and weight, Ivan Vavak's most distinguishing feature was a scar that started just under his left eye, slashed across his cheek like a purple lightning flash, and ended at the corner of his mouth. The scar was the result of an errant halyard during a storm at sea. Born Ivan Vavaklonski in Poland, fifty-five years ago, he had gone to sea when he was fourteen. Six years later, when his ship made port at Galveston, Texas, he came ashore. Shortening his name to Vavak, he went back to sea, this time as a sailor on one of Endicott Williams's ships. When the war started, Ivan Vavak left the sea for good, joining with General Hood's Texas Cavalry.

Captured at Vicksburg, Vavak was taken to Camp Douglas, Illinois. Endicott Williams, then a Colonel in the Union Army, learning of the incarceration of his old employee, arranged for Vavak's parole. Giving his word not to bear arms against the North anymore, Vavak returned to Texas, there to begin working for Williams on his Texas ranch. It was a decision he never regretted.

"Harold, all the shopping lists, you are sure you have?" Vavak asked.

Though Vavak's Polish accent was well enough controlled that he could be easily understood, he still had problems with sentence structure.

"I have everything, Mr. Vavak," Harold said, patting his shirt pocket.

"Good, good. The mail, do not forget."

"No, sir, I won't."

Vavak started back toward the house, then turned just as Harold started driving away. "And drunk do not get!"

"Damn, Mr. Vavak, you take away all the fun," Harold called back in a teasing voice.

It was nearly supper by the time Harold got back from town, and the cook mustered all the other cowboys to help unload the wagon. Alice Vavak came out to get her own purchases, a bolt of cloth and some lace and thread, then took it back to her sewing room, pleased with the prospect of starting a new dress.

The most important thing to Vavak was the mail, and he took the little packet into the house where he settled down in his large, leather chair to go through all the letters and packages. A couple of the letters were for Roselyn, missives from friends she had made at school.

Roselyn was laughing over a story one of her friends had written when she heard her father groan.

"Oh, no," he said in a tight voice.

Puzzled, she looked toward him. "Papa?"

To her surprise, Vavak's head was bowed forward, and he was gripping the bridge of his nose between his thumb and forefinger.

"Papa, are you all right?" Roselyn asked, a little anxious, now.

"Mr. Williams is dead," Vavak said.

"Oh, no. When? How?"

"Now it is three weeks before," Vavak said.

"Oh, Papa, I'm so sorry. I know how much you thought of him."

"Yes," Vavak said. "A fine man he was." He looked at the letter again. "To his son now belongs the ranch."

"Surely, nothing will change," Alice said. "I mean, if Mr. Williams was happy with the way you were running the ranch, don't you think the son will be as well?"

"I don't think you will have to worry about Todd Williams changing anything," Roselyn said, derisively. "As long as he can play his games and go to his parties, he will be satisfied to leave everything just as it is."

Vavak continued to read the letter until he came to a part that confused him. "Roselyn, this, I do not know the meaning of. You read for me."

Taking the letter from her father, Roselyn cleared her throat, then began to read.

" 'Dr. Bill Todd will be arriving in Sierra Blanca, Texas, on June 1st. Please arrange to have someone meet him, and take him out to the ranch where, I trust, you will show him every possible kindness.

" 'It is my intention to introduce a new breed of cow to the Texas range and Dr. Todd, who is a veterinarian, will be overseeing this operation.' The letter is signed Todd Williams," she concluded.

"A new breed of cow?" Alice asked, confused. "What do you suppose that means?"

"I do not know, Alice," Vavak said. "I think we will have to wait and see."

When Roselyn attended the South Texas Finishing School for Young Women in San Antonio, she had been one of two students from the Sierra Blanca Valley. The other student was Cindy Murchison, daughter of Tom Murchison, Sierra Blanca's only lawyer. Learning that her father would be sending someone into Sierra Blanca to pick up their visitor, Roselyn asked permission to ride into town with the surrey.

"Whoever Papa sends after the tenderfoot will have to spend the night in town, because the train doesn't arrive until nearly ten. That means if I went with him, I could stay the night with Cindy. She and

I would have such a lovely time together," Roselyn said to her mother. "Please say I can go."

"Of course you can go, darling," Alice replied. "I'll have your father write a letter to Mr. Murchison, asking him to extend the courtesy of his home to you. And of course we will offer the same courtesy to Cindy, should she care to return the visit."

Out in the bunkhouse there was some concern being expressed among the cowboys as they discussed the tenderfoot who was coming to spend some time at the ranch. Nearly all of them had heard stories of Eastern dudes coming West. In truth, most of the stories were apocryphal, but they didn't know that, and wouldn't have known what that meant if someone had made the accusation. What made this particular situation troubling was the fact that this tenderfoot was not only coming to Trailback, he was to be the instrument of some sort of change. And as a general rule, the cowboys didn't like change.

Vavak had put a good face on the idea, but Harold was pretty sure that he, like nearly everyone else on the ranch, wondered just what this new breed of cow was to be, and why young Mr. Williams was so intent to have it in the first place?

"Seems to me like Longhorns has done just fine," Dewayne Blackwell said, speaking for the others. "I mean they ain't no hardier creature alive than a Longhorn. You can turn one of them critters loose and it'll purt' nigh raise itself. What does someone want to go messin' with a good thing for?"

"Has anybody ever seen one of these here Herefords?"

"I have," Don said. "They was some on the farm next to ours."

"What are they like?"

"Well, their horns are short, and they're shaped something like a milk cow," Don said.

The other cowboys laughed. "A milk cow? We're goin' to be nursemaid'n' us a herd of milk cows?"

"I said they were something *like* a milk cow. They aren't milk cows."

"Wonder which one of us will be goin' into town to get 'im?" John asked.

"Prob'ly won't be you," Dewayne said. "You'd more'n likely get yourself all drunked up."

"That'd be better than you lyin' with some soiled dove and forgetting what you come for," John replied.

71

"It'll more'n likely be Don. He's the onliest one of us that don't drink, or lie with women."

"Ha!" Harold said. "Iffen Don saw a woman, he'd like as not run away."

"I doubt that," Crites said. "Don is the quiet type. It's been my experience that they're the ones you have to keep your eye on."

Don looked over at Crites and smiled, appreciating the fact that the cook had boosted his status among the others. As the oldest, and most experienced, everyone paid attention to whatever Ken Crites had to say.

Monday, June 1st, Sierra Blanca, Texas:

Sierra Blanca, Texas, owed its existence to the competition that surrounded the construction of the nation's second transcontinental railroad. Collis P. Huntington's Southern Pacific Railroad began building eastward from the Pacific in 1869, while Jay Gould's Texas and Pacific Railway began west from central Texas in 1872. In December of 1881, the two roads connected, seven miles southeast of Sierra Blanca Mountain, in what was called the Sierra Blanca Valley, and the town of

Sierra Blanca was born. Transcontinental rail service began immediately, and Sierra Blanca, which was 80 miles southeast of the county seat of El Paso, and connected by rail to that community, quickly grew into the most important commercial center in the valley, providing stockyards and a railhead for local ranchers, as well as a shipping center for salt.

The task of picking up the tenderfoot fell to Harold Shedd. He helped Roselyn up onto the seat, then slapped the reins against the back of his team. The surrey started forward. It was hot, and Harold pushed his hat back to let it hang around his neck by its rawhide thong. That action exposed his hair, which was dark and so curly that a few people had tried to give him that nickname. It never stuck though, primarily because Harold considered "Curly" sort of a sissified nickname, and wouldn't answer to it.

If Trailback had a horse to be broken, the job fell to Harold. He was not only the best horseman on the ranch, he was also the best cowboy. He could drop a lariat over the horns of a steer in full gallop, then jerk the steer down and tie his legs together to make branding easy. He was also quite good with a pistol. He spent a lot of money on ammunition and would often practice in the open area just behind the cookhouse.

"How long have you known Mr. Crites?" Harold asked, as he drove Roselyn into town.

"I've known him a long time," Roselyn said. "Since I was about seven years old, I think."

"Where did he come from?"

"Oh, I couldn't answer that. In all the years I've known him, I don't think I've ever heard him say where he was from. I'll say this, though: He sure is a good cook. I don't guess I knew what a good cook he was until I had to eat that food at the finishing school."

"He is a good cook," Harold agreed. "Most cowboys judge a ranch by how good the cook is, and having him makes Trailback the best ranch to work for in the county. Maybe even in the whole state of Texas. But he's more than that."

"What do you mean?" Roselyn asked, though she knew perfectly well what Harold meant. She just wanted to hear what he thought.

"Well, for example, most of us call each other by our first names, or sometimes just the last name. But nobody calls Mr. Crites anything but Mr. Crites. And it ain't that he's asked us to, or that anyone has ever said we should. It's just that way."

"That's true," Roselyn said. "And it has been that way for as long as I've known him. Even Papa calls him Mr. Crites."

"And he's smart," Harold added. "He's maybe the smartest man I know. And I don't mean no disrespect to your pa, who is also real smart," Harold said, quickly. "But no matter what question you ask him, seems like he knows the answer. And he's always readin', which means he's just getting smarter."

Roselyn laughed, recalling the poem he had quoted for her shortly after she returned from school. And she was well aware of the cook's penchant for books. While she was away, Mr. Crites was always sending her money with a request that she buy some book for him, books being more available in San Antonio than in Sierra Blanca.

For the rest of the trip into town, they speculated about the tenderfoot veterinarian they were to pick up.

"More'n likely, he's some sawed-off little feller with no hair, and them glasses that just kind'a perch on the end of your nose, like this," Harold said, making lenses with his thumb and forefinger and demonstrating.

"And buck teeth," Roselyn added, laughing, and Harold caused her to laugh harder when he rolled his lip back to approximate buck teeth.

"Now, Harold, you have to promise me something," Roselyn said.

"What's that, ma'am?"

"Don't be mean to him. I know how you boys like to treat newcomers. Especially a tenderfoot from the East. I remember the awful way Timmy was treated."

"Yes, ma'am, but Timmy's one of us now," Harold said. "If a fella's got a little gumption in him, some teasin' ain't goin' to hurt him. It'll just make him stronger, like it did Timmy."

"Yes, but remember, Dr. Todd isn't coming out here to be a cowboy. He may not have the gumption you are talking about. And, with Mr. Williams gone now, well, it wouldn't look good for papa if there was some incident over the veterinarian they sent out here."

"All right," Harold said. "I'll tell the others to go easy on him."

"Thanks, I appreciate that. Oh, there's Cindy's house. You can let me off here."

"Yes, ma'am," Harold said. "I'll pick you

up tomorrow mornin', right after break-fast."

After Harold let Roselyn off, he went down to the livery where he put the surrey and team away. With that taken care of, he walked back out onto the board sidewalk in front of the livery stable where he stood for a moment, rubbing his hands together in eager anticipation of doing a night on the town.

The boardwalk ran the length of the town on both sides of the street, which was called Ranch Road. At the end of each block there were planks laid across the road to allow pedestrians to cross over without having to walk in the dirt or mud. Harold waited patiently at one of them while he watched a lady cross, daintily holding her skirt up above her ankles to keep the hem from soiling, then he stepped onto the plank himself.

Just as he started across the street though, he saw Roselyn and Cindy on their way downtown to do some shopping, so he stepped back and walked in the opposite direction. The young cowboy had been intending to cross the street to go into the Brown Dirt Cowboy, the town's biggest and best saloon, but he didn't want

Roselyn to see him. It isn't that he had to hide his actions from her — she probably suspected he would visit a saloon anyway — it was just that he didn't want to be quite so blatant about it.

Walking around town for a bit more, Harold stopped and stared in the window of a leather goods shop to contemplate a pair of boots. They were good-looking boots, and he would love to have them, but the boots he owned weren't worn out yet, and it didn't make sense to spend good money for something he didn't really need.

Harold strolled all the way up one side of the street and down the other, finally winding up at the Brown Dirt Cowboy Saloon. Pushing his way through the bat-wing doors, he stepped up to the bar.

"Well, if it ain't old Harold Shedd," a tall, thin cowboy said.

"Slim Posey, you mean you ain't in jail yet?" Harold asked

Posey laughed. "Barkeep, give that poor lost creature a drink, on me," he said, slapping a coin down on the bar. "Comes to my mind I may owe him a drink."

"Comes to my mind, you may owe me a lot of drinks," Harold said. "But I'll take this one on account."

"Name your poison," the barkeep said as

he moved down the bar to stand in front of Harold. He carried a damp rag with him, which he used to wipe the bar just in front of Harold. The rag reeked with a sour stench.

"Whiskey," Harold replied.

The glass was set before Harold and he took it, then turned with his back to the bar to survey the room. The evening customers were just beginning to gather, and the soiled doves were moving about the room like bees working in a field of wild flowers, going from table to table to ply their wares.

Slim Posey was a cowboy for the Metzger Land and Cattle Company, another very large ranch in the valley. In fact, Metzger Land and Cattle was second in size only to Trailback.

Posey moved down the bar to have a couple of drinks with Harold, and to share the latest jokes with him. The two young men had known each other for years, and were friendly competitors. Slim was as good with horses and the lariat as Harold, and there had been a few impromptu competitions between them.

"One more drink, and I have to go," Posey said. "By the way, what's brung you to town?"

"I've come to pick up a tenderfoot from back East," Harold said.

"Haw! Wish I could stay in town long enough to help you razz him some. He some Eastern dude wantin' to cowboy?"

"No, he's comin' out here to change all the cattle."

"What do you mean, change all the cattle?"

"He wants to get rid of all the Longhorns and start raisin' somethin' called a Hereford."

"What for?" Posey asked.

"Damned if I know," Harold replied. "But Mr. Williams, the fella that owns Trailback, wants to do it, I suppose. That is, Mr. Williams's son. Old Mr. Williams died about a month ago."

"Did you ever meet the fella that owned Trailback?" Posey asked.

Harold shook his head. "Nope, I never did. Far as I'm concerned, Mr. Vavak is my boss."

"Yeah, I reckon that's the way I would figure it, too," Posey said. "Well, I have to go. Take it easy, Pard, don't drink all the whiskey, and don't be too rough on the women."

By the time Posey left the saloon, the tables were filled with drinking, laughing customers, and at one of the tables, a card game was in progress. As Harold watched, one of the players left one of the games, and Harold walked over to the table.

"Mind if I join you?" he asked.

"Your money's good," a tall man with a handlebar mustache said, pushing a chair out with his foot.

40 Miles East of Sierra Blanca:

Todd James Williams, who had bought his ticket as William J. Todd, DVM, shifted positions in the hard seat of the day-coach, then looked through the window at the wide open spaces outside. No more than one hundred yards away he saw a herd of wild horses, their manes and tails flying in the wind as they ran parallel with the track, actually outpacing the train. He was four days out of New York, having changed trains in Chicago, St. Louis, Memphis, Houston, and San Antonio. For much of the trip he had enjoyed the comfort of Pullman cars, or Wagner Parlor cars. But there were no such amenities on this train, and for the last twelve hours Todd had tried, with little success, to accommodate his large frame to the cramped passenger seats.

It was, at that, much better than the last time he had made this trip. He was twelve years old then, and there was no train service to Trailback. The last three days of that trip had been by stagecoach. Still, it had been very exciting for a young boy, and Todd smiled as he recalled that trip.

He remembered, also, that Mr. Vavak had a daughter. Roselyn was two years younger than he was, and Todd wondered what she was like today. Was she pretty? As he recalled, she had been a pretty little girl. He laughed at his thought. That analysis had been from the perspective of a 12-year-old boy, not a grown man.

She was probably married, anyway. It had been his observation that young women who grew up in a rural environment generally married at a much earlier age than women from an urban environment.

Todd's stomach growled. He was hungry. The trains he had taken on the first part of the trip had dining cars with menus as extensive as could be found in a New York restaurant. Not realizing that this train had no such amenities, he missed breakfast, thinking he would be able to eat in the dining car. He barely managed lunch, gulping it down during the brief stop in Del Rio, Texas. The fare was beef-steak, fried potatoes, and fried eggs, and the passengers were given a total of twenty minutes to detrain, order their lunch, then get back on the train.

The conductor passed through the car and Todd called out to him.

"Conductor?"

"Yes, Dr. Todd," the conductor replied.

"How much longer until we reach Sierra Blanca?"

The conductor took a watch from his pocket, opened the case and examined it.

"Let's see, it's just after seven. About two more hours, sir," he said.

"Nine o'clock."

"Yes, sir."

"Will we have an opportunity to stop for supper before then?"

"Before then?" The conductor shook his head. "I'm afraid not, sir. We had our supper stop at six, if you will recall."

"That was the supper stop? The only thing they had was beans and bacon."

"Yes, sir, the fare there is generally quite meager. I'm sure you will be able to get something in Sierra Blanca, though."

"Thanks," Todd said, settling back in his seat.

It grew dark outside, and Todd turned

his thoughts away from his hunger to concentrate on the task before him, that of introducing Hereford cattle onto the range. Having gotten the idea to raise Herefords while still a student at Princeton, Todd prepared a paper on the subject, exactly as if he were doing a class assignment. And though he had read the paper many times, he pulled it out now for one last perusal before reaching his destination. Reaching up to the kerosene lantern on the wall beside him, he turned the light up high enough to be able to read the papers.

Herefords came to the United States in 1817 when the great statesman Henry Clay of Kentucky made the first importation of a bull and two females. These cattle and their offspring attracted considerable attention, but they were eventually absorbed by the local cattle population and disappeared from permanent identity.

The first breeding herd in America was established in 1840 by William H. Sotham and Erastus Corning of Albany, New York, where they have proved to be a superior beef-producing breed. As Herefords thrive on grass, it is believed that the large scale introduction of this breed into the cattle growing areas of Texas, and the American West, would be successful, and their greater weight and superior beef would make the operation very profitable.

"Sierra Blanca," the conductor called, walking through the car. "Our next stop is Sierra Blanca."

Surprised at how quickly the last two hours had passed, Todd folded up the papers and put them back into his inside jacket pocket. Then he turned off the lantern so he could see outside. There was nothing to see but a black, seemingly empty maw, interspersed with low-lying brush that grew alongside the track, illuminated for a brief moment by light cast from the windows of the train, then disappearing back into the darkness. Not until the train had slowed considerably did Todd see any indication of life — a few low-lying, unpainted wooden buildings of such mean construction that, had he not seen dim lights shining from within, he would have thought them unoccupied.

"Todd, what have you gotten yourself into?" he said under his breath.

With a rattling of couplings and a squeal of brakes, the train gradually came to a jerking halt. Looking through the window of the car, Todd saw a brick building with a small, black-on-white sign that read SIERRA BLANCA, TEXAS.

He recalled the moments just before kickoff in a football game; the nervous anticipation, the excitement, and even a little fear. Oddly, he felt that very thing right now.

FIVE

A few minutes earlier, Harold left the saloon and walked down to the railroad depot in the dark. He had not had that much money to start with, and any hopes he might have had of running it up into enough to have a pleasant night on the town were dashed by his run of bad luck.

If it was bad luck.

Halfway through the game Harold began to suspect that the man with the handlebar mustache and one of the other men at the table were working in cahoots to cheat him. But if they were cheating, they were good at it. They were so good, in fact, that he knew he wouldn't be able to prove it, and an unsubstantiated accusation of cheating wasn't a smart move. Therefore, Harold had no choice but to grit his teeth and bear it.

One of the most exciting events in any Western town was the arrival and departure of the train. Many would come to watch the trains even if they had no personal stake in them. As the townspeople began to gather, the crowd would take on a carnival atmosphere, with a great deal of laughing and joking. Harold found a place away from the jostling crowd, then, leaning against the depot wall he rolled a cigarette, lit it, and smoked quietly as he waited.

"Here comes the train!" someone shouted.

Immediately upon the heels of the shout, came the sound of the train whistle, announcing its arrival.

"It's right on time tonight," another said.

The laughing and joking ceased as everyone grew quiet to await the train's arrival.

Harold watched as the people on the platform moved closer to the track to stare in the direction from which the train would come. In the distance they could see the headlamp, which was a gas flame and mirror reflector, casting a long, bright beam.

The train could be heard quite clearly now, not only the whistle but the hollow sounds of the puffing steam coming from the engine, then rolling back as an echo from the surrounding hillsides. As the train drew even closer, Harold could see glowing sparks spewing out from the smoke-stack, whipped up into by the billowing clouds of smoke.

The train pounded into the station with sparks flying from the drive wheels and glowing hot embers dripping from its firebox. Following the engine and tender were the golden patches of light that were the windows of the passenger cars. The train squealed to a halt, then, through the windows of the car Harold could see the people who would be getting off here beginning to move toward the exits at the end of the cars. Others, those who were through passengers, simply stared tiredly through the windows.

Because he was in no particular hurry to meet the new tenderfoot, Harold just stood quietly until everyone was off the train. Most of the passengers were being met, but there were several who weren't, most of whom were traveling salesmen. These were called drummers, and they were easily identified by the samples cases they were carrying. Sierra Blanca was part of their route.

One of those who got off the train was a rather small, prim-looking man. He was wearing spectacles, and he took them off, polished them industriously, then put them back on, fitting them carefully over one ear at a time. He glanced around the depot, as if looking for someone.

With a sigh, Harold started toward him. He was sure this would be the tenderfoot vet he was to meet.

"Would you be the fella I'm supposed to meet?" Harold asked, as he approached him.

The man looked at him with a confused expression on his face. "You're here to meet me?" he asked.

"Yep. Where's your grip? I'll grab it for you."

"Percy? Percy, I'm over here!" a woman's voice called out.

"Martha," the little man replied.

"I'm sorry I'm late," Martha said, approaching Percy. "I couldn't get the team harnessed." She looked at Harold. "Who is this?"

"I've no idea," Percy said. "Some man who said he was here to meet me."

Realizing now that this wasn't the person he was to meet, Harold touched the brim of his hat. "Sorry, my mistake," he said.

"I do believe he wanted to steal my grip," Harold heard Percy say as he and Martha started toward the surrey she had driven to the station.

Shaking his head, Harold walked back to stand against the wall of the depot. He would have sworn that man to be the tenderfoot, but the experience just reinforced the old adage that things aren't always what they seem.

By now the departing passengers were boarding the train. Then the conductor called out, "All aboard!" moved his lantern up and down a couple of times, and stepped up onto the car. With a gush of steam and two whistles, the train jerked, rattled, strained, and began moving forward. Harold watched the train pull away, then turned to leave. His tenderfoot hadn't showed up.

"I beg your pardon, sir," a man called to him.

The man who called to him was big, at least six feet five inches tall, and he probably weighed two hundred forty pounds. He had wide shoulders and long, powerful-looking arms.

"Yes?" Harold replied.

"Would you know the way to Trailback Ranch?" the man asked.

Harold pushed his hat back and studied the man. Surely this couldn't be his tenderfoot.

"You headed for Trailback?"

"I am indeed, and I was led to understand that someone would be here to meet me."

"Yes, well, I reckon that would be me," Harold said. "Only I didn't expect . . ." he paused in mid-sentence.

"You didn't expect what?"

"I didn't expect so damn much of you. Are you Dr. Todd?"

The big man nodded, and stuck out his hand. "Yes," he said. "And you would be . . . ?"

"Harold Shedd."

"Do you have some sort of conveyance?"

"What?"

"A carriage of some sort?"

"Oh, yeah, a surrey," Harold said. "But it's over in the livery."

Todd walked over to the baggage cart and picked up a large trunk which two men were struggling with, lifting it easily to his shoulder. "Why don't you lead me to it?" he asked.

Harold looked at him, amazed over how easily he had hoisted the trunk to his shoulder.

"Uh, that's pretty far for you to carry that trunk," Harold said. "If you want, you can wait here and I'll go hook up the team and come back for the trunk."

"No need to go to all that trouble," Todd said easily. "Just lead the way."

As the two men walked toward the livery, Todd kept up an easy conversation for the entire distance, showing absolutely no strain from carrying the trunk. When they reached the livery, Harold showed Todd the surrey and Todd set his load down easily. The surrey sagged under the weight.

"Now," Todd said, brushing his hands together. "What do you say we get something to eat? I'm starved."

"I have some jerky here in the surrey," Harold said.

"Jerky? Well, I guess that would be an interesting introduction to the West, all right. But I was thinking of something a little more substantial. There is a place where we could eat, isn't there?"

"Well, there's the Brown Dirt," Harold said.

Todd fought the urge to chuckle. "There is actually a place to eat called the Brown Dirt?"

"The Brown Dirt Cowboy," Harold said. "It's more of a saloon, but most of the time, they got food there."

"What kind of food?"

"You can purt' near always get beans there. Couple of tortillas," Harold said.

"Anyplace else, some place maybe with a little more variety?"

"The City Pig stays open 'til eleven," Harold said. "But it's more for the high-tone folks."

"High-tone?"

"Yes. You know, people with money," Harold said. "And that's somethin' I ain't got none of. I lost it all tonight."

"How did that happen?"

Harold shrugged. "Beats me. I was just killin' time a'fore I come to meet you, so I decided to play a little poker. Trouble was, it wasn't an honest table. Turns out they was a couple of . . . well, I don't know what you would call them, but out here we call them low-down, side-windin' card cheats."

Todd chuckled. "Yes, we call them the same thing. You'll have to show me the men you were playing with. I'll want to be sure and avoid them if I get into any poker games."

"Yeah," Harold said. "Yeah, I'd say that would be a pretty good idea."

"Now, seeing as how you came into town to pick me up, and you just gave me some good advice on watching who I play cards with, it seems to me that the least I could do would be buy your dinner at the City Pig."

94

Harold shook his head. "You don't need to do that. I told you, it ain't cheap. I'll just show you where to go."

"Nonsense. I want to buy your dinner. Now, what do you say?"

Harold smiled, broadly. "I say I'd appreciate that."

Half an hour later Harold pushed his plate away, so stuffed that he could scarcely breathe. Todd had eaten half a dozen eggs, a heaping plate of potatoes, several pieces of ham, more biscuits than Harold could count, and was still going.

"If you aren't going to eat any more of those biscuits, would you pass them this way?" Todd asked, and Harold, amazed at Todd's appetite, pushed the plate of biscuits across to Todd.

"How long has it been since you ate?" Harold asked.

"Not since lunch," Todd replied, as he spread butter and jelly onto one of the biscuits.

"I ain't never seen anyone eat like you."

"That's what the fellas on the football team used to say."

"Football team?"

"Yes, I played football at college. Have you never heard of football?"

"Well, yes, but I thought it was mostly something kids played. Didn't know grown men did it."

Todd laughed. "Well, you might say that those of us who play the game have never quite grown up."

"Whoowee," Harold said. "I sure hope you don't grow no more. You're big as a tree now."

At that moment a couple of men came in through the front door. Harold glanced toward them and saw that they were the two men he had suspected of cheating at poker. The fact that they were together now, talking and joking, proved that they weren't casual acquaintances who just happened to meet in the game, though they had carried on that front while the game was in progress.

"Hey, Doc," Harold said, nodding toward the two men, "that there's them, the fellas I lost my money to."

One was tall and wore a handlebar mustache. The other was short, rather fat, and clean-shaven. Both were wearing city-style clothes. Their laughter was low and evil, and Harold intuitively knew that it wasn't the kind of light banter he was used to with the cowboys.

"What'd that fella say that pretty

woman's name was again?" the tall one asked.

"Roselyn," the other answered. "Course, that prob'ly isn't her real name. Most whores don't use their real names."

"Roselyn. Haw, wouldn't she be good for warmin' a man's bed on a cold night?"

Both men laughed, raucously.

"What do you reckon a whore like that would cost?"

Without saying a word, Harold got up and walked over to the table where the two men had sat. He glared down at them.

"You got something on your mind, Cowboy?" the short fat one asked.

"Mister, I'm going to ask you to mind your tongue," Harold said in a low and ominous voice. "I'll not listen to that kind of talk about Miss Vavak."

"Miss Vavak? Who is Miss Vavak?"

"The lady you two was jawin' about."

"Hey, Luke," the short, fat man said to his partner. "You ever hear tell of a whore with a name like Miss Vavak?"

"She's no whore. She is the daughter of our ranch manager and she is as fine a young woman as there is to be found in these parts."

"She's the daughter of the ranch manager, is she?" Luke asked. "So, you been visitin' her in the hayloft, have you?"

Suddenly, and unexpectedly, Harold brought the back of his hand across Luke's face so hard that it sounded like someone clapping hands.

"Why, you upstart turd, you hit me!" Luke said in surprise, running his fingers across his cheek, which was now showing a red welt.

"You're damned right I hit you, and I'm about to do it again if you don't apologize for those remarks about Miss Vavak." Harold drew back, making a fist this time, but he just let it hang there when he saw a small derringer suddenly appear in Luke's hand.

"No, I don't think you will," the tall gambler said menacingly. He raised his hand to fire, but before he could, Todd, who had come over to see what was going on, grabbed the gambler's wrist. He squeezed the wrist so hard that Luke let out a yelp of pain, and the gun clattered harmlessly to the floor.

"Let go of his wrist, mister, or I'll put a bullet in your brain!" the short, fat man said. Now, he, too, was armed. But he was too busy watching Todd to notice that Harold had picked up a chair. The cowboy brought the chair crashing down on the short, fat gambler, and the gambler fell like a sack of potatoes. Todd increased the pressure on Luke's wrist until the tall man sank to his knees, crying out in pain. Finally Todd released him.

"You damn fool. . . . I think you broke my arm!" Luke said, his voice laced with pain.

"I didn't break it," Todd said. "But if I had wanted to, I could have done so quite easily. Take off your jacket."

"What?" the gambler replied. "Are you crazy? I'm not going to take off my jacket."

"I don't need the whole jacket off to see what is under this sleeve," Todd said. Putting one hand on the gambler's shoulder and grabbing the sleeve cuff with his other, Todd gave a jerk, and the sleeve came off. When it did so, it revealed a clamp and an accordion-like device strapped to his arm.

"I thought so," Todd said.

"What the . . . ? What is that contraption?" Harold asked.

"I've read about such things," Todd said. "It is called a sleeve holdout."

"What does it do?"

"It's a small machine, arranged to allow him to slip a card into the palm of his hand anytime he needs it."

"Then he *was* cheating, wasn't he?"

"I'd say so," Todd replied.

"Mister, you owe me two dollars and fifty cents," Harold said.

Slowly, painfully, the gambler reached into his vest pocket and pulled out a handful of money. He dropped the wad of bills on the floor in front of him.

"Here!" he said. "Take it. Take it all. Just, for God's sake, get this giant away from me!"

"I don't want it all," Harold said. "I want only what is mine." Harold picked up his share of the money and put it in his pocket. At that moment the other gambler was coming around, and Harold looked over at him. "I suggest that you and your friend stay out of our sight for the rest of the time we're in town."

"Don't you worry none about that," the gambler said as he helped the other man to his feet. "If I ever see either one of you again, it will be too soon for me."

"Wait a minute. I want to know where you saw Miss Vavak?"

"At the mercantile," Luke answered. "She was there with the lawyer's daughter."

"You saw her at the mercantile, and you started spouting off filth about her?"

"I didn't mean no harm, I was just

funning, that's all."

"In addition to the money you owed my friend, I think you also owe an apology," Todd said.

Looking at the powerful young man who had inflicted such pain on him, merely by squeezing his wrist, Luke's eyes grew wide with fear.

"I apologize!" he said quickly. "I'm sorry I spoke about the young lady in such a way."

"You're sorry all right, but I don't accept your damn apology," Harold said. He made a waving motion with his hand. "Just get the hell out of here."

Both gamblers hurried out of the restaurant while Todd set the chair back up and carefully rearranged the tables to the way they were. He looked over at the proprietor of the restaurant, who, when the trouble began, had moved with the other customers to the far side of the room.

"I'm sorry for the disturbance," Todd said. "I hope you will forgive us."

"Mister, those two hyenas have been nothing but trouble ever since they came into town," the restaurant owner said. "Believe me, it does my heart good to see them run off. You don't have my forgiveness, for none is needed. You have my thanks."

"Come on, Doc," Harold said, now grinning broadly. "Seein' as how I've got my poke back, I can show you how to have a little fun in this town."

So far Todd had seen Sierra Blanca only by the golden glow of the lamps and lanterns which splashed patches of light onto the street. He was enjoying it because it was all new and strange to him, and he was absorbing new experiences. As he and Harold made the rounds of the saloons, Todd watched the bargirls and the gamblers and the cowboys with an intense, though guarded interest. Guarded, because he didn't want to make anyone uneasy by his observation.

The bargirls fluttered to the cowboys like moths to a flame, moving to a new one as soon as someone else came into the saloon. They were drawn to Todd by his size, and to Harold by the hope that he would be generous enough to spread some of his money around. When they discovered that Todd wasn't interested in anything they had for sale and that Harold was doing a maximum amount of drinking on a minimum investment, the girls left them alone. At midnight, Todd suggested that they take rooms in the Morning Star

Hotel, offering to pay for the rooms himself.

"Why are you wantin' to go to bed now? The night's just gettin' started," Harold complained.

"Because I've had several days on the train and I'm tired. But you go ahead and enjoy yourself," Todd said. "When you're ready, come on to the hotel. I'll go ahead and pay for your room, just ask the clerk for the key."

"You aim to pay for it?" Harold asked.

"Yes."

Harold rubbed his chin. "Doc, if it's all the same to you, could you just let me have the money the room would cost? That way I can spend it on havin' fun, and I'll bunk down in the livery stable for the night."

"You're going to sleep in the livery stable? Won't that be terribly uncomfortable?"

"Not at all," Harold insisted. "It ain't near as confining as a hotel room. And if a feller's got clean straw, why, he can settle down in there as snug as a bug in a rug."

"All right," Todd said, laughing, as he handed over the money. "Have a good time."

"Oh, I plan to," Harold replied.

Todd watched as Harold hurried down the street toward the Brown Dirt Cowboy, then he checked himself into the hotel.

When Todd lit the lantern in the hotel room, half a dozen roaches skittered across the floor to get out of the light. For a moment, he thought that perhaps Harold's idea of sleeping in the livery might not be crazy after all. The room consisted of an iron bedstead with linen that he was sure hadn't been changed in a couple of weeks. A chest of drawers set against a wall that was covered with wall-paper that may have been yellow at one time, but was now a dull, cream color, decorated with large, blue, flowers. On top of the chest of drawers sat a pitcher of water and a porcelain basin. There was no towel. Alongside the basin was a chamber pot that, while mercifully empty, reeked of urine. The dark-green window shade was badly torn, and the window pane was cracked.

Fully clothed, Todd lay on the bed without turning down the bedspread. The window was up about two inches and through it, he could hear the sounds of night revelry: a woman's scream, not of terror but of excitement, followed by her high-pitched laugh, a man's low guffaw, and the tinkling of a piano. Evidently Harold had been correct when he said that the night was just beginning.

SIX

Todd was awakened by a totally different concert of sounds from those that he heard last night. Gone was the laughter, the boisterous conversation, and the piano music.

In its place were the sounds of a town at commerce — the ringing of a smithy shaping iron at his forge, the scratching sound of a shopkeeper sweeping his front porch, a carpenter sawing wood, and the squeaking wheel of a freight wagon rolling down the street. From a nearby laundry, he heard the sing-song language of the Chinese as they went about their business.

Todd washed his face and hands in the water provided by the pitcher, then went downstairs to inquire about breakfast. The hotel had no dining room, but the clerk recommended the same restaurant in which Todd had eaten dinner last evening.

He was having his breakfast when Harold came in. The young cowboy was

105

disheveled and bristling with little pieces of straw.

"The man over at the hotel told me you was in here," Harold said.

"Yes," Todd answered with a chuckle. "I see you made good on your promise to spend the night in the stable."

"What do you mean?"

Todd picked a dangling straw off Harold's arm. "I should have joined you," he said.

"Yeah, I told you the night was just getting started. I had me a fine old time last night."

"No, I mean . . ." Todd started to explain that he meant the stable was probably preferable to the hotel room, but decided it would be impolite to criticize something that, to Harold, was probably very routine. "Never mind. So, you had a good time, did you?"

"Well, I reckon I did," Harold said. He rubbed his head. "Only thing is, I'm thinkin' maybe a horse stepped on my head during the night."

"Don't blame the horse for that. You brought that on yourself, I'm afraid. Even before I left you, you had already put away a prodigious amount of whiskey."

"What did I do?" Harold asked, not

understanding the word.

"You drank a lot," Todd said simply.

Harold smiled. "Well, that's good. I was stone-broke this morning, so I was sure hoping that I spent it all on whiskey. It would be a cryin' shame to think the money went to waste."

Todd laughed. "If the governing criteria is spending all of your money on drink, then it didn't go to waste."

"Damn, you talk smart. I can't wait for you to meet our cook. He's real smart, too. I got a feelin' the two of you are goin' to get along just fine."

"Well, I hope I get along with everyone," Todd said.

Harold chuckled. "Doc, if you don't mind my sayin' so, I can't imagine anyone settin' out to get on your bad side. You're about the *biggest* son of a bitch —" Harold stopped in mid-sentence and his eyes grew wide. He held out his hand. "I didn't mean nothin' by that," he said quickly. "I wasn't really callin' you no son of a bitch, it was just . . ."

Todd smiled. "No offense taken," he said.

"Whew. I'm some glad for that."

At that moment Todd's breakfast was brought to the table. It consisted of half a dozen eggs, a pound of bacon, and a huge stack of pancakes.

"As long as you're here, how about joining me for breakfast?" Todd invited.

"Breakfast?" Harold moaned and shook his head. "No, thank you."

"Come on, it'll do you good," Todd invited. "You can start on some of these pancakes and I'll order some more." He moved several of the pancakes onto his egg plate, then pushed the plate with the rest of the pancakes across the table in front of Harold.

Harold looked down at the pancakes with a pained expression on his face. His skin was the color of candle tallow. Closing his eyes, he pushed the plate back.

"No, but thank you kindly," he mumbled.

"Go on, eat. You'll feel better," Todd insisted, pushing the plate toward Harold again.

Harold opened his eyes and glared at Todd. "Tenderfoot, if you don't quit shovin' that food in my face, I swear to God I'm going to shoot you right where you are sitting."

"Really?" Todd replied with a chuckle. "You're going to just shoot me down before I've even had a chance to finish my breakfast?" He poured syrup on his pancakes.

"Well, maybe I won't shoot you. I'll just strangle you with my bare hands, and . . . ," Harold started, then, looking at Todd and his size, he stopped in mid-sentence and groaned. "Oh, please, Doc, can't you just have mercy on me?"

"All right," Todd laughed. "I won't insist that you eat breakfast. But I hope you don't mind if I do." Todd took a bite of his eggs.

"No, you go ahead, only I ain't plannin' on stayin' around to watch," Harold said. "I'm goin' on over to the stable to get the team hitched up for the drive back out to the ranch. You might want to come over there soon as you're finished. I reckon Miss Vavak will be about ready to go back home and it wouldn't be good to keep the boss's daughter waitin'."

"I'll be right over," Todd promised, mopping up some of the egg yellow with a syrup-covered pancake.

Groaning at the sight, Harold turned away and hurried out of the restaurant.

Roselyn and Cindy were waiting for Harold in the front parlor of the Murchison house.

"You will come to Trailback and visit me?" Roselyn said.

"Of course," Cindy replied.

"But not just for a day, you must come and stay several days."

"I wouldn't want to be a burden on your family."

"Nonsense, they would love to have you come." Roselyn looked up at the clock on the wall. "I don't understand what's keeping Harold. He should be here by now."

"I'm sure he will be along shortly."

"If he didn't get drunk last night," Roselyn said.

"Heavens, is that a possibility?"

"Possibility? It is more a probability," Roselyn said, and both girls laughed.

"Oh, here comes someone now," Cindy said, looking out the window. "Yes, that's him, for I recognize him from when he dropped you off yesterday. Oh, my!" she said.

"What? What is it?" Roselyn asked.

"Oh, my, who is that with him?"

Roselyn chuckled. "Probably the tenderfoot he came to pick up. He's a veterinarian. What is he, some little pipsqueak of a fellow?"

"Hardly that," Cindy said. "Come look."

110

Curious by Cindy's strange reaction, Roselyn walked over to the front window and looked out. She saw Harold stop the surrey, then step down and loop the reins over the hitching rail. But Harold was only in the periphery of her view, for what really caught her attention was the man sitting in the back seat. He was one of the biggest men she had ever seen. And one of the most handsome.

"I'm sure that isn't him," Roselyn said.

"Why are you sure? Have you ever seen this veterinarian before?"

"No, but, come on, Cindy. Does that look like a little pipsqueak of a tenderfoot to you?"

Cindy laughed. "Well, he might be a tenderfoot. But he is certainly no pipsqueak."

There was a knock on the front door, and Cindy opened it.

"Mornin', Miss Murchison," Harold said, touching the brim of his hat. "Is Miss Vavak here?"

"I'm right here, Harold," Roselyn called. "Would you mind collecting my luggage for me? I have some things from shopping, as well."

"Yes, ma'am, I'll be glad to gather them for you," Harold said, coming inside.

"Harold, who is that man in the surrey?"

111

"Why, that's Doc."

"Doc?"

"Doctor Bill Todd, the fella we come to town to get, Miss Vavak."

"*That* is Doctor Todd?"

"Yes, ma'am, that's him all right. It's some surprisin', ain't it? I mean, he sure don't look like no veterinarian I ever seen before. And he for sure don't look like no tenderfoot."

Harold walked outside with two bags, and several packages, with Roselyn following him. Seeing them coming up the brick walk, Todd got down from the surrey and hurried to relieve Harold of the two suitcases.

"Allow me," he said, taking both of them, and handling them with ease. He put them on the surrey behind the second seat, alongside his trunk. Then, as Harold was loading the packages, Todd turned and offered his hand to help Roselyn climb up.

"Thank you," Roselyn said. "I take it, you are Doctor Bill Todd?"

"Yes, ma'am," Todd replied.

"Well, welcome to Texas, Dr. Todd."

"Thank you," Todd said.

Ivan Vavak met the surrey when it pulled

to a stop in front of the house. Todd had seen him once, years ago, and recognized him immediately. Then, when he saw the curious way Vavak was looking at him, he had a moment's apprehension that he might be recognized as well.

"Dr. Todd?" Vavak asked.

"Yes."

"It is welcome, you are, to Trailback," Vavak said, extending his hand. Todd shook it.

"Thank you, sir."

"Roselyn, your visit with your friend, it was good?"

"Yes, Papa. It was good. I bought a few things," she said, nodding toward the packages in the back of the surrey.

Vavak chuckled. "I think it is many things you have bought. I hope all of my money you did not spend."

Todd reached for Roselyn's bags but Harold waved him off, saying some of the other hands would take care of it. "You got your own trunk to take care of," Vavak said.

"Where do I go?" Todd asked.

"Dr. Todd, in the bunkhouse there is place for you if, with the cowboys, you don't mind sleeping," Vavak said.

"I don't mind at all," Todd replied,

picking up his trunk and putting it on his shoulder.

Vavak looked on in surprise, then glanced over at Harold. Harold chuckled.

"Somethin' maybe you ought to know about this fella," Harold said. "He's a strong one."

"Oh, and Dr. Todd," Vavak called. "It is dinner with our family you will have tonight?"

Todd nodded. "Yes, thank you. That's very nice of you."

John Harder was in the bunkhouse when Todd stepped inside. Like Harold before him, he was somewhat taken back by Todd's size. Most cowboys were relatively small in stature. Smaller men were generally more nimble, could get in and out of tight spots, and could work a herd of cattle easier than larger men. Their smaller size was also good for the endurance of the horse they rode, especially if they were going to spend many hours in the saddle. As a result, larger men were uncommon on a ranch, and a man as large as Todd was rare indeed.

"I was told I would be bunking in here," Todd said.

"Uh, yeah," John replied. He pointed to a bunk in the corner. "I reckon that one would be yours. If it's big enough," he added.

Todd chuckled. "Thanks, I'm used to making do," he said. He put his trunk down at the foot of the bed, then came over and extended his hand to John. "Bill Todd," he said.

"You that veterinarian Harold went to pick up?"

"Yes."

"You're the one that's going to change all our cows?"

"If you're talking about selling off the Longhorns, and bringing in Herefords, the answer is yes. That's my job."

"That's what Mr. Vavak wants to do, is it?"

"Well, it's what Mr. Williams wants to do," Todd said.

"I thought Mr. Williams died."

"I'm talking about his son."

"Humph," John snorted. "If you ask me, his snot-nosed son should just leave well enough alone. We've been doin' just fine with Longhorns all this time. Why change now?"

"I take it you aren't in favor of switching to Herefords?"

"No, I ain't," John said. "And there ain't nobody on this here ranch who is.

Includin' Mr. Vavak."

"Well then, it appears that I will have my work cut out in trying to change everyone's mind, doesn't it?" Todd said.

The subject came up again over the dinner table that night.

"What about Mr. Williams?" Roselyn asked. "Is this something he wanted to do?"

"You would be talking about Endicott Williams?" Todd asked.

"Well, I'm certainly not talking about that wastrel son of his."

"Wastrel?" Todd asked, surprised by the unflattering reference. "What makes you think Todd Williams is a wastrel?"

"Well, let's see, he races yachts, he's made a grand tour of Europe, and I've heard that there is scarcely a party in New York that he doesn't attend. He seems hell bent on spending his father's money as fast as he can. I can hardly imagine him taking any interest in Trailback."

"Have you ever met him?" Todd asked, wondering if she remembered when he came to Texas with his father.

"Once, many years ago," Roselyn said.

"What did you think of him then?"

"I didn't think of him, one way or the

other," Roselyn replied.

"Oh?" Alice said, with a little laugh. "Seems to me you moped around here after he left, certain that you were in love with him."

"Mama!" Roselyn said. "That was the crush of a foolish ten-year-old girl."

"True, but you can't tell Doctor Todd that you didn't think of young Mr. Williams one way or the other," Alice said.

"That was a long time ago."

"So, Mr. Williams came out here for a visit, did he?" Todd asked.

"Yes. The young Williams we met when with his father he came to visit," Vavak explained. "He was a good boy."

"That's the problem," Roselyn said. "He is still a boy, with the games he plays. He is someone who has never had to work a day in his life, yet he has absolutely no hesitation about disrupting our lives with this insane notion of introducing a new breed of cattle. Why couldn't he just leave well enough alone? He should go race a yacht or something."

"Oh, I don't think he's as bad as all that," Todd said.

"You have met him?" Roselyn asked.

"Yes."

"Yes, of course you would have met him,

you are out here to do his dirty work for him."

"Roselyn," Vavak said. "He is our guest, Dr. Todd."

Roselyn shook her head, then held up her hand. "I'm sorry, Dr. Todd, you are just a man who is hired to do a job. I have no right taking all this out on you. Please forgive me."

"Why should someone have to be forgiven for expressing her honest opinion?" Todd replied. "I know that my job here is going to be difficult. But, I sincerely believe I can win all of you over to my side."

"Your side?" Roselyn asked, looking at him suspiciously. "Wait a minute, was this all your idea? This crazy notion to introduce a new breed of cattle onto the range?"

"I plead guilty to the charge," Todd replied.

"What gives you the right to interfere like that?" Roselyn demanded. "Have you ever spent one day on a ranch?"

"Once, many years ago."

"So you weren't raised on a ranch?"

"No."

"I didn't think so. So, where did you come up with the idea to replace Longhorns with Herefords? Was that something you learned in veterinarian school?"

"That's where I first got the idea, yes."

"Then you aren't just a man doing a job, are you? You are a man on a mission, a personal mission, as it turns out. I can see now that my anger was misdirected. I shouldn't be mad at the young Mr. Williams. No doubt he is off enjoying himself somewhere right now. You are the one I should be angry with, for taking advantage of his naiveté and our vulnerability. What a disingenuous person you turned out to be."

"Roselyn! We don't speak to our dinner guests in such a way," Alice said, obviously upset with Roselyn's behavior.

"Again, I apologize," Roselyn said. She stood up. "However, it seems that I've lost my appetite. I think it would be better if I went to my room. Please excuse me."

When Roselyn stood, Todd stood as well.

"A scalawag with manners," Roselyn said when he stood. "How quaint."

For someone brought up in affluence, Todd's introduction to the bunkhouse was quite an awakening. Dimly lit by two kerosene-burning lanterns, the entire room was in shadows. The cowboys' spare clothes were hanging from nails by each bunk, though a surprising number of clothes were lying on the floor.

The room reeked of kerosene, boots, dirty clothes, chewing tobacco, and the sour stench of bodies too long between baths. And though the odor was almost overwhelming, none of the cowboys seemed to notice.

"This here is my pard," Harold said, introducing Todd to the other cowboys. "He's a good man, and I wouldn't take too kindly to anyone who starts trying to razz him 'cause he's a tenderfoot."

"Hell, Harold, who's goin' to be crazy enough to try 'n razz a fella who is the size of a grizzly bear?" John asked, and the others laughed.

"So, you had dinner with the boss man, did you?" Dewayne asked. "Mr. Vavak is a good man. I hope you were on your best manners."

Recalling Roselyn's comment about a "scalawag with manners," Todd smiled. "I tried to be," he said.

"What did Mr. Vavak think about you wantin' to change ever'thing all around?" Don asked.

"You mean sell off the Longhorn and

introduce Herefords?"

"Yeah."

"I think he's going to go along with it."

"Well, I ain't in favor of it," Don said.

"Why not?" Todd asked.

"Herdin' a bunch of milk cows? We're goin' to wind up the laughing stock of the range," Don said.

"They aren't exactly milk cows," Todd said. "In fact, the Hereford is bigger than the Longhorn."

"Yeah, well, even so, it ain't somethin' I'm looking forward to," Dewayne said.

"Do all of you feel like that?" Todd asked. He looked at Harold.

"I reckon we do," Don said. "But that don't mean we ain't goin' to go along with it. If that's what Mr. Vavak wants us to do, why, I reckon we'll do it."

"One thing for sure, we won't have to be worryin' 'bout no cattle rustlers," Harold said. "Won't nobody want them things."

The others laughed.

"Have you ever had to deal with rustlers?" Todd asked.

"We haven't had no real problems," Harold replied. He took out his pistol and began spinning the cylinder. "I reckon they know that we could handle things if they tried."

"Yeah, you're quite the gunman, you are," John said derisively.

"Well, I ain't no Lucien Shardeen, if that's what you mean. But I reckon I could handle myself if it come right down to it."

"Lucien Shardeen? Who, or what, is Lucien Shardeen?" Todd asked.

"He's about the deadliest gunman there ever was," Harold said. "That's who he is."

"Shardeen couldn't hold a candle to Cold Blood Collier," John said.

"And who is that?"

"His real name was Cole Collier," Harold replied.

"Was?"

"Don't nobody know if he is alive or not," John explained. "Some time ago, he had a shootout up in Puxico, that's a town no more'n fifty miles from here. He went up against four men at the same time, and killed them all. Ain't nobody else ever done nothin' like that. Includin' not even Lucien Shardeen," he added, looking at Harold.

"Maybe. And maybe Collier could beat him, if he was still around. But the two ain't never run into each other which is why I don't think he's still alive."

"Why doesn't anyone know?" Todd asked.

"That big shootout up in Puxico I told you about? Cold Blood Collier ain't never been heard from again since then."

"I think he's dead," Don said.

"He ain't dead," Dewayne said.

"He was shot in that fight," Harold said. "Folks say he was shot up real bad. He rode out of town, holding his guts in with his hand."

"Wasn't all that bad," Dewayne insisted.

"Nevertheless, nobody's heard from him since that time."

"Whoowee, wouldn't it be somethin' if he was still alive and him 'n Shardeen went up against each other?" Harold said. "Man oh man, would I like to see that happen."

"Who would you want to win?" Don asked.

Harold thought for a moment before he replied. "Collier, I reckon," he said.

"Why is that?" Todd asked.

"Because Shardeen is an evil man."

"Sounds to me like they are both evil men. I mean, if they are both killers, how could they be anything else?" Todd asked.

"I don't know as I'd say Collier was an evil man," Harold said. "I mean, he done his share of stealin', rustlin', and killin', that's for sure. But don't know as he ever

123

killed anyone who wasn't tryin' to kill him."

"What about Shardeen?"

Harold shook his head. "He's killed a lot of men, maybe even more'n Collier. But it seems like Shardeen enjoys it. They say he's always goadin' someone into goin' up against him."

"So, if they was to go up against each other, who do you think would be faster?" Dewayne asked. "Shardeen or Collier?"

"I don't know," Harold answered. "In his prime, I don't think anybody could'a beat Cold Blood Collier. But, if he's still alive, he has to be gettin' some old, now. He probably don't have the speed he used to have. I guess I'd have to say Shardeen would beat him."

"If that's the case, then I don't want to see them go against each other," Don said. "I wouldn't want to see Shardeen kill Collier."

At that moment a small, almost bent, man came into the bunkhouse.

"Hey, Mr. Crites," Harold called to him. "Who do you think would be the fastest? Cold Blood Collier or Lucien Shardeen?"

"It doesn't matter," Crites answered.

"What do you mean, it doesn't matter?"

"It doesn't matter because they aren't fighting," Crites said.

"Well, we know that. But we was just wonderin' who would be the fastest, is all."

"How many fairies can dance on the head of a pin?" Crites replied.

"What?"

Todd laughed. "I think what Mr. Crites has just told you is that you are attempting to fathom the unfathomable."

"You must be the veterinarian, Dr. Todd," Crites said, looking at Todd.

"I am," Todd said.

"Except you can just call him Doc," Harold said.

"I would not do that until invited to do so," Crites replied.

"By all means, address me in whatever way is most comfortable for you," Todd said.

"Where did you go to school?" Crites asked.

"Princeton."

"Young Mr. Williams went there, as well, didn't he?" Crites asked.

"Yes, that's where we met."

"I believe Princeton was started as a Presbyterian seminary," Crites said. "Does it still serve that purpose?"

"Yes, it does. Though, it has expanded

far beyond that now," Todd said.

"So I have heard. It seems that many schools that started as seminaries have expanded into more disciplines," Crites said. "Though one can't help but wonder if deteriorated would not be a better description."

"There are those who would make that case," Todd said, surprised to find himself in such a conversation with a ranch cook.

"And indeed, I count myself in that number," Crites replied. "Welcome to Trailback, Dr. Todd. I hope your stay here is enjoyable."

"Thank you," Todd said.

With a nod, Crites turned, and walked to the far end of the bunkhouse, then passed through a door that Todd noticed for the first time.

"Whooee, that Mr. Crites is somethin', ain't he, Doc? You ever met anyone as smart as he is?"

Todd shook his head. "I don't know," he said. "I'm not sure that I have." He pointed to the door. "Where does that door go?"

"It goes into Mr. Crites's room," Harold said.

"The cook has his own room?"

"You bet he does. And there don't nobody ever go in there either, but what they are invited."

SEVEN

In his room, Crites opened the trunk at the foot of his bed. Prominent in the trunk, and quite noticeable because of their juxtaposition, were an ecclesiastic stole and a Colt .44 pistol, tucked into an unadorned and well-worn leather holster.

Moving the pistol to one side, Crites picked up the stole, held it to his lips, kissed it, then draped it around his neck. Kneeling at the side of his bunk, Crites began to pray. It was a prayer of contrition, the General Confession, taken from the Episcopal Book of Common Prayer. It was the same prayer he had said every day for twenty-seven years, since August 21st, 1858.

Almighty God, Father of our Lord Jesus Christ, maker of all things, judge of all men; I acknowledge and bewail my manifold sins and wickedness which I, from time to time, most grievously have committed, by thought, word and deed, against thy Divine Majesty, provoking most justly thy wrath and indignation against me. I do earnestly repent, and am heartily sorry for these my misdoings. The burden of them is intolerable. Have mercy upon me. Have mercy upon me, most merciful Father; for thy Son our Lord Jesus Christ's sake. Forgive me all that is past; and grant that I may ever hereafter serve and please thee in newness of life, to the honor and glory of thy name; through Jesus Christ our Lord. Amen.

Finished with the prayer, Crites returned the stole to the trunk, then took out a copy of Ralph Waldo Emerson's *The Conduct of Life*. Crites was a man looking for answers. More than that, he was looking for absolution. Would he find it in the writings of this one-time Unitarian minister turned Transcendentalist?

He read until his eyelids grew heavy. Lowering the book to his chest, he decided he would rest . . . just for a moment.

Lawrence, Kansas, Friday, August 21st, 1858:

More than four-hundred men had ridden through the star-filled, moonless night. They were Quantrill's Raiders, though those who feared them most called them Bushwhackers and that became a sobriquet that the men wore as a badge of pride. At the head of the column was their leader, William Clark Quantrill. Quantrill called himself a lieutenant colonel in the Confederate Army, though no such rank had ever been officially bestowed upon him.

Just as the sun was coming up, a red disc on the horizon behind them, they arrived at the outskirts of the small town of Lawrence, Kansas. Quantrill held up his hand, bringing the column to a halt.

For a moment, the riders were quiet, staring down at the just awakening town.

A rooster crowed.

A dog barked.

A baby cried.

Bill Anderson, Quantrill's second-in-command, rode up alongside his leader, spit out a wad of tobacco, then wiped his mouth with the back of his hand.

"Look down there," Quantrill said. "They don't suspect a thing. They are ripe for the picking."

"Could be they're waitin' on us," Anderson said.

The door opened at the rear of one of the homes and a man started across the backyard toward the outhouse, adjusting his galluses as he walked.

"Does it look to you like they are waiting on us?" Quantrill asked, as the man went inside and closed the door.

"Well, they're not going to be hangin' out welcome signs to let us know they're waitin' on us, are they?" Anderson replied. "If they're planning on ambushing us, why I reckon this is the way they'd want the town to look."

Quantrill looked at his second-in-command, then, with an evil, twisted smile, he pulled his pistol.

"Charge!" he shouted, firing the pistol into the air.

The four-hundred men started forward at a gallop.

On the outer edge of town, a middle-aged man was heading to his barn with a milking stool in one hand and the milk bucket in the other. Curious about the sound of thundering hooves, he put the stool and bucket down, then walked out to the front gate to see what was going on.

"Kill him!" Quantrill shouted, pointing to the man as the raiders galloped by.

Several of the riders fired at the same time and the man paid for his curiosity, dying from more than a dozen bullet wounds.

A small Union Army detachment was encamped in the middle of Main Street. Like the man with the milk pail, they were more curious than alarmed by the unusual activity of hundreds of riders coming into town. More experienced soldiers would have sensed danger and armed themselves, but these were not experienced soldiers. These were men recently mustered into the service, waiting to be sent east to join the fighting, and they came out of their tents, half-dressed, rubbing the sleep from their eyes.

"Yankees!" Quantrill shouted, and he began firing at the soldiers. The other Bushwhackers followed suit and the young, inexperienced soldiers were cut down like sheep in a slaughtering pen.

A few of the townspeople came out into the street, many still in their nightgowns, and seeing what was happening, retreated back into their houses.

With most of the Union soldiers now lying in the street dead, or gravely wounded, Quantrill turned his attention to the townspeople.

"People of Lawrence!" he shouted. "Turn out! Turn out into the street, now!"

No one came.

Quantrill nodded at Anderson, who

tossed a flaming brand onto the shake roof of the apothecary. The roof caught fire and, within a few moments, the entire building was ablaze.

"I'm going to burn every house and building in Lawrence, whether anyone is in them or not," Quantrill shouted. "So, if you don't want to get roasted alive, you'd better come out now."

With that shout, several came outside.

"Now, that's more like it," Quantrill said. Looking around, he saw that he was in front of the hotel. "Where's the manager of this hotel?" he asked.

"I'm right here, sir," a man said, stepping down from the porch. Unlike most of the others, he was dressed, and he finished buttoning his vest, even as he approached Quantrill.

"I want you to prepare breakfast," Quantrill said.

The hotel manager looked at Quantrill's army and blanched.

"For all these men, sir?"

"No, just for me," Quantrill replied. "The rest of my men will fend for themselves." He twisted in his saddle, then yelled out at the town. "Townspeople! My men will be your guests for breakfast. Give them anything they want."

"If you think my wife is going to fix breakfast for any of you Rebel trash, you're crazy," someone said.

Quantrill nodded to one of his men, and the protesting citizen was shot down.

"Anyone else have anything to say?" Quantrill asked.

The townspeople were silent.

"Men," Quantrill said, addressing his own soldiers. "I want you to visit every store and select the best merchandise the store has to offer. Visit every house, eat breakfast where you wish, and take all the jewels and money you can find. If anyone protests, kill them. Bill, you go to the bank. Have the banker open his vault and clean it out. Clean out the cash drawers, too."

"Right," Anderson said.

As the men started to carry out Quantrill's orders, Quantrill called Archie Clement over to him. Archie was his third-in-command.

"Archie, I have a special job for you."

"What job is that, Charley?" Archie replied, using the name by which Quantrill's men called him.

"I want every male between the ages of fifteen and sixty, killed. See to it."

Archie grinned. "Yeah," he said. "That'll be fun."

"I thought you might like that."

"Hold on, Colonel, are you sure you want to do that?" one of Quantrill's lieutenants asked.

Quantrill looked at the young lieutenant. "If we don't, who is to say the men of this town wouldn't organize, and try to ambush us on the way out of town. I'm just looking out for my men, that's all."

"But, every *one*, between fifteen and sixty? That seems unnecessarily harsh. The Yankee press is already having a field day with us. What do you think they are going to do with this?"

"This is war. People get killed in war."

The lieutenant stood there for a long moment, staring at Quantrill.

"Are you going to disobey my orders, Lieutenant?"

"No."

Quantrill smiled, and put his hand on the young lieutenant's shoulder. "I didn't think you would. Don't worry, you can pray over them, if you want," he said. "There's probably some prayer already written for just such a thing. Look in that prayer book you carry."

The lieutenant shook his head. "I don't think there is a prayer for massacre," he said.

The systematic killing began, and as word spread of what was going on, the men tried to run. For the most part, running did nothing to save them, but merely provided additional entertainment for Quantrill's Raiders. Bushwhackers on horseback would chase the men down, then kill them, sometimes by shooting, sometimes by clubbing, and sometimes by saber thrusts.

The lieutenant began firing as well, but he killed only two and he justified the shootings by the fact that the two he killed were armed. However, he didn't let himself carry that logic to its next step — the realization that they were armed only because they were trying to defend themselves.

The lieutenant spurred his horse into a gallop and darted between two houses. In the back of the house he saw a woman and two young girls backed up against the side of a stone cistern. The mother and her daughters were holding their skirts out, trying to form a screen, but the screen wasn't effective. Behind their skirts the lieutenant could quite easily see a man, holding a young boy close to him.

The lieutenant pointed his pistol toward them, motioning for the woman and her daughters to step aside. With a look of fear and defiance, the woman shook her head, no.

The lieutenant stared at her for a long moment, then fired two shots into the air. The woman screamed.

"You two," he said to the man and boy. "Lie down on your stomach and play dead. You," he said to the woman, "cry over them."

For a moment, no one moved.

"You need any help back there, lieutenant?" one of the Bushwhackers called from the front.

"No, I just killed two of them," the lieutenant replied. Then he looked at the man and the boy. "If you want to live, do what I said," he ordered harshly.

Hesitantly, and with fear obvious in his face, the man came out from behind the women and got down on his stomach. He was joined a second later by the boy.

"Don't move until we are gone," the lieutenant said.

"God bless you," the woman said, now realizing what he was doing.

"Bless me, madam?" the lieutenant replied. He shook his head. "On the contrary. God has damned me for all time."

From somewhere on the street, one of the Bushwhackers laughed loudly.

★ ★ ★

Crites was jarred awake by a loud laugh coming from the bunkhouse.

"Damn, Harold, if that ain't about the funniest thing I ever heard!" Dewayne was saying. "What happened next?"

"Well, then Posey said . . ." Harold continued with his story, but Crites could hear only the low mumble of his voice. Whatever story Harold was relating elicited another loud laugh, just like the one that had awakened him.

Crites held his hands out in front of him, examining them closely. "Out, out, damned spot," he said, quietly.

Over the next several days Trailback was a beehive of activity, getting ready for the big changeover. The first thing they had to do was bring in the cattle from the free range, weed out the ones that weren't wearing their brand and pen them up for their rightful owners. They also put on the Trailback brand, which was a backward slanting curly line, representing a trail.

The round-up was exciting. Thousands of hooves churned up the ground so that the air was thick with dust, and redolent of the musk of the hot sun beating down on the skin of the cattle. On the first day,

Todd watched it all from the back of a horse. He was amazed by the adroitness of the cowboys as they darted about, moving as one with their horse, almost as if they and the animal shared the same musculature.

Amazingly, Roselyn was riding with the cowboys, and she seemed as quick and athletic as any of them.

"Hear! Hear cow!" Roselyn called, darting after one maverick that broke away from the others and started trotting off on his own. Guiding Pepper only by pressure from her knees, Roselyn leaned forward in her saddle, whirling the lariat over her head to keep the loop open. When she was close enough, she tossed it toward the fleeing animal. The rope dropped over the calf's head, and Roselyn twisted her end around her saddle horn. Pepper came to a stop, hunkering down on his back legs. The calf was jerked off its feet, then it got up, shook its head, and trotted back toward the herd.

"She's something, isn't she, Doc?" a voice said from behind Todd. Twisting in his saddle, he saw that Ken Crites had brought the chuck wagon out.

"What?" Todd asked.

"Miss Vavak," Crites said. "I saw you

watching her."

"Uh, yes," Todd said. "I'm amazed at her skill as a rider."

"You shouldn't be. She grew up here, and could sit a horse before she could walk. How's your backside holding out?"

"I beg your pardon?"

"It is no secret that sitting in a saddle all day long, especially if one isn't used to it, can cause quite a bit of discomfort in the posterior," Crites said.

"Posterior discomfort," Todd said. Smiling he stood up in his stirrups and rubbed his backside. It felt raw. "A most astute observation, Mr. Crites."

"It doesn't take a great deal of perception to see that you are hurting. Why don't you tie your horse onto the back of the wagon and stay here?" Crites invited. "When I go back, you can ride with me. This isn't a king's carriage, you understand, but I promise you, it will be considerably more comfortable for you than sitting in a saddle all day." Crites smiled. "And, considering your size, I think it more than likely that your horse will appreciate it as well."

"Thanks," Todd said. He swung down from the saddle and tied the horse onto the back of the chuck wagon. "And you may be right about the horse."

Of all the ranch hands, Todd found Ken Crites to be the most intriguing. His job as cook was the least adventurous of any on the ranch, yet all the cowboys seemed to have a great deal of respect for the little, bandy-legged man. He was sometimes their arbitrator, often their counselor, and always their teacher. And while he was older than all the ranch hands, Todd got the idea that his position of respect was earned by more than seniority.

"Can you lay a fire?" Crites asked.

"Yes."

"Get one started right there," Crites said, pointing.

Todd rounded up the wood, laid it out where Crites indicated, then got the fire started. Crites erected a steel frame over the fire then hung the coffee pot. After that, he went around to the back of the wagon and began rolling out biscuits.

"If you are of a mind to help, you might peel some potatoes and carrots," Crites said. "I plan to make a stew for lunch."

"Be glad to," Todd said.

The two men worked together in silence for a while, then Todd pointed toward the coffee pot. "May I have a cup of coffee?"

"Yes, you may. And I appreciate your

141

asking," Crites said. "Most would've just tried to help themselves."

"Tried to help themselves?" Todd asked.

"Without success," Crites replied simply.

Todd poured himself a cup of coffee, then, when he turned around, he saw that Crites was offering him something else.

"I made some sinkers fresh this morning," he said. "They go good with coffee."

Todd looked at the pastry, then chuckled. "Back home, we call these doughnuts."

"Yes, I know they are called that," Crites said. "But I thought you might appreciate knowing our name for them."

"I do appreciate it, thanks." Todd broke the doughnut in half, and dunked one end into the coffee before he took a bite. "Uhmm, good," he said.

"There was once a range war fought over a cook who could make good sinkers," Crites said.

"Really? You aren't the cook they were fighting over, are you?"

Crites chuckled. "No, I don't flatter myself that these are good enough to start a range war."

"You don't talk like the others I've met out here," Todd said.

"You mean because I don't fracture grammar?"

"Something like that, I guess," Todd said. "Have you always been a cook?"

"No."

"What else have you done?"

"I've done more things than I care to talk about," Crites answered, and Todd was perceptive enough to know that this was a courteous way of letting him know that he wasn't ready to share that information. Todd changed the subject.

"Looks like everyone is coming around to the new plan," Todd suggested, nodding toward Roselyn and the cowboys who were busily working the herd.

"They aren't coming around at all," Crites said.

"What do you mean? Look at them. They're working hard as they can."

"They're working hard because they are loyal to Mr. Vavak, and he asked them to," Crites said. "But if you want them to really get behind the plan, you need to win them over."

"How would I do that?"

"Tell me something about the Hereford," Crites said. "Why are you so hell-bent on getting rid of the Longhorns and raising the Herefords?"

"They are a more desirable breed of cow."

"Desirable? You mean they are hardier than the Longhorn? They're more likely to take care of themselves?"

"Well, no," Todd said. "Fact is, the Longhorn is a little more self-sufficient. The Herefords will probably mean more work for the cowboys."

"If that's the case, what is so desirable about them?"

"Well, for one thing, the meat is a whole lot better. And for another, each cow weighs almost twice as much as the average Longhorn. Also, they bring a higher price per pound. That means the ranch will make more money."

"For Mr. Williams," Crites said.

"For Mr. Williams, yes," Todd agreed. "After all, it is his ranch."

"Uh-huh."

"But for Mr. Vavak as well," Todd added quickly. "He's on shares, so the more the ranch makes, the more he will make."

"I see."

"I thought you might. I just wish the cowboys could see it."

"Look at it the way the cowboys are looking at it," Crites suggested. "What you are telling them is, they are to get rid of the

Longhorn and replace it with a cow that's bigger, but not nearly as hardy."

"Yes."

"But this bigger cow is going to make better meat, so some fat gentleman will have a better steak in some fancy New York restaurant."

"That's pretty much the size of it, yes."

"And all this is going to make Mr. Williams and Mr. Vavak a lot of money."

"Yes, I, uh, I think I see what you're getting at," Todd said. "There's really nothing in it for the cowboy, is there?"

"I'm not saying that," Crites said. "Fact is, there is something to be said for knowing your job will still be here. Ranches that don't make money can't afford cowboys. That means everyone on the ranch, from Mr. Williams to Mr. Vavak, all the way down to young Don Walton, want what's best for the ranch."

"That's good to know," Todd said.

At lunchtime, Todd came in for some good-natured ribbing from the cowboys, because he had obviously abandoned his horse for the chuck wagon.

Over the next few days of the round-up, Todd made no effort to ride a horse. Instead, he went out every day with Crites. But he wasn't just a freeloader; he made himself useful, gathering wood and building the fires, washing pots and pans, peeling potatoes, and generally handling any job Crites gave him.

Just before lunch one day, Vavak rode out to the cow camp. Swinging down from his horse, he walked over to pour himself a cup of coffee.

"Dr. Todd, his work is good?" Vavak asked, nodding toward Todd, who was peeling potatoes.

"Yes, sir, it is," Crites said. "Most new hands are more trouble than they're worth. You have to go behind them to clean up their mistakes. But Doc doesn't make many mistakes. And he doesn't complain. That's all the more surprising because he's not here to be a hired hand, he's here to be a vet. He's a good man, Mr. Vavak."

"I am glad he is not trouble for you."

"Mr. Vavak! Mr. Vavak!"

Looking toward the sound, they saw Dewayne Blackwell, bent forward in the saddle, slapping the reins from side to side as he urged his animal on. The horse was at a full gallop with clods of dirt flying up from its drumming hooves.

Vavak, Todd, and Crites hurried out to meet him.

"Here, Dewayne, what is wrong?" Vavak asked.

"It's Timmy Baker, Mr. Vavak," Dewayne said, "He's got hisself in a heap of trouble."

"What has happened?" Crites asked.

"A fallen tree has rolled over on him."

"Is he hurt?" Vavak asked.

"I think he's got a broke leg," Dewayne said. "But we can't get him out."

"I will come."

"Doc, I know you're a vet and not a people doctor, but I reckon you know something about broke bones, don't you?" Dewayne said to Todd.

"Yes, a little," Todd said.

"Then, maybe it'd be good if you would come, too."

"I'll need a way there. I came out in the chuck wagon today."

"Take my horse," Dewayne said. "I'll get another one from the remuda."

"Thanks," Todd said, climbing into the saddle of Dewayne's horse.

It took Todd and Vavak about five minutes to reach the place where the accident happened. It wasn't hard to find, nearly all the cowboys in the round-up were standing around a rent in the earth, looking down into a deep gulley. Roselyn was there, as well, the expression on her face showing her concern over the young man in trouble.

"Papa," Roselyn said when Todd and Vavak arrived. "We've got to do something. Poor Timmy is suffering so."

Dismounting, Todd and Vavak hurried over to the edge of the ravine and looked down. What they saw was a large log at the bottom of the gulley, with Timmy Baker pinned beneath it.

Todd had met Timmy Baker the first day he arrived. Only Don was younger than Timmy. Todd and Timmy had gotten on right away, because, like Todd, Timmy was from the East. His father was a policeman in Philadelphia, and Timmy had been to New York several times so he and Todd were able to share stories about the city.

Timmy was popular with the other men as well, even though he was from the East. He had adapted quickly, and he worked hard without complaint which was all a man needed to do to be accepted by the others.

"Timmy, are you in pain?" Todd called down.

"It hurt some when it first happened," Timmy replied. "But to tell the truth, it ain't hurtin' all that much now."

"How did this happen?" Todd asked.

"That there log was up here on the edge of the gulley," John explained. "And they was a maverick that somehow got hung up in it, so Timmy tried to get the critter loose. Well, the next thing you know, the log rolled down to the bottom and took Timmy with it."

"Can't we lift the log off him?" Todd asked.

John shook his head. "We done tried. But the bottom is so narrow that we can't get more'n two men down there, and that log is just too heavy for two men to lift."

"What about tie rope and pull?" Vavak asked.

"We ain't got a rope long enough to reach," Harold said.

"Maybe if we tie two or three ropes together?" Roselyn suggested.

"If we do that, and the ropes come undone, why, the log could fall back on him," John said. "And that would make things worse than they are now."

"What if we doubled the rope," Roselyn suggested. "That way, if one of them comes undone, the other would hold it."

"That's an idea. What do you think about that, Doc?" John asked. But when he looked around, Todd was halfway down the gully.

"What's he doin'?" John asked.

"He's a doctor. Maybe he just wants a closer look," Harold said.

"Well, he ain't a people doctor," Don said. "He's an animal doctor."

"Animals has got bones, too, ain't they?" Harold asked.

The men and Roselyn moved a little closer to the edge of the gulley so they could get a better view. By now, Todd had reached the bottom.

"Well, Timmy, you seem to have gotten yourself in quite a fix," Todd said, as he squatted alongside the log for a closer look.

"I reckon I have," Timmy replied.

"It's not exactly like being on Market Street in Philadelphia, is it?"

Despite his situation, Timmy chuckled. "No, it ain't. Listen, you fellas goin' to be able to get me out of here, or what?"

"Oh, I think we'll get you out, all right," Todd said, reassuringly. He reached down to feel Timmy's leg, then jerked his hand back when he felt the bone protruding. Timmy had suffered a compound fracture. He put his hand back and pressed against the wound. "Can you feel that?" he asked.

"Feel what?" Timmy asked.

The leg was numb. Although it kept Timmy from being in unbearable pain, it was a bad sign because it meant all the circulation was cut off. Todd knew that if they didn't get him out soon, it could become gangrenous, and if that happened, Timmy would lose his leg, or worse.

Todd studied the log that held him pinned down.

"I couldn't get myself pinned under a little branch," Timmy said, when he noticed what Todd was looking at. "No, sir, I had to pick a tree. And not a little tree, either. Like as not, you could get enough lumber from this one tree to build an entire house."

"Oh, it's not all that bad," Todd said as he continued to examine the log. Then he found what he was looking for, a place where he could not only grab hold, but also have good purchase with his legs. He bent down and grabbed the log.

"What you doin'?" Timmy asked.

"When I lift this log, I want you to scoot out from under it," Todd said. "It's going to be hard because you won't be able to use this leg. But you are going to have to get out from under the log."

"Damn, Doc, they can't no two men can

lift this log. You ain't plannin' on tryin' to do it all by yourself, are you?"

"Get ready," Todd said.

"What the hell? What if you can't do it, and you just get it up far enough to drop it on me again?"

Todd didn't answer. Instead, he strained, grunted, and lifted. The log came up.

"You done it!" Timmy said.

"Crawl out from under there," Todd said, his voice strained with the effort of holding up the log.

"Oh, shit, that leg won't move," Timmy said.

"Use your other leg, your arms, and hands," Todd said. "But get out of there, now!"

Suddenly Harold appeared, having climbed down when he saw what was going on. Harold reached down, grabbed Timmy under the arms, then he pulled the young cowboy free.

"He's out!" Harold said.

Todd wanted to drop the log, but he was afraid if he did, it would roll again, and this time trap Timmy and Harold. That meant he had to set it down gently. Feeling it in his back, legs, and arms, he put the log down, then, straightened up with a relieved sigh.

"How are we going to get him back up?" Harold asked.

Without another word, Todd picked Timmy up and draped him across his shoulder.

"Drop a rope down here!" Harold called, and a rope was lowered immediately. Although the rope wasn't long enough to tie around the log, it did fall far enough down into the gulley to reach. Todd grabbed it with one hand and started to climb, then noticed, gratefully, that there were people on the other side, pulling on the rope, helping him with his climb.

By the time Todd reached the top, Crites had brought the chuck wagon to the scene. Todd laid Timmy down, then tore off the cowboy's trouser leg.

"Damn, Doc, what're you doin'? I ain't got me but one more pair of pants," Timmy complained.

"Don't worry, Timmy, Mama and I will sew this pants leg back on for you and the trousers will be as good as new, I promise," Roselyn said.

"Well, now, wearin' somethin' you sewed," Timmy said. "That'd be real nice. Yes, ma'am, that'd be just real nice. Go ahead, Doc. You can tear the other leg off, too, if you want."

Todd laughed. "I don't think that will be necessary."

Todd examined the leg closely. The break was in the tibia, halfway between the knee and the ankle. The wound was bloody, red, and blue, where the bone stuck out.

"Oh, that looks bad, don't it, Doc?" Don asked. "We goin' to have to cut that leg off?"

"What?" Timmy shouted in alarm.

"Don!" Roselyn said, glaring at the young cowboy.

"I don't think it's that bad," Todd said in a calming voice. "There is no arterial or venous hemorrhaging. The bleeding appears to be capillary, and that's good."

"You hear all those big words he's usin', Don?" Timmy asked. "Those are doctor's words. I guess he knows more about it than you do, and he said it wasn't all that bad."

"I didn't mean nothin' by it, Timmy," Don said. "I was just worried some, that's all."

"Well, don't you be worryin' about it. I guess my leg will heal up enough for me to kick you in the ass whenever you need it," Timmy said, and the others, including Don, laughed.

"Mr. Crites?" Todd said.

"Yes, Doc?"

"Would you bring me some vinegar and baking soda, please?"

Crites hurried the items over to him. Todd sprinkled generous amounts of baking soda over the wound, then he poured vinegar onto the baking soda. The solution began bubbling and boiling over the wound.

"Oh, good idea," Crites said.

"Good idea? Look at that! What's happening?" Harold asked.

"Vinegar is a mild acid, baking soda is a base," Crites explained. "Doc is using the chemical reaction between them to clean out the wound."

Todd waited until the reaction subsided, then, gently, he brushed away the residue. The result was a much cleaner wound. Todd poured more vinegar onto the end of the bone, then he pushed the tibia back into the leg. After the bone was back inside, he reset it. Timmy cried out in pain, just before he passed out.

"Oh!" Roselyn said, calling out in involuntary empathy.

Todd looked up at her. "The worst part is over," he said. "And I'm glad I hurt him."

"You're glad?" Roselyn asked, shocked at his comment.

Todd nodded. "Yes. If he could feel it, it means gangrene hasn't set in. I'm pretty sure we got to him in time."

"We didn't do it, Doc. You did," Harold said.

Todd shook his head. "No. There's no way I could have gotten him out from under there, and up here, without help. I'm going to need two boards about this long," he added holding his hands apart. "We'll put a temporary splint over his leg now, and when we get him back home, we'll make a more permanent splint, using plaster of Paris."

The boards were presented, along with pieces of rope to hold them in place and, expertly, Todd applied the splint.

Timmy came to, just as Todd finished the splint. He looked down at his leg. "Thanks, Doc," he said. "I guess I'm lucky you're a vet."

Todd chuckled. "I don't know about that," he said. "Think about it. What do you do when a horse breaks its leg?"

"You . . . whoa, Doc! You weren't thinkin' about shootin' me, were you?"

"I did give it a passing thought," Todd said.

For a moment, everyone looked at Todd in surprise, then, realizing he was teasing, they roared with laughter. It wasn't really all that funny, but the laughter released their tension.

EIGHT

Metzger Land and Cattle Company Ranch, Texas, Monday, June 15th:

Lon Metzger bit the end off his cigar and licked it along each side. Firing a match, he held up the flame, puffing until the tip of the cigar began to glow. He was standing in the drawing room of his Spanish-style hacienda, and as he squinted through the wreathing smoke, he made a count of the other ranch owners who were present.

Metzger, who was president of the Ranch Owners Association, had called the members together in an impromptu meeting, suggesting that they meet at his house instead of at the Morning Star Hotel in Sierra Blanca where they normally gathered. His note explained that they had a subject of great importance to discuss, and he believed it would be better if they held the discussion in a less public place.

The response had been better than he hoped, and twelve ranch owners were gathered in Metzger's parlor, with extra chairs brought in from the dining room to accommodate all who had come. It was a warm night and the windows were up to catch the night breeze. Moths, drawn to the light of the dozen or so lanterns inside, fluttered against the window-screens, their wings leaving a powdery residue on the wire mesh.

More than half the men were smoking, and those who weren't smoking were chewing tobacco. To accommodate the latter, three brass spittoons had been strategically positioned to receive the expectorations.

Lon Metzger liked to claim that his father was an early Texas pioneer who had fought by Sam Houston's side at the battle of San Jacento and received a land grant doled as a result of his service. In truth, Metzger had no idea who his father was. His mother, Fancy D'Garneau, had been a beautiful octoroon, a prize New Orleans whore who died of consumption when Metzger was fifteen years old. Metzger shifted for himself for the next five years.

When he was twenty years old, Metzger was working in a New Orleans saloon when he saw a man lose the deed to some Texas land in a poker game. Later, the winner of the deed, a visiting gambler from the North, went out behind the saloon to relieve himself.

The gambler paid no attention to the shadowy figure who was lurking around the outhouse. He should have. Metzger had been waiting for him, and he hit the gambler in the back of the head with a shovel. The man went down, and Metzger robbed him, taking the title to the land, as well as the gambler's money.

Metzger left New Orleans, neither knowing, nor caring whether he had killed the gambler. The gambler had not been killed, but was knocked so senseless that he not only couldn't tell who his attacker was, he didn't even know what was stolen from him. Metzger had gotten away cleanly.

The deed Metzger had stolen was for just over four thousand acres of land located in West Texas. Shortly after arriving in the Sierra Blanca Valley, Metzger married Emma Bowen, whose family was one of the "Old 300." Their land had come by way of a grant from Stephen Austin in the earliest days of Texas settlement.

With his stolen land, and the legitimacy provided by marrying a true Texas pioneer, Metzger set about building the empire of Metzger Land and Cattle Company, by the sweat of his own brow, and with the blood of the Mexicans and Indians who got in his way.

Emma Bowen was appalled by her husband's ruthlessness and greed, but she was a good woman who would never think to tell her family what Lon Metzger was really like. Adhering to the Biblical injunction to honor and obey her husband, she lived her short, married life without complaint as a shadow within the shadows. Emma died bearing Metzger a son. Metzger named the boy Galen, after Emma's father, not out of any respect for the old man, but to maintain some ties with him, and for the legitimacy the family connection gave him.

Emma didn't live to see her son grow up, and Galen was the worse for it. Perhaps the ameliorating influence of a good mother would have made him a good man, instead of the pompous bully he became.

Metzger looked over toward his son. Like his father, Galen had dark hair and eyes, but beyond that, he was more like his mother; a narrow nose, high cheekbones, and a full mouth. There were times when Metzger thought Galen was too handsome, almost to the point of looking effeminate. But that was only on first glance. There was something about Galen, a manner and perpetual sneer, that more than offset his fair features.

Galen was standing by the liquor cabinet, leaning back against the wall, looking out over the gathering. His arms were folded across his chest, and his hat was pushed back on his head. He was chewing on a small piece of rawhide, and it dangled from his mouth. Even in this, in the way he was leaning against the wall looking out over his father's guests, there was a degree of arrogance to his demeanor that was almost palpable.

Metzger was glad that a life of affluence had not softened Galen. His son was self-centered and conceited, yes, but those weren't necessarily bad traits for someone who would, one day, run an operation as large as the Metzger Land and Cattle Company.

Though big, the Metzger Land and Cattle Company wasn't the biggest ranch in El Paso County. That distinction fell to Trailback. But both Metzger and Galen were driven to make the Metzger Land and Cattle Company not only bigger than Trailback, but bigger and more productive than any other ranch in the entire state of Texas.

Steve Warren and Carl Phillips were also present at the meeting. Both were lifetime residents of Texas. Warren's ranch, which he called Lariat, was only slightly smaller than the Metzger Land and Cattle Company, and the Flying P, which belonged to Carl Phillips, was just a little smaller than Lariat. Though not part of the Old 300, Warren's and Phillips's ranches were exactly what Metzger claimed his ranch was — the result of land grants given in appreciation for services rendered during the Texas Revolution. At one time both ranches were larger than the Metzger Land and Cattle Company. It was only when Metzger started an aggressive program of expanding his ranch by buying out smaller, neighboring ranches, that he overtook Lariat and the Flying P.

"Lon, what's all this about? I'd like to get back home before midnight," Warren said. Of all the ranchers gathered, only Steve Warren and Carl Phillips, by virtue of the size of their ranches, had the temerity to address Metzger by his first name.

"Yeah, what's all the secrecy? I mean why are we meeting here, instead of at the Morning Star at our usual time?" one of the other ranch owners asked.

"I reckon enough of you came to take

163

care of what we need to take care of," Metzger said. "So, if you'll all get settled, we'll get started."

While waiting for the meeting to start, the visiting ranchers had gathered into conversational groupings to exchange pleasantries and information. With Metzger's call to them, the little groups broke up and everyone started looking for a place to sit. Warren and Phillips, as was their due, sat in the front row in the two most comfortable chairs. The other ranch owners sat where they could find a seat. Metzger waited until all were settled and quiet, before he continued.

"Some of you may have seen all the goin's on over at Trailback Ranch," Metzger said.

"Yeah, I've seen it," Steve Warren said. "They've been roundin' up cattle like they was goin' to do a drive or somethin'. Only it ain't round-up time, so I've been wonderin' what it was all about."

"Well, I'm about to tell you," Metzger said. "That is, my son will tell you. I reckon you all know Galen." He pointed to the tall, slim young man who was still leaning against the wall, still chewing on the piece of rawhide. Galen took the rawhide from his mouth and nodded in acknowledgment of the several greetings offered by the gathered ranchers.

"We're listenin'," Phillips said.

Galen moved to the front of the room, then looked out over the gathered faces.

"I don't know if all of you know it yet, but Endicott Williams, the fella that owned Trailback, died."

Most of the men did know it but a few didn't, and for a moment there was a general buzz as they reacted to the news.

"The old man died and his son is running the show now," Galen continued, calling attention back to himself.

"Is young Williams moving out here?" one of the others asked. "Is that what this is all about?"

"*Haw!*" Galen snorted. "I don't reckon it's very likely that he'll be comin' out here. Young Mr. Williams don't want to give up his social life, back in New York City. So, what he done was send some Eastern dude out here to run things for him."

"Run things for him? Wait, you mean, Vavak is being replaced?" Andrew Peters asked. Peters owned one of the smaller ranches.

"I'd hate to see Vavak replaced. He is a pretty good man," Bill Johnson said. Johnson, too, was one of the smaller ranchers.

"Vavak is a weasel," Lon Metzger said with a snarl.

"I don't know as I would call him a weasel. He's always done right by me," Brad Simmons said.

"He's a foreigner who is nothin' more than a hired hand," Metzger insisted. "And, anyhow, this tenderfoot that Galen is talkin' about didn't come here to replace Vavak."

"Then, what did he mean, when he said he come out here to run things?" Peters asked.

"If all you folks would just shut your traps and listen, I'll tell you what this new fella is out here for," Galen said.

Galen's smart-mouthed retort caused a few of the ranch owners to seethe, but they did so inwardly. They knew they were in no position to talk back to him, not only because Galen was the son of the biggest ranch owner, but also because he was known to have a temper. He had taken a whip to one of his cowboys once, had beaten a man half to death in a bar fight in Sierra Blanca, and was even rumored to have killed a Mexican in a shoot-out in El Paso.

"Now, getting back to what Pop said, I'm sure you've seen all the activity goin'

166

on over at Trailback. This fella that young Williams sent out here is a veterinarian, and what he's plannin' on doin' is introducin' Hereford cattle out at Trailback."

"Hereford cattle?"

"Yes. And we've got to stop it," Galen replied.

"Why do we need to stop it? I mean, if Trailback wants to run a few head of Hereford cattle, what does that have to do with us?"

"What it has to do with us is . . . ," Galen started to reply, but his father interrupted him.

"It ain't just a few head of cattle," Metzger said. "They're plannin' on bringin' in an entire herd. And that means that the first thing they will have to do is get rid of the Longhorn they've already got." Metzger paused for effect. "Do you understand what I'm saying? They will sell off the entire herd and when they do that, the price of our beeves is going to go down."

"Well, hell, Mr. Metzger, that happens ever now and then anyway," Peters said. "You know how it is. Anytime one of our herds get too large for the grass or water, we have to sell 'em off. Hell, ranchers has been doin' that as long as there's been cows."

"Yeah, what's new about that?" Johnson asked. "The market drops a little when that happens, but it always recovers. Besides, like Andy says, it's all just a part of the cattle business."

"Alright, Johnson, I will tell you what is new about this," Metzger replied in slow, measured words. "When Trailback replaces all their Longhorns with Herefords, nobody is going to want to buy Longhorns anymore. This will be much, much more than a normal drop in prices, because the market is going to be flooded with Longhorns that nobody will want. What they are trying to do over there is take the market away from us completely," Metzger said. "Hell, by the time this is over, we'll be lucky to get two dollars a head."

"Two dollars a head? It cost more'n that to raise 'em!" one of the smaller ranch owners said.

The last announcement got the response Metzger had been looking for as all the ranch owners, big and small, reacted angrily.

"What are we going to do about it?" one of the ranchers asked.

"A better question is, what *can* we do

about it?" Steve Warren asked.

"Well, the first thing we can do, is all stick together," Metzger said. "Nobody can pull off an operation as large as the one they're trying over at Trailback, without the support of others. Like as not, Vavak, or one of his cowboys, is going to be coming to some of you to ask for help in something. It might be as little a thing as asking to borrow some of your tools, or as big a thing as asking you to lend 'em some of your cowhands to help out. If anyone does that, you tell them no."

"Wait a minute, now, Mr. Metzger. We purt' near always help one another out durin' round-up, if for no other reason than to get all the stray cows back where they belong," one of the smaller ranchers said. "If they're wantin' to bring some of my own cows back to me, I don't have all that many that I can turn them away. Besides, it just ain't neighborly to say no. I've always give out a helpin' hand whenever someone asks for it. It just goes agin' my grain, not to."

"You say that, Cleetus, even though what they are doing over there at Trailback will destroy you?" Metzger asked.

"Well, I . . . ," Cleetus Bowman started to respond.

"Look, Cleetus," Metzger said. "There's nobody that understands range etiquette any better than I do. Ordinarily, I wouldn't turn anyone down if they come to me for help and believe me, it hurts me to tell you to turn Vavak down if he comes to you. But, if we don't do this, if we don't fight back, some of you fellas are going to be hurt, and you are going to be hurt bad. Metzger Land and Cattle Company will make it. So will Lariat and the Flying P. Fact is, we might even grow stronger because some of you smaller ranchers aren't going to make it and we'll be able to move in and buy you out."

"Like you did Carson and Michaels during the blizzard?" Bill Johnson asked.

There was an audible gasp from the crowd. During the blizzard of 1882, Lon Metzger had taken over some of the ranchers who couldn't make it, buying the paper on their ranches, then evicting the ranch owners so he could annex their land to his. His action hadn't set well with everyone, and Johnson's remark was an outright challenge.

"Yes," Metzger answered, meeting his challenge with a steely gaze. "If the folks over at Trailback get away with it, it could well be exactly the way it was then. Your bad luck will produce opportunities for the bigger outfits, like Metzger Land and Cattle Company."

"I don't know about you, Johnson, but looks to me like Mr. Metzger is trying to play it straight with us," one of the other ranchers said. "I, for one, think we ought to listen to him."

"So do I," another rancher said and, after a general expression of assent, Metzger continued.

"Here is the long and short of it, men. If Trailback introduces Herefords, it will kill the market for Longhorns. You'd all be forced to get rid of your herds. Can you imagine what it will be like if all of you sold out at the same time? A moment ago I said cattle prices would drop to two dollars per head. That's if you are lucky. Chances are you'd wind up having to pay folks to take the cattle off your hands."

"Seems to me like Lon is making a good point here," Phillips said to the others.

"So, what can we do about it?" Cleetus asked.

"We've got to do everything we can to discourage Vavak from going through with this," Metzger said.

"Vavak don't have no say so in it, does

he?" Steve Warren asked. "I mean, he's just managing the ranch. According to Galen, it's young Williams that's behind it."

"Do you know anything about young Williams?" Metzger asked.

"No, don't know anything about him."

"Well, I've taken the trouble to find out about him," Metzger said. "When Galen said young Williams wouldn't want to give up his social life, he wasn't just flappin' his jaws. Turns out, Mr. Todd Williams is a ne'er-do-well, a wastrel who has spent his entire life spending his pa's money. He . . . sails yachts and attends teas," Metzger said, setting the last words apart from the rest of the sentence and assuming a false, cultured accent.

The others laughed at his mimicry.

"From everything I've gathered, Todd Williams is as worthless as tits on a boar hog," Metzger added.

The ranchers laughed again.

"I don't know where young Williams came up with this idea of introducing Herefords," Metzger continued. "No doubt he read about it in some book somewhere. But the point is, he's too busy with high society back in New York to pay that much attention to what's happening out here. That means he can't do this without Vavak."

"So all we have to do is discourage Vavak, and maybe a few of the Trailback cowboys," Galen put in quickly. He smiled. "If we show Vavak and his cowboys the error of their ways, word is going to get back to Williams and he'll drop the entire thing."

"What do you mean by discourage?" Peters asked.

"Discourage is discourage," Galen said enigmatically.

"Well, look, maybe we ought to invite Vavak to a meeting of the ROA," Phillips suggested. "Like Johnson said, I've always found Vavak to be a good man. I think if we explain the situation to him, and get him to see it our way, he might be able to put a stop to it."

"That might've worked if we'd found out about it in time," Metzger said. "But we didn't, and now it's already started. We're going to have to come up with some other way to stop him."

"What way is that?" Andrew Peters asked.

"You let me handle that."

"Well, I'm with Andy, here," Brad Simmons said. "I'd like to know what you're plannin' on doin'. Galen here said discourage is discourage. That don't tell us nothin'. What exactly do you plan to do?"

"I plan on doing whatever it takes to keep Metzger Land and Cattle Company, and all the other ranches in this part of Texas, from going under."

"Well, yeah, I'm for that. But I wouldn't be in favor of doing anything that's . . ." Simmons started, but he let the sentence hang.

"You wouldn't be in favor of doing anything that's what?" Carl Phillips asked.

"I wouldn't want to do anything that was wrong."

"The biggest wrong would be if we let this go on without doing anything about it," Metzger said.

"I don't know about the rest of you fellas," Cleetus Bowman said. "But if it's as bad as Mr. Metzger says it is, and he's got me convinced that it is, I'd have to sell everything I own. I know I've got one of the smallest ranches here, but I've worked too hard for what little I have got. I don't aim to just stand by and watch some New York son of a bitch, who wouldn't know a Longhorn from a coyote, bankrupt me. I'm behind you, Mr. Metzger. And you too,

Galen. Whatever needs to be done." He paused for a moment then said, pointedly, "*Whatever* you have to do . . . why, I say go ahead and do it."

"I appreciate that, Cleetus," Metzger said. "What about the rest of you?"

"You know," Phillips said, "I reckon that when you get right down to it, this isn't much different from a war. And in a war, you do things you wouldn't do otherwise. You've got my backing, Lon."

"Why don't we just put this thing to a vote now," Warren said. "All in favor, raise your hand." Steve Warren was the first to raise his hand and Carl Phillips's hand went up immediately thereafter.

The commitment of the two biggest ranchers convinced most of the others, and several, but not all, hands went up quickly. Then, after a few seconds of contemplation, the remaining hands went up as well. By a unanimous vote, Lon Metzger was given carte blanche to do whatever he thought necessary to stop Trailback from introducing Herefords onto the range.

Metzger smiled broadly. "I thank you," he said. He pointed to his liquor cabinet. "Galen, break out the whiskey. Boys, let's have a drink."

Galen Metzger stopped the surrey in front of the bank, let his father off, then drove down to the saloon where he parked it and went inside.

"Hey, Galen, what you doin' on wheels?" one of the patrons teased. "Get throwed by your horse, did ya'?"

"The horse hasn't been born that can throw me," Galen replied haughtily.

"I don't know 'bout that," one of the other patrons said. "You know what they say. Ain't a horse that can't be rode, ain't a cowboy that can't be throwed."

"Whoever said that, hasn't met me," Galen replied. The others guffawed at his bravado. "Pete," Galen said. "You got a couple of kegs of beer I can take back to the ranch with me?"

"I reckon I do," the bartender answered. "You got that big a thirst, have you?"

"No, I just want it for the hired hands."

"Whoa, Galen, when did the Metzgers become that generous? Hell, if you goin' to be givin' beer away, I might come out there and work for you my ownself."

"You may have to," Galen said.

"What do you mean?"

"If the New York son of a bitch who

176

owns Trailback has his way, you'll more'n likely be out of a job. They're plannin' on sellin' out their entire herd of Longhorns and bringing in a new breed. That's going to cause a lot of ranchers to go out of business."

"Huh. I never heard of nothin' like that. But anyway, what does that have to do with me? I sell leather goods."

"Tell me, Dolan, where do you get your leather?" Galen asked. "And who are your customers?"

"Well, I get it from . . ." Dolan started, then he stopped. "Yeah, I see what you mean," he said. "If the ranchers go out of business, so will I."

"So will you, Ted," Galen said to one of the other men. "Not much need of an apothecary if there aren't any people around to buy the potions you sell. And Able Clark, that dress shop that your wife runs, who's she goin' to sell dresses to?"

One by one, Galen went around the saloon, pointing out to the patrons how they were being threatened by what Trailback was doing.

"Damn, if that's true, somebody ought to do something about it," one of the patrons said.

Galen smiled. "Somebody is ᐧ doing

something about it," he said.

In the back of the bank, in the two-room office of the Texas Water Management Commission, a meeting was in progress. Jay Jensen, the Water Commissioner in charge of Sierra Blanca Valley, was chairing the meeting of the Board of Directors, which was an advisory committee made up of ranch owners from within the county.

Jensen had not expected to hold a meeting today and was caught off guard when the entire Board of Directors showed up in his office demanding a special meeting. And, because it was the policy of the Texas Water Management Commission to have their field offices run by local boards, Jensen had no choice but to acquiesce. Right now he was listening to a presentation from Lon Metzger.

"Jensen, we had a meeting of the Ranch Owners Association the other day to discuss a problem that has come up."

"You had a meeting of the ROA?" Jensen asked. "Why didn't I know anything about it? I'm generally invited to your meetings."

"As a courtesy, and a courtesy only, you are generally invited to them, and that's a fact," Metzger said. "But this was a special meeting in which we discussed the Trailback problem."

"The Trailback problem? What is the Trailback problem?"

In response to Jensen's question, Metzger laid out the situation, much as he had laid it out to the ranch owners when they met at his house. The Water Management Commissioner listened attentively, then when Metzger was finished, Jensen took off his glasses and polished them before he responded.

"I think you men may be overreacting," he said. "I've read about these Herefords. There are some areas where Herefords have already been introduced, and there has been very little economic impact on the local economy. In fact, in some cases, the local economy has improved because of it."

"Where would that be?" Metzger asked.

"Well, in upstate New York, for example. They've been running Herefords there now for . . ."

"New York?" Metzger said, then he laughed, and the others laughed with him.

"I don't understand," Jensen said. "What is so funny?"

"Sonny, we aren't talking about New York here," Metzger said. "This is Texas.

Why, I reckon just the ones of us who are here in this room have more cows than you'll find in the entire state of New York."

"I was only pointing out that you may be overestimating the economic impact," Jensen said.

"You are comparing a pin prick to a saber slash," Metzger said. "The truth is, if Trailback starts selling off all their cows, some others are going to have no choice but to sell theirs as well, then it's going to be like a prairie fire. Even you know what a prairie fire is like, don't you? Once it gets started, you can't stop it. Unless we stop it now."

"And how do you propose to do that?"

"I've got a plan," Metzger said.

Half an hour later, Metzger and his son were driving back to Metzger Land and Cattle Company. Two kegs of beer sat on the back of the surrey.

"How did it go with the meeting?" Galen asked.

"I got what I wanted," Metzger replied. "How did it go with you?"

Galen smiled. "By tomorrow, there won't be a man, woman, or child in town who wouldn't be happy to see Trailback burned to the ground."

"Good. It's good to have the towns-people on our side. But we also need our own hands on our side. This could get dirty before it's all over, and if it comes to a shooting war, we're going to need to know we can count on our men."

"You let me handle that, Pop," Galen said. "By the time I get through with them, they'll be ready to hold a pocket knife in their teeth, go over to Trailback, and charge the big house itself."

NINE

When Harold, Dewayne, John, Don, and the other cowboys at Trailback came in after a day's work, they were greeted with the aroma of cooking meat. Investigating the source, they found a quarter of a beef on a spit, dripping juice onto glowing mesquite coals. Todd was slowly turning the spit, while Ken Crites was brushing some sort of sauce onto the brown, glistening meat.

"Hey," Harold said, reaching out to pull off a piece of the meat. "Is it somebody's birthday?"

"You pull off any of that meat and I'll cut off your hand," Crites said, and though Harold knew he was joking, there was enough seriousness in the remark to cause Harold to jerk his hand back.

"I just wanted a taste."

"You'll get a taste," Crites said. "You'll get all you want at dinner time."

As Harold started toward the bunkhouse

he looked over toward a spreading oak tree. On a grassy glade, in the shade of the tree, was a long table, covered with a white cloth, and set with real china and silver.

"What? What is that for?" Harold asked, pointing to the table.

"That's where we're going to eat dinner," Crites said.

"Oh. You mean Mr. Vavak is having company?"

"No," Todd said. "When he says we, he means us. Cowboys included."

"I'll be damned," Harold said. He walked over to the table and reached out to touch the tablecloth, pulling his hand back at the last moment because he didn't want to soil it. He looked at the plates, white, with dark blue and gold trim, and at the glistening silverware. Awestruck, he walked back over to where Todd and Crites were cooking the beef.

"What do you think?" Todd asked.

"I don't think I've ever eaten off anything as elegant as that," Harold said.

"Yeah, well, you just tell the other boys to mind their manners tonight," Crites said. "Because Mr. and Mrs. Vavak and Miss Vavak are going to eat with us tonight."

Without a word to the others, Harold

went straight to his bunk, reached up to the nails where his spare clothes hung, and took down his Sunday-meeting shirt and trousers.

"What are you doin', Harold?" Don asked.

"I aim to get myself cleaned up for dinner," Harold said.

"*Haw!*" Dewayne laughed. "You gone high-falutin' on us?"

"No," Harold said. "I just want to be cleaned up for this dinner."

Harold was the only one who had gone over to the area between the cookhouse and the big house to investigate, so he was the only one who had seen the elegantly set table. But now, curious, Dewayne walked over to look at it as well. When he came back to the bunkhouse, he, like Harold, got a clean change of clothes then started out the back door, headed toward the big watering trough that sat under the windmill in the corner of the corral.

"I'll be damned," Don said. "Dewayne's taking a bath, too."

John went over to get his own clothes. "You too?" Don asked.

"Well, I sure don't intend to sit there all dirty, if they are cleaned up," John said as he headed toward the back door.

"Well, hey, wait for me!" Don shouted as he hurried to get his own change of clothes.

Several minutes later, Todd heard a loud shout, followed by laughter, and leaving the spit for a moment, he walked around behind the bunkhouse to see what was going on. That's when he saw the cowboys in the watering trough, naked, and splashing each other with water.

Smiling, he returned to the spit. "I hope Miss Vavak doesn't wander over by the watering trough," he said.

Crites pointed to a sawhorse that was set up alongside the bunkhouse. "See that?" he asked.

"That sawhorse?"

"That's a signal to the ladies that someone is back there, taking a bath," he said.

"Oh. Good idea," Todd said.

"Your idea of having a party for the men is a good idea, too," Crites said. "They've been working hard for several days now."

"Well, there's a method to my madness," Todd said. "The quarter of beef you're cooking came from a Hereford. I want them to get a taste of this new breed, so they'll know what I'm talking about."

Crites nodded. "I thought it must be. I never saw this much meat off a Longhorn quarter before."

"I think maybe I'd better go get cleaned up, as well," Todd said. "That is, if you don't need me to help finish up here."

"Go ahead," Crites said.

Everyone on Trailback turned out for the dinner, including Timmy, who hobbled up to the table on crutches. The cowboys were dressed in their best clothes, including shirts with collars, and in a couple of cases, even a jacket. Todd had dressed for the occasion as well, and was wearing a brown suit, complete with vest, shirt and collar, and tie.

But it wasn't just the cowboys who had dressed for dinner. The ladies, in particular, brought elegance to the table, Alice in a dress that was white and demure and Roselyn in a gown that was blue and regal.

"Mr. Crites," Vavak said, when all were gathered around the table. "Would you say the blessing, please?"

All bowed their heads, as Crites began to pray: "Oh most merciful Father, who hast blessed the labors of the husbandman in the returns of the fruits of the earth; We give thee humble and hearty thanks for this thy bounty; beseeching thee to continue thy loving kindness to us, that our land may still yield her increase, to thy glory and our comfort; through Jesus Christ our Lord. Amen."

Todd looked toward Crites in surprise. This, a prayer from the Episcopal Book of Common Prayer, had been delivered without falter. It wasn't exactly something he would have expected from a ranch cook.

"Damn, that was just a real nice prayer, Mr. Crites," Don said.

"I don't think you should be saying damn and prayer in the same sentence," John said, and the others laughed.

The cowboys were on their best behavior, waiting patiently for Vavak, Alice, and Roselyn to be served first. Then, they presented their plates to Crites, who carved generous portions of the meat for them.

For the next few moments, there was little conversation around the table as everyone enjoyed the meal.

"Whooee, what'd you do to this here beef?" Harold asked, putting into words what everyone was thinking. "This here's the best tastin' meat I ever ate."

"It's the sauce," Don said. "What kind of

sauce are you usin'?"

"The sauce is nothing but vinegar, lemon juice, brown sugar, and some ground cayenne," Crites said. "That's the same sauce I always use."

"Well you've done somethin' different."

"Ask Doc," Crites said, pointing to Todd.

"I seen you turnin' the spit," Harold said. "Did you do something to this meat?"

Todd shook his head. "It's not how it's cooked," Todd answered. "It's what is cooked. The beef you are eating came from a Hereford cow."

"The hell you say," John said. He looked at the meat on his plate. "And this here is what you say we're going to be raising?"

"Yes."

"Well, I'll give you this, Doc. This here is some better tastin' than Longhorn, that's for sure."

"Now, let me ask you something," Todd said. "If you were going into a fancy restaurant in New York, and you had your choice of buying a steak cut from a Longhorn or a Hereford, which would you want?"

"Hell, Doc, that ain't no poser," Dewayne said. "I'd take Hereford."

"Would you pay more for it?"

"Hell, yes, I would."

"Now, you understand why Mr. Williams wants to switch over to Hereford cattle. The cows weigh more, and they'll bring more per pound at the market."

"I can see that," Don said.

"And can you also see that Mr. Williams will make more money," Todd said.

"I reckon he will," John said.

"Yeah, he's going to make more money, but we're goin' to have to work harder," Dewayne said. "You said yourself, these Hereford cows ain't as hardy, and are going to take more looking after."

"Yes, but look at it this way," John said to Dewayne. "If Mr. Williams makes more money, then that means our jobs is going to be here as long as we want them."

"Yeah," Dewayne said. "Yeah, I reckon there is that to be said about it."

"I'm glad you men see it that way," Todd said. "But, there's another reason why this is good for you, other than just making sure your jobs will always be here."

"What reason is that?"

"I can tell you what it is," Harold said. He held up his fork. "We'll get to eat more meat like this."

Todd laughed. "That's true," he said. "But, I also have it on good authority that

Mr. Williams plans to put ten percent of the increased profit into an escrow account to be divided equally among you."

"What kind of account did you say?" Harold asked. The confused look on his face was mirrored in the faces of all the other cowboys.

Todd chuckled. "Escrow account. That is a bank account that is set up for a specific purpose. And the purpose of this escrow account will be to provide a bonus for each of you, in addition to your regular salary."

"A bonus? How much?" Dewayne asked.

"There is no way of knowing exactly, but I'd say that the bonus should just about equal what you are being paid now."

"Doc, wait a minute, are you sayin' that these here Hereford cows is goin' to double the amount of money we're makin' now?" Harold asked.

Todd smiled and nodded. "Yes, that's exactly what I am saying."

"Yahoo! Boys, I don't know about you, but I say, bring them Herefords on!"

Laughing and shouting, the cowboys left the table, then began horsing around with each other. While they were playing, Todd started clearing the table, and Roselyn came over to help.

"Look at them," Todd said, laughing. "They're like a bunch of kids. Of course, most of them are practically kids anyway. John's older, of course."

"I don't think cowboys ever really grow up," Roselyn said.

"Why should they? They work hard. I see nothing wrong with them playing hard as well."

"You know, Doc, when you had dinner with us that first night, it may be that I was wrong about what I said to you," she said.

Todd chuckled. "Oh. You mean I *don't* have manners?"

Roselyn looked at him in confusion for a moment, then she realized what he meant.

"A scalawag with manners," she said. "I did say that, didn't I?" She laughed, and shook her head. "No, Doc, I wasn't wrong about the manners part. But I no longer think of you as a scalawag."

"Why, I thank you, ma'am," Todd said, graciously.

"Doc, when you were in New York, did you ever go to any balls?"

"What?" Back in New York, Todd had been very active socially, attending several coming out parties over the last few years. He wondered if Roselyn had learned his identity and was now trying to trap him.

"What do you mean?" he asked cautiously.

"Dances," Roselyn said. "The reason I asked is, there is going to be an Independence Day Dance in Sierra Blanca on the 4th of July. I was just wondering if you planned to attend."

Todd smiled, broadly. "Absolutely I plan to attend," he said. "And, although I'm sure your dance card will be full, I have every intention of putting my name on it. That is, if you will allow me."

"I suppose I could find room for you," Roselyn replied, coyly.

"Hey, what the hell?"

The sudden shout from Harold arrested not only Todd and Roselyn's conversation, but the conversations of all the others as well.

"Harold, what are you yellin' about?" John asked.

"Look over there! Look at Duck Creek!"

"What about Duck Creek?" John asked.

"There ain't no Duck Creek," Harold answered.

With Harold's pronouncement, several rushed over to the creek bank.

Normally a swiftly flowing stream of clear water, perhaps two feet deep and twenty feet wide, there was nothing there now but a bottom filled with water-polished rocks and a very tiny trickle of water.

"What the hell? What happened to the water?" Don asked.

"How can that happen?" Dewayne asked. "It was there this afternoon. Streams don't just dry up that quick, do they?"

"They do if someone shuts the sluice gate," John said. "And it looks to me like that's what they done."

"Where is the sluice gate?" Todd asked.

"It's on Metzger's ranch," Roselyn said. "Duck Creek flows through his property before it reaches Trailback."

"And he has a gate he can close anytime he wants?"

"The gate, I do not think he will close," Vavak said. "Permission he must have from the Water Management Commission."

"Well, somethin's happened," Harold said. "We sure ain't gettin' no water."

"Papa, don't think he wouldn't do it in a minute. He has never been a friend of ours," Roselyn said. "Don't forget, he is the one who has kept you from being a part of the ROA."

"ROA?" Todd asked.

"That's the Ranch Owners Association," Roselyn said. "Nearly every law that has to do with ranching is enforced by the Texas Water Management Commission, and the

Commission is controlled by a board of directors."

"And this Water Management Commission can order the gate closed?"

"Yes. It is supposed to be a way of regulating the water during floods or droughts."

"Who makes up the board of directors?"

"The board of directors comes from the ROA," Roselyn said.

"And you say that this man, Metzger, is keeping your father out of the ROA? Why?"

"Metzger is president of the ROA, and he is interpreting the term owner very literally. Papa doesn't own Trailback."

"But, surely, as Mr. Williams's representative, they would make him a member," Todd said.

Roselyn shook her head. "Before Metzger, Papa did belong as Mr. Williams's representative. But Trailback is the biggest ranch in this part of the state, and I think Metzger is afraid of the influence we might have, the influence we *should* have, if we were allowed to belong."

"Well, I don't know about the rest of you fellas, but I'm going to go see what has happened to our water," Dewayne said.

"I'll go with you," Don said.

"Me, too," Harold put in. "But first, I want to get heeled." Harold started toward the bunkhouse.

Crites stepped out in front of Harold, and held up his hand. "Harold, don't go over to the Metzger Land and Cattle Company wearing a gun," he said.

"What? Why not?"

"I think it would be better if you don't," Crites repeated.

Harold stared at Crites for a moment, then nodded. "All right, if you say so."

The three cowboys went out to the stable, saddled their horses, and a moment later, rode out, following the creek bed north.

"What was all that about?" Todd asked Crites. "The business about not wearing a gun."

"I don't have a good feeling about this," Crites replied as he started cleaning up the pots and pans.

"Yes, well, you are probably right. Oh, the prayer you gave for the blessing? That was right out of the Episcopal Book of Common Prayer, wasn't it?"

"It was," Crites answered without elaboration.

"I didn't know you were Episcopalian."

"I'm not."

"Oh. What are you?"

"I'm a sinner," Crites said.

Todd chuckled. "Well, to hear the preachers and the priests tell it, I'm a sinner, too. We're all sinners."

Crites shook his head. "We are all sinners in the abstract," he said. "I'm a sinner in fact."

As Galen Metzger took a leak against a low-lying mesquite tree, he caught a hapless lizard with his urine stream, and laughed as the creature scurried off. Galen, Wade Babcock, who was foreman of the Metzger Land and Cattle Company, plus Roy Croft, Lou Shannon, Slim Posey, and Jack Spence, four of the men who worked for his father, were at the extreme southeast end, very near where Metzger Land and Cattle Company and Trailback connected. They were near the spillway, where, even now, water was pooling into a widening lake behind gate number one. The lake was filling as a result of a directive from the Texas Water Management Commission ordering gate number one closed. Closing the gate stopped the creek from flowing onto Trailback.

Closing the gate was done only under

the most unusual of conditions. Normally, the gate was left open, allowing Duck Creek to provide water for both Metzger Land and Cattle Company Ranch and Trailback. But, as Duck Creek was the largest of all the natural streams in the Sierra Blanca Valley, it could also be used during drier times to provide water for some of the other ranches, as well. This was accomplished through a network of three sluice gates which would not only create an equitable sharing of water during the dry months, but would divert the water during freshet stages.

Galen buttoned his pants, and walked back over to stand beside Wade Babcock.

"See anything yet?" Galen asked.

Babcock spit a wad of tobacco before he answered. "Nope," he said. "I'm not sure he'll come."

"Oh, he'll be here, all right. Either Vavak or some of his men," Galen insisted. "He isn't going to like the fact that Pop shut off his water supply."

"No, I don't reckon anyone would much care for that," Babcock agreed.

"Yeah, well Vavak can squeal all he wants, but Pop has authorization from the Water Management Commission, so there's nothing he can do about it.

Nothing legal, that is. That means that if he, or any of his men, show up, it can only be to cause us trouble. And remember, when they do arrive, they will be trespassing, which means we have every right to shoot them down."

"Hey, Galen," Shannon shouted. "Looks like we've got company comin'."

Looking in the direction indicated by the cowboy, Galen saw three riders approaching.

"Alright, you fellas stay out of sight," Galen said to the cowboys. "Have your rifles loaded and ready. If I give the signal, shoot 'em."

"Shoot at them?" Posey asked.

"I mean shoot them down. Remember, they won't be here for any reason but to make trouble."

The cowboys looked at each other.

"Do it, and there's a hundred dollars in it for each of you," Galen said.

Jack Spence smiled broadly, then jacked a shell into the chamber of his rifle. "Hell, Galen," he said. "For a hundred dollars, I'll go into town and kill the preacher." He started toward a small outcropping of rocks.

"What about you two?" Galen asked the others.

"That's a hundred dollars for each of us?" Shannon asked.

"Yes, for each of you," Galen confirmed.

"I reckon I'll shoot 'em for you," he said.

Posey joined the other two and, as the three cowboys got out of sight behind the rocks, Galen and Babcock walked out to the middle of the road. They just stood there, waiting until the riders came to within hailing distance.

"That's far enough!" Galen called out, holding his hand up to stop the riders. "You are trespassing on Metzger Land and Cattle Company property."

"Trespassing? What do you mean, we're trespassing. Galen, we've never been none too particular about crossing from one ranch to the other before. Hell, we've done brung your pa fifteen or twenty of your cows that's strayed over onto Trailback, just in the last few days."

"Times are changing," Galen said. "What are you doing here?"

Harold pointed to the closed gate. "What for did you shut off the creek?"

"Not our doin'," Galen replied. "The Texas Water Management Commission ordered it so as to divert some water to the other ranches because of the drought."

"Drought? What the hell drought are

you talkin' about?" Dewayne asked. "There ain't no drought."

"So you say. But the Water Management Commission sees it some different," Galen said. "Now, get off my property."

"When are you going to open that gate?" Harold asked.

"When am I going to open it? When hell freezes over. That's when I'm going to open it," Galen replied.

"You got no right to keep this gate closed, no matter what that damned Commission says."

"Get off my land," Galen ordered.

"We ain't goin' nowhere until you open that gate."

"Don't say you wasn't warned," Galen said. He held up his hand, ready to drop it as a signal to his men to open fire. But, at that moment his foreman, Babcock, noticed that none of the three Trailback riders were carrying guns.

"Better hold off there, Galen," Babcock hissed. "Them boys ain't armed."

"That's their problem," Galen replied.

"Could be ours, too. If we shoot 'em now, it'll be murder, pure and simple," Babcock said under his breath. "That could get your pa in a lot of trouble."

Galen pulled his hand back down slowly,

while at the same time Babcock turned toward the three concealed men and held his hands out, shaking his head in a signal that they shouldn't fire.

Don started toward the gate.

"Where do you think you're going, cowboy?" Galen asked.

"I aim to open that gate."

Galen turned toward the concealed men. "Boys," he said.

The men stood up. All three of them were holding rifles, pointed at Harold, Dewayne, and Don.

Harold stuck his hand out to pull Don back. "No, Don, wait," he said.

"I think you boys better get on back where you belong," Galen said, menacingly. "And tell Vavak that if he has a problem with this, he should take it up with the Water Management Commission."

"Slim? Slim, are you goin' along with this?" Harold asked.

"I'm just doin' my job," Posey called back.

"Doin' your job? Hell, Galen here was about to have you fellas shoot us. Me'n you been friends a long time, Slim."

"Your boss is tryin' to put all the other ranches out of business," Posey said. "If there ain't no ranches to work at, there ain't no cowboys. I don't aim to let that happen."

Harold stared at Posey for a long, pained moment, then he looked over at the two men he had come with. "Let's go," he said.

"I'm sorry about your friend," Dewayne said.

"That son of a bitch ain't no friend of mine," Harold replied. "Not anymore. Not if he was ready to shoot me."

"We should'a brought our guns," Don grumbled as they rode away.

"No, I don't think so," Dewayne said. "I think if we had been wearin' guns when we rode in here today, they would've shot us down without so much as a by-your-leave."

"Mr. Crites was right," Harold said. "He told us not to come over here wearin' guns."

"How do you think he knew?"

"I don't know," Harold said. "All I know is, Mr. Crites knows things like that."

TEN

Trailback Ranch, Friday, June 19th:

When Ivan Vavak decided to go into Sierra Blanca to talk to the Commission about the diverted water, Alice asked him to take the surrey so she could go as well.

"To the Water Management Commission you wish to speak?" Vavak asked.

"Now, what would I have say to a bunch of stuffy old men?" she replied.

"Believe me, I would have plenty to say if I could speak to them," Roselyn said.

Alice chuckled. "I'm sure you would. But I think it would be better if you just went with me. I want to pick up a few things in town."

"All right, the surrey we will take," Vavak said. "The team I must harness."

"Papa, would you have someone saddle Pepper for me?" Roselyn asked. "I'll go into town with you and mama, but I'd rather ride."

Vavak nodded affirmatively as he left.

★ ★ ★

Todd came out of the bunkhouse at about the same time Vavak finished harnessing the team to the surrey. Todd had already planned to go before the Water Management Commission with Vavak, but, until he saw the surrey, he thought he was going to have to ride a horse. He brightened a little at the sight of the wheeled vehicle.

"You're taking the surrey into town?" he asked.

"Yes. Like you, Alice does not like to ride a horse. So, I take the surrey."

Todd smiled. "Good, good," he said. "I think the surrey will be better."

Alice and Roselyn came out of the house then, and Todd helped Alice climb into the front seat. He then turned toward Roselyn to help her up as well, but before he could do so, he saw that Don was leading Pepper, who was already saddled, out from the barn.

"Doc, how are we ever going to make a cowboy out of you, if you won't ride a horse?" Roselyn asked.

"Maybe if I had a horse as easy to ride as Pepper, I could do it," Todd said.

"As easy to ride as Pepper?" Roselyn replied. She offered the reins to him.

"Well, be my guest."

"Not a good idea, Doc," Don said. "Pepper is pretty much a one-woman horse."

"Really? Well, then, perhaps I'd better pass, this time," Todd said.

"Smart move, Doc," Roselyn said as she swung easily into the saddle.

Ken Crites was also going to go to town, but because he would be picking up supplies for the kitchen, he would be taking a wagon. At the moment, he was in front of the barn, hitching up the team. Harold, who was going into town to help Crites load the wagon, was standing close by, holding his horse's reins.

"Hey, Mr. Crites, do you mind if I ride along with them?" Harold asked, nodding toward Vavak and the others. "You can catch up with me, once you get to town."

"I don't mind," Crites said.

"Thanks."

"Just don't get yourself so drunk that you can't help me load the wagon."

"I won't," Harold replied. "I promise, I'll be there when you need me."

As the surrey passed by, Harold swung into his saddle to join them. "See you in town, Mr. Crites!" he shouted as he rode alongside the surrey.

Crites nodded, then went back to his work. The windmill in the corral, answering a breeze, creaked and swung into the wind. The thirty-six blades whirled into life, and the piston began rattling and clanking as the pump started its up-and-down motion.

By the time he had the team hitched, then loaded the empty barrels he would need for the produce he was buying, the surrey was well out of sight.

"All right, boys, I'm pulling out now," Crites shouted toward the bunkhouse. "If any of you have dealings in town you want me to take care of, now's the time to let me know."

As he expected, the cowboys in the bunkhouse hurried outside, crowding around him to press money into his hands and tell him what they wanted him to buy for them. Graciously, Crites accepted every order.

It was a warm day, and as Todd sat in the back seat of the surrey, he felt himself becoming very drowsy. The aroma of sun-bleached wood and leather, the warmth of the morning, and the gentle rhythm of the slow-moving surrey had a very relaxing effect, and Todd drifted off to sleep.

"Hey, Doc, how's your backside holdin' out?" Harold asked. The sudden intrusion into Todd's subconscious caused his head to jerk forward, and his eyes to snap open.

"What?"

Harold laughed when he saw that he had awakened Todd. "Your backside," he repeated. "How's it doin'?"

"Oh, uh, my backside is just fine, thank you for your concern," Todd replied.

"I didn't figure it was botherin' you none too much," Harold said. "Seein' as how you was sittin' there sleepin'."

"I wasn't asleep, I was just thinking about a few things," Todd said.

"And Rip Van Winkle was just counting blades of grass," Roselyn said.

"Rip Van Winkle *was* just counting the blades of grass," Todd said, accepting the tease with good nature. "I know that to be true, because it just so happens that he was from my part of the country."

Roselyn laughed. "I'll have to give you this, Doc: You're a hard man to get one over on." Slapping her legs against the side of her horse, she galloped on ahead of the surrey by twenty feet or so. After a few more minutes, Todd was, once again, fighting the urge to fall asleep.

Sierra Blanca:

Galen Metzger was holding forth in the Brown Dirt Cowboy Saloon. But he was preaching to the choir because six of the patrons were cowboys from the Metzger Land and Cattle Company. In addition, he had added to his appreciative audience by setting up everyone else in the saloon with drinks.

"Drink up and enjoy yourselves, boys," Galen said. "And just thank your lucky stars you ain't on Trailback 'cause, unless I miss my guess, folks out there are goin' to be getting' pretty thirsty about now."

"I hope shuttin' off their water works," Dolan said. "But I've known Mr. Vavak for a long time. He don't seem like the kind that you can persuade to change his mind."

"Hell, he don't have to change his mind," Galen said. "What he's goin' to wind up with is a bunch of dead cows. And since you can't sell dead cows, there's not much chance of him killin' the market, is there?"

"No, I guess not," Dolan said. "Still, I wouldn't be writin' off a man like Vavak."

"A man like Vavak," Galen said with a snarl. "That foreign son of a bitch can't even speak English good. 'Why my water you have cut off?' " Galen said, mimicking Vavak's fractured speech.

"Damn, Galen, if that don't sound just like him," Ted said.

"Let's have three cheers for Galen, boys," one of the Metzger Land and Cattle Company cowboys said. He held up his glass, and everyone in the saloon held their glasses up to join him.

"Hip, hip!" the cowboy said.

"Hooray!"

"Hip, hip!"

"Hooray!"

"Hip, hip!"

"Hooray!"

The three cheers were followed by everyone draining their glasses.

"Pete!" Galen shouted.

"Yes, sir, Mr. Metzger?"

"Fill them up again."

"Yes, sir, Mr. Metzger."

Every patron in the saloon rushed to the bar, holding their glasses out to be refilled.

On the Trail:

As Trailback was about ten miles south of Sierra Blanca, it took just over an hour to make the trip. This would be Todd's first trip back to town since he arrived and when he wasn't dozing off, he was enjoying the vistas of the wide open country.

There were some things about New York that Todd missed. He missed having nice restaurants nearby, and shops where one could buy items of every description. He missed the fascination of being near a seaport and listening to the cacophony of a dozen foreign languages being spoken by sailors whose ships arrived daily from exotic ports all over the world. He also missed the sheer excitement of living in a city with a population of nearly two million people.

But those things were always there, and he could see them anytime he visited. He knew now that visiting was the only way he would be seeing New York from now on because he was never going back there to live. He had fallen in love with this magnificent West, and once he got the Hereford cattle introduced onto the range, he intended to make his real identity known, and stay here from now on.

Ahead of them Sierra Blanca seemed to rise from the horizon, looking at first like nothing more than irregular hillocks in the prairie. Gradually the lumps took shape to become buildings of rip-sawed lumber, adobe, and brick. A dog ran out to meet the surrey, then escorted them on into town, yapping at the spinning wheels before it retreated.

Sierra Blanca was laid out like a cross. The vertical bar was Range Road, and it ran north and south with the ends of the street trailing off into roads that disappeared in the plains. The horizontal bar of the cross was Front Street, and it ran east and west, parallel with the railroad track. Approaching the town from the south, they passed a cluster of private dwellings. In an empty field near the houses, several young boys were playing football. As the surrey passed by, Todd turned in his seat to look at the sandlot game. It was the first time he had thought about football in a long time, and for a moment he felt a small pang of regret over the fact that he couldn't go over to the boys and provide them with a few pointers.

Beyond the houses was a high-steepled church, and beyond that a mortuary. When they reached the commercial part of town, Vavak headed the team toward Belding's General Store, then stopped in front.

"Here, I will leave surrey," he said to Alice. "My business, I think, will not take too long."

"Take as long as you want, Roselyn and I will be fine," Alice said, nodding toward the store. "Don't you be hurrying on our account."

"Take what time you need," Vavak said. "I will not make you hurry."

"Mr. Vavak, if you don't need me for anything, I thought I might wander on over to the Brown Dirt Cowboy while I'm waitin' for Mr. Crites," Harold said.

"I hope trouble you will not have," Vavak said.

Harold held his hands up. "I'll be as innocent as a lamb."

"As innocent as lamb," Vavak said. He chuckled. "To slaughter I hope you are not led."

"You comin' with me, Doc?" Harold asked.

"I think I'd rather go with Mr. Vavak, if he doesn't mind having me tag along," Todd said.

"Yes, it will be good to have you with me," Vavak said.

"Uh, maybe I should come as well," Harold suggested, though it was obvious by the tone of his voice that he was making the offer only. He did not believe he was necessary, nor did he want his offer to be accepted.

"Better you wait for Mr. Crites," Vavak said.

"Yeah, I guess so. Uh, like I said, I'll wait for him at the Brown Dirt, but, I'll be here if you need me."

Todd watched Harold ride toward the saloon, urging his horse into an impatient trot.

"Poor Harold," Roselyn said with a little laugh. "I think for a minute there he was afraid you might actually take him up on his offer to come with you."

Alice, Vavak, and Todd laughed at her comment.

Tying her horse off at the hitching rail, Roselyn went into Belding's General Store with her mother while Todd and Vavak started toward the Water Management Commission office.

The Water Management Commission office was located in the back of the Sierra Blanca Bank, which, along with the rail-road depot, was one of only two brick buildings in town. It sat across the street and about halfway down the block from the General Store. Todd and Vavak picked their way across the dirt road, through a mine-field of horse droppings, and around a kiosk that displayed about a half-dozen signs advertising products from beer to washboards.

Entering the bank, they passed the teller's cage and walked to the rear. There, on the frosted glass of a closed door, was a painted sign, lettered in black, and outlined in gold.

TEXAS WATER MANAGEMENT COMMISSION
JAY JENSEN, COMMISSIONER

Vavak knocked on the door.

"Come in!" a voice called from inside.

Todd opened the door, then stepped to one side, allowing Vavak to enter first. The office actually consisted of two rooms. A counter divided the front room, while the back room, visible through an open door, was dominated by a large conference table and chairs. Behind the counter was a roll-top desk with the top rolled up. Sitting at the desk was a smallish man, bald, with rimless glasses. He was wearing a suit with a vest, starched shirt, collar, and tie.

"Mr. Jensen, with you I would like to speak," Vavak said.

"Yes, Mr. Vavak, what can I do for you today?"

"Duck Creek has no water. Did you give orders the gate to be closed?" Vavak asked.

Jensen paused for a second, stroking his chin before he answered. "I gave those orders, yes."

"Now, no water I have. It is not right for you to do such a thing, Mr. Jensen," Vavak said.

"Well, now, hold on there, Mr. Vavak," Jensen replied. "I sure hope you don't think I just took it on myself to do it. I can't do anything without the approval of the board, you know that. And the board ordered me to close the gate to help with the drought."

"Drought?" Todd said, coming down hard on the word. "What drought are you talking about? There's no drought."

"Well, if there is no drought, then you shouldn't be having a problem with water," Jensen said. He looked at Todd. "And, who might you be?" he asked.

"The name is Todd. Bill Todd."

"Are you that veterinarian from the East that's causing all the trouble?" Jensen asked.

"Trouble?" Todd asked, surprised by the question. "What do you mean, I'm causing trouble?"

"Aren't you the tenderfoot who has come out here with the idea of raising Herefords?"

"Well, yes, but, why would that be trouble?"

"Have you stopped to think that when you do that, it will send the price of all the other cattle down so far that the ranchers won't be able to survive?" Jensen asked.

"No," Todd said, genuinely surprised by the observation. "No, I never thought about that. In fact, I don't believe it. There is still a demand for beef, and the country is a long way away from raising enough Herefords to meet that demand. Hereford beef will bring a higher price, yes, but I think that Longhorns will continue to be quite marketable, for some time, at their current price."

"Do you now?" Jensen replied sarcastically. "Are you working for Mr. Vavak?"

"I am."

"Well, Mister, I want you to know that you haven't done your boss any favors," Jensen said. "I imagine that right now Mr. Vavak is about the second most unpopular man in El Paso County. You being the first."

"What about the sluice gate?" Todd asked, ignoring Jensen's comment. "When are you going to open it so we can have water again?"

"I told you I don't make the decision to

close or open the spillway gates. The Board of Directors ordered the gate closed, and it is the board who will have to make the decision to open it."

"How often does the board meet?"

"This was a special, called meeting," Jensen said. "But there will be a regularly scheduled meeting Monday afternoon at one o'clock."

"Well, if they've just had a special meeting, will they have the regular one?"

"Yes. There are other things to discuss besides the condition of the spillway gates."

"Closing of the spillway gates is the only thing we care to discuss. We'll be here Monday at one."

Jensen shook his head. "It won't do you any good," he said.

"Why is that?"

"Because only a ranch owner can petition the board." He looked at Vavak. "And, in case you don't know it, Mr. Vavak here isn't a ranch owner. He is just a ranch manager."

"*Just* a ranch manager?" Todd repeated. "He ramrods Trailback, which is the biggest ranch out here. And, as such, he is the direct representative of Mr. Williams. Are you telling me that the biggest ranch here has no right to petition the Water Management Commission?"

"The Water Management Commission is for land owners, not land renters," Jensen explained. "It doesn't matter how big or how small Trailback is. You still have the same problem. Only the owner of Trailback can appear before the Commission. Mr. Vavak does not qualify."

"Come, Doc. Here time we waste," Vavak said.

The two men started to leave the office but just as they reached the door, Todd turned back toward Jensen. "It doesn't matter how small the ranch is?"

"It does not matter," Jensen said.

"So that means that Mr. Vavak cannot make an appeal to the board of directors, but the owner of the smallest ranch in the Valley can?"

"If the smallest ranch is directly effected by an action taken by the Board of Directors, then yes, that ranch owner may petition the Board," Jensen explained. "But, it must be a land owner." He pointed at Vavak. "And Mr. Vavak is not a land owner."

"That isn't right," Todd said.

"I don't make the rules, Mister," Jensen replied. "I'm just a public servant, appointed by the governor of the state of Texas, and following orders the board gives me."

"A public servant," Todd said. "That's good to know."

ELEVEN

When Harold Shedd went into the Brown Dirt, Galen Metzger and the six men who had come with him were sitting in the back corner of the saloon. They had pulled two tables together and, because Galen was being rather generous with his money, all of the bar girls were gathered around the table.

The talk and laughter was loud and some of the men were getting a little heavy-handed with the girls. As a result, one of the bar girls walked away from the others, adjusting her dress as she did so.

"Are they having a party back there?" Harold asked, nodding toward the table.

"If they are, it's not a party I want to go to," the girl said.

"Could I buy you a drink?" Harold offered.

The girl smiled at him. "Sure, Mister," she said, moving down the bar to stand beside him.

"I don't think I've seen you in here before," Harold said.

The girl shook her head. "No, I just got

off the train yesterday. The name is Belle," she said, sticking out her hand. "Belle Sinclair."

"My name is Harold. You've got a pretty name."

"Thanks," Belle said. "I made it up myself. I've been told that girls who work in this business should never use their real names."

"That's probably a pretty good idea," Harold said. "Where did you come from?"

"Missouri," Belle said. "My pa had a farm but the bank took it when he died. My ma tried to make it for a while, takin' in laundry and such, but she up and died last winter."

"I'm sorry to hear that," Harold said.

"Yes. Well, I tried to carry on with what ma was doin', taking in laundry, but I could never do it to satisfy anyone. And, like as not, after a full day's work, they'd say they didn't like it, and they wouldn't pay me."

Harold let the girl talk. He didn't know if it was a story she had practiced, or if it was the truth and she just needed someone to talk to. He would give her this. She was prettier than most of the soiled doves. She was young and fresh, not dissipated looking at all. The work had not yet taken its toll of her.

"I can see why you would want to get out of that situation," Harold said. "Have you had any . . . uh, experience?" he asked, unable to word his question any more delicately.

Belle laughed. "Do you mean am I a virgin?"

"Well, somethin' like that, yeah," Harold said.

Belle shook her head, then put her hand on Harold's. It was cool. Funny, Harold thought, how a cool hand could heat the blood so. "I'm no virgin, cowboy. I've been around a bit." She looked back toward the table where Galen and his boisterous cowboys were holding court. "I just hope I don't run into many like that bunch."

"We're not all like that," Harold said.

"I can see that, now," Belle said, looking directly into Harold's eyes.

"Uh, look, I can't stay long, I've got to help load a wagon," he said. "But, maybe I can come back and see you sometime?"

"Of course you can, honey. That's why I'm here," Belle answered.

"Oh, yes, I suppose it is, isn't it?"

Belle realized then that she had made a faux pas, and smiling at him, she leaned forward and kissed him a soft, almost chaste kiss, on the lips. Then, pulling away from him, she smiled up at the shocked expression on his face.

"In this business, we sometimes have people we call our specials," she said. "Would you be my special, Harold?"

"Yes, ma'am," Harold said, his voice husky. "Wouldn't nothin' give me more pleasure."

One of the cowboys who had ridden in with Galen was Slim Posey, and he yelled out. "Hey, Belle! Get your ass back over here! When we buy the drinks, we expect the women to stay with us!"

"I don't want any more of your drinks," Belle replied.

"Yeah? Well you get back over here, or I'll come drag you back."

"Ease up on her, Slim," Harold said. "You fellas have all the other women over there. You ought to leave at least one for the rest of us." Harold ameliorated his comment with a smile.

"You stay out of this, Harold. This ain't none of your concern," Posey said.

"The girl's with me, now," Harold said.

"Yes, leave me alone," Belle said. "I'm with him."

"Listen, whore, I told you to get back over there with us, and by god that's what I mean!" Posey said, moving quickly to her. He grabbed Belle by the shoulder, but that was as far as he got before Harold hit him.

Posey had made the mistake of coming up from the left rear, which gave Harold an open shot at him with his right hand, and Harold made the most of his opportunity. He caught Posey on the point of his chin, and Posey went down.

Harold pushed Belle back out of the way and, with a little scream of fear, she ran down the length of the bar, then halfway up the stairs before she turned to see what was going on. Harold was standing just over Posey now, looking down at him, his fists at the ready.

"Slim, this ain't like you," Harold scolded. "This ain't like you a'tall."

Posey lay on the floor for a moment, rubbing his chin.

"No need in me'n you fightin' like this," Harold continued. "Hell, me'n you wintered together a few years back. We been friends too long to let something come between us."

"I ain't friends with the likes of you, Harold Shedd," Posey said as he got up.

As Todd and Vavak approached Belding's, Alice and Roselyn were just coming out of the store. Because both women were loaded down with packages, Todd hurried over to relieve them of their burden.

"How did the meeting with Mr. Jensen go?" Alice asked.

"The meeting went not good," Vavak said.

"Well, did he tell you why the water was shut off?"

"The board of directors seems to be under the mistaken impression that we are experiencing a drought," Todd said.

"Drought, my foot," Roselyn said. "There is no drought, and they know it. This is all Lon Metzger's doing. He has never been what you would call a good neighbor, but this seems a bit far, even for him."

"Why is there such animosity between Trailback and Metzger?" Todd asked.

"Metzger Land and Cattle Company is a very large ranch," Roselyn said. "It isn't as large as Trailback, but it is quite large, and it got bigger during the great blizzard three years ago."

"Really? I thought the blizzard hurt the ranchers," Todd said.

"It did hurt the ranchers," Roselyn answered. "Especially the smaller ranchers. A lot of them were unable to meet their loan obligations, so Metzger bought up the paper, then forced them off their land with no compensation at all. When Papa found out what Metzger was doing, he wrote to Mr. Williams, and Mr. Williams bought the remaining notes, not to force the ranchers off their land, but to hold them until the ranchers were on their feet again. I think Metzger felt that we had cheated him out of acquiring even more land."

"You helped some of the smaller ranchers?" Todd asked. "That was very nice of you."

"Mr. Williams helped them," Vavak said.

"Yes, but because you asked him to," Roselyn said. "Papa, maybe now we can get one of those ranchers to pay you back."

"All have paid back the money," Vavak said.

"Not the money, the favor," Roselyn replied.

"I do not understand."

"Since only a land owner can go before the Water Management Commission, get one of them to plead your case," Roselyn suggested.

"Yes," Todd said. "That is a good idea. But we will need one who is directly affected by Duck Creek."

Roselyn shook her head. "Well, then,

that kills that idea. Duck Creek flows only on two ranches. Metzger's and Trailback."

"What about the diversionary channels? I mean, when the gates are in place, where does the run-off water go?"

"One goes to Lariat, the other to Flying P."

"Who owns those ranches?"

"Steve Warren owns Lariat, and Carl Phillips owns the Flying P," Roselyn said. "But don't count on any help from them. Lon Metzger has them in his hip pocket."

"Close friends?" Todd asked.

Roselyn chuckled. "I don't think Lon Metzger has any close friends. Warren and Phillips are allied with him, because they don't want him for an enemy."

"Well, according to Jensen, only a land owner who is directly affected by the water from Duck Creek can intercede on our behalf. And if I understand you correctly, only Metzger Land and Cattle Company, Trailback, and, by extension, the Warren and Phillips ranches are involved."

"Which means Metzger pretty much has us tied up," Roselyn said. "What I don't understand is why he has done this. I mean, we've had an uneasy truce for the last couple of years, why would he do this now?"

"I believe it is because of the Hereford cows," Todd said.

"The Herefords?"

"Evidently the Ranch Owners Association thinks that once we get the Herefords in place, the price of Longhorns will plummet."

"Will they?"

"Not right away," Todd said. "But, as more and more Herefords are introduced across the country, the demand for Longhorns is going to go way down and then, the prices, will drop."

Roselyn was silent and Todd thought for a moment that she was about to turn on him again. Instead, she just nodded.

"I can see how that might happen," she said. "But as far as I'm concerned, that's all the more reason we need to do it now. If we don't, someone else will," she said. "Someone who may be less benevolent than Trailback."

Todd smiled, then ran his hand through his hair. "I'm glad you see it that way," he said. "I mean, when you get right down to it, I guess I am the cause of all this. You have every right to be resentful of me for coming in here and disturbing the status quo."

"The status quo," Roselyn said, chuckling. "Only a college-educated dude from the East would use such a term out here."

"I guess I had better start watching that, if I want to blend in," Todd said.

Roselyn laughed. "Blend in? Oh, yes, I can see that, Doc. You are a six-foot five-inch, 250-pound man who speaks with a Northern, cultured accent, in a world of small to average-sized cowboys who speak only Texan. Yes, I think you will blend in quite easily."

Todd laughed at her observation.

"In the meantime, we still have a problem. We have no water, and we have better than 15,000 cows who are going to get awfully thirsty," Roselyn said.

"What about the well?" Todd asked. "You have a windmill. Does it produce enough water?"

"That will work for a while," Roselyn said. "But the well won't produce enough water for the entire herd."

"Mr. Vavak, what about the board of directors? Is it stacked against us? What I mean is, if you could go before the Board, do you think you would get a fair hearing?"

"I cannot go."

"As things stand right now, I know you can't," Todd said. "But I'm curious as to the makeup of the board. If you *could* go before the board, would you get a fair hearing?"

Vavak thought for a moment, then nodded his head. "I don't know. Peters, Johnson, and Simmons are good men. To them if I could talk, I think perhaps they would listen."

"How many are on the board?"

"Six."

"So, we might be able to get to half of them? What happens if it is a tie vote?"

"Jensen can vote only if it is a tie vote."

"Jensen would never vote for us," Roselyn said.

"I'm not so sure," Todd said. "If he is forced to vote against us, it will show his true colors. He told us that he had no hand in this. This could force his hand."

"What if it did force his hand? What good would that do us?"

"He holds his position by gubernatorial appointment," Todd said. "The governor might be interested in hearing about one of his appointees who uses the excuse of a nonexistent drought to deprive Trailback of water. I happen to know, by the way, that Mr. Williams contributed generously to Governor 'Oxcart John' Ireland's gubernatorial campaign."

"What good does that do us?" Roselyn asked. "Knowing Mr. Todd Williams, he is probably in Paris with some lady of the evening."

"I thought you didn't know him," Todd said.

"I don't know him, but I know all about him," Roselyn said. "And I know we can't count on him for any help. No, sir, I'd say we are up the creek right now." Roselyn laughed, bitterly. "And, as it so happens, it is a dry creek."

"Ivan, can we stay in town a little longer?" Alice asked. "I have some material I want to take to Mrs. Clark, so she can make a new dress."

"Yes, we can stay," Vavak said. "Come, Doc. We will drink beer with Harold, and keep him out of trouble until Mr. Crites comes."

"Who is going to keep the two of you out of trouble?" Alice asked.

"I will watch out for him," Vavak said.

"And I will watch out for him," Todd added.

Alice chuckled. "Now, that is a comforting thought, the two of you keeping each other out of trouble. Come, Roselyn."

Alice and Roselyn started toward Mrs. Able Clark's Dress Making Shop, while

Vavak and Todd went in the opposite direction, toward the Brown Dirt Cowboy. Just before they went inside though, Todd put his hand on Vavak's shoulder.

"I'll be back in a couple of minutes," he said. "I have something I need to do."

"All right," Vavak said. "I will find Harold."

As Vavak pushed through the batwing doors to go into the saloon, he saw Harold looking down at a cowboy sprawled on the floor.

"Harold, what is this?" Vavak asked.

"Nothing, Mr. Vavak," Harold said, walking toward him. "Just a little difference of opinion is all."

Suddenly, and totally unexpectedly, someone came up behind Harold and hit him over the head with the butt of his pistol. Harold went down in a heap.

"Harold!" Vavak shouted, starting toward him.

"Grab him, boys," Galen said.

Lou Shannon and Jack Spence came toward Vavak, one grabbing him from each side.

"What is this?" Vavak asked. "Why you do this?"

"Take him over to the bar," Galen said.

The two men dragged Vavak, who was protesting and fighting against them, over to the bar. Galen stepped up in front of him, and smiled at him, a crooked, evil smile.

"Well now, Mr. Ivan Vavak," Galen said. "I think it is time you and I had a little talk."

"With you, I have nothing to say," Vavak said.

Galen turned to the others. "Wit you, I hov nutting to say," he mimicked. The two men holding Vavak, and the other cowboys who had come with Vavak, including Slim Posey, who, by now, had regained his feet, laughed at Galen's mimicry. Most of the others in the saloon looked on in nervous silence, clearly not agreeing with what Galen was doing, but frightened to do anything to stop it.

"Let me go," Vavak said, struggling with the men who held him. "About Harold I wish to see."

"About Harold you wish to see?" Galen sneered. Suddenly, and brutally, he brought the back of his hand across Vavak's face. It popped loudly in the saloon and, almost immediately, blood began coming from Vavak's lip. "If you are going to live here, you should learn to talk good English," Galen said.

Vavak glared at him.

"Now, Mr. Vavak, here is the deal I have to offer you. You send your tenderfoot back to New York to tell Williams that you don't want to raise Herefords. If you do that, I think we can be good neighbors."

Galen smiled at him again, and again, it was a smile without mirth.

"What do you say, Mr. Vavak? What can I tell my father?"

"Your father you can tell, go to hell!" Vavak said, punctuating his reply by spitting in Galen's face.

"You son of a bitch!" Galen shouted and he swung at Vavak, but, just as he did so, Vavak ducked. As a result, Galen hit Shannon in the face. As Shannon's knees buckled he loosened his grip, allowing Vavak to jerk his arm away. With his arm free, Vavak hit Galen, catching him square on his nose. Galen's nose went flat and started bleeding.

"Grab him! Grab him!" Galen shouted, and Shannon and Spence managed, once more, to get Vavak under control.

Galen took a handkerchief from his pocket and put it to his nose. He held it there for a moment, then pulled it away.

"I think you broke my nose," he said in

quiet anger. "Hold him up. I'm going to teach the son of a bitch a lesson he won't forget anytime soon."

After Vavak went into the Brown Dirt Cowboy, Todd continued down the street until he reached the railroad depot, where he stepped into the telegraph office to send a message. Writing the message on a sheet of yellow lined paper that was provided specifically for this purpose, he tore it from the tablet, then handed it to the telegrapher.

"I expect a response to this by no later than tomorrow morning," he said. "And when it comes back, I want you to have it delivered to me at Trailback Ranch. Deliver it right away, as soon as you get it."

"Trailback is a long way out of town. Delivering it out there will cost you a dollar extra," the telegrapher said.

Todd paid him a dollar. The telegrapher put the dollar in his pocket.

"And it will cost another dollar, if you want an immediate delivery."

Todd looked at the telegrapher long enough to make the telegrapher uneasy, then he pulled out a second dollar and handed it to him.

"The telegram had better be punctual

and accurate," he said, "or I'm coming after you."

"Yes, sir," the telegrapher replied. "Punctual and accurate. It will be, sir, I can promise you that."

Satisfied that he had made his point, Todd left the depot, and walked back down to the Brown Dirt Cowboy. Even before he got there though, he knew something was happening inside. He hadn't heard anything, it was just . . . that was it! He hadn't heard anything: no loud talk, no laughter, no piano. The saloon was strangely quiet.

Quickening his pace, Todd pushed through the front doors, then looked around the place. He was right, something was wrong. There was no drinking or easy banter, and there were no women going from table to table. Instead, the women were gathered on the stairs at the back of the room, looking on in horror at the scene being played out before them. Everyone else was quiet, ashen-faced, and looking toward the far end of the bar.

Harold Shedd was on his knees, shaking his head, trying to get up from the floor. Vavak was on his feet, being held up by two men. Vavak's left eye was black, and swollen nearly shut. His lip was bloody. A

236

younger man was standing in front of Vavak. Having never met Galen, Todd didn't recognize him, but he did see that the man was about to hit Vavak again.

Quicker than anyone would have thought possible for a big man to move, Todd was across the room. Before Galen could deliver his blow, Todd grabbed him by the scruff of his neck and the seat of his pants, then lifted him up over his head.

"Hey! What the hell?" Galen shouted in shock and fear, when he suddenly, and unexpectedly, found himself being held high over the floor of the saloon.

Galen tried to reach for his pistol, but he couldn't get to it before Todd threw him as one would a sack of flour. In an explosion of glass, Galen crashed through the front window of the saloon, then fell, unconscious, to the wooden porch out front. With Galen out of the way, Todd turned his attention to the two men who were still holding Vavak. Like everyone else in the saloon, they were so shocked by what they had just seen that they hadn't even moved since Todd came into the room. Then, suddenly realizing that they were about to be his next victims, they let Vavak go and tried to run.

"Jesus, Lou! Let's get the hell out of

here!" Spence shouted, and both started to run, but Todd caught them.

"Hey, what are you doing? Let go of me, you big son of a bitch!"

Cupping his big hands on opposite sides of their heads, he slammed the heads together. Both men went down and out.

"Doc! Look out for Babcock!" Vavak shouted.

Vavak's warning referred to the chair in Wade Babcock's hands. Todd spun around just as Babcock was bringing the chair down on him. But, thanks to Vavak's warning, Todd managed to protect his head by putting up his left arm. That arm shattered the chair and deflected the blow. At the same time, the heel of Todd's open right hand struck a hammer-like blow to Babcock's chest. The blow knocked the wind from the startled foreman, and sent him sprawling back until he hit the bar. He slid down to the floor, winding up in a sitting position, trying desperately to draw a breath.

Behind Todd, and unseen by him, three men drew their pistols. Suddenly the room echoed with the explosion of gunfire.

Startled by the gunshot, Todd spun around. That was when he saw Ken Crites standing just inside the doors, holding a double-barrel shotgun. A little wisp of smoke curled up from one of the barrels, and he was pointing the gun toward the three men who had drawn their pistols.

"Drop your guns, right now, or I'll drop you," Crites said.

"Now, how are you goin' to do that, old man?" Slim Posey sneered. "You got only one shot left in that scatter gun."

"Sonny, this is a ten-gauge Greener, double-aught," Crites said. "There is enough charge here to kill one of you, and do some serious hurt to one more of you."

"Yeah, well that still leaves one of us to kill you, doesn't it, old man?" the arrogant young man said.

"That's right," Crites said.

The three men looked at each other, a smug grin spreading across their faces.

"Which one of you will be left standing, do you think?" Crites asked, easily.

The men stood there for a moment longer, then they dropped their grins and their pistols. The revolvers landed with loud clumps on the floor.

With the immediate danger over, Todd turned toward Vavak. "Mr. Vavak, are you all right?" he asked.

"I'm fine," Vavak said, holding a handkerchief to his lip. "See about Harold."

Harold had managed to get all the way up to his feet. With the immediate danger now over, Belle had left her position on the stairs and was now attending to Harold. Blood was streaming down his forehead and there was a large, very visible lump on back of his head. It was also matted with blood, and Todd went over to look at it.

"I need a cloth and some whiskey," Todd said.

Without hesitation, Belle held up her silk underskirt. "Will this do?" she asked.

"Yes, thank you," Todd replied. He tore a large piece from the underskirt and, soaking it in the whiskey the bartender provided, began wiping away the blood.

In the meantime, the sound of Crites's gunshot had alerted the town marshal, and now he came rushing into the saloon with his own gun drawn. Seeing Crites standing there holding a shotgun, the marshal pointed his pistol toward him.

"You want to lower that scattergun, Crites?" he asked.

"I'll do that," Crites replied, "now that you're here to keep things under control." He lowered the gun.

"I'd feel a mite better, if you'd break it open," the marshal said.

"All right," Crites said, complying with

the marshal's request. He broke the gun open, then pulled out the two shells. He tossed the expended shell into a nearby spittoon, but the good shell, he dropped into his pocket.

"Now, how about somebody tellin' me what is goin' on here?" the marshal asked.

Harold started to answer, then he chuckled and shook his head. "Damned if I know," he said. "All I know is, I was standing at the bar, having a drink and some conversation with Belle, when Slim there," he pointed to Posey, who was one of the three cowboys Crites had disarmed, "come over to palaver with me. The palaverin' got a little out of hand, and I think I hit him." He put his hand to the wound on the back of his head. "But I don't have any idea how I got this."

"Who hit him?" the marshal asked. When nobody answered, he looked over at the bartender.

"Pete, did you see anything?" he asked.

"Now, Marshal Tanner, you know I can't afford to get mixed up in any brawls that go on in here."

"You can't afford to have your place shut down either, can you? Now, who hit him?"

"Well, in that case, I reckon you'll find

him lyin' out there on the front porch," Pete said.

"Yeah, who is that? I didn't get much of a look at him, being as he's belly down."

"That's Galen Metzger," Wade Babcock said. Like Harold, Babcock had regained his feet and he was standing there, leaning back against the bar, still gasping for breath.

"Galen Metzger? Holy shit! You mean Lon Metzger's boy?"

"That's right, Marshal," Babcock said. He looked over at Todd. "And Mister, I don't think Mr. Metzger's going to be none too happy about the way you treated his son."

"You're Metzger's ramrod, ain't you?" the marshal asked Babcock.

"That's right."

"And you fellas," he said, indicating the three men Crites had disarmed, as well as the two men who had been holding Vavak, who had now regained their feet to join their friends. "All of you work for Metzger?"

"We do," Slim Posey answered.

"Uh, huh," Marshal Tanner replied. He stroked his chin. "And this fella works for you, doesn't he, Mr. Vavak?" He pointed to Harold.

242

"Yes," Vavak said.

"And I know Mr. Crites works for you," the marshal said. He looked over at Todd. "You must be that big tree of a tenderfoot I been hearing about. You've come here to get rid of all the Longhorns, I believe?"

"Just the Longhorns on Trailback," Todd replied. "We are replacing them with Herefords."

"So I've heard," Marshal Tanner said. "Though why in hell you would want to come out here and make that kind of trouble is beyond me."

"We aren't doing it to make trouble," Todd said. "Herefords are a better breed of cattle than the Longhorn, but that doesn't mean the other ranchers are going to go out of business. At least, not if they are smart."

"You son of a bitch!" Galen suddenly shouted, rushing in through the batwing doors at that moment, brandishing his pistol. "I'm going to kill you!"

Nearly everyone in the saloon let out a shout of alarm because Galen was waving his pistol around and was clearly about to open fire on someone, even if he wasn't sure who.

Crites was the only one who didn't start running away from Galen. Instead, he took a step toward him, then brought the double barrels of his shotgun down, hard, on Galen's head. Galen went down again and the gun he was carrying went scooting across the floor. Vavak reached down to pick it up.

"I'd appreciate it, if you would give that gun to me, Mr. Vavak," the marshal said, holding out his hand.

Without a word of protest, Vavak did so.

"Thanks," Marshal Tanner said. He stuck Galen's pistol down his belt, then sighed. "I'm telling you boys that whatever you have going on between you, keep it between you. I won't have it coming into my town. Do you understand that?"

"You're a big man, mister," Babcock said, pointing to Todd. "But you ain't so big that a bullet can't stop you."

"Well, now, you wouldn't be threatening him, would you, Babcock?" Marshal Tanner asked.

Babcock's eyes blinked a couple of times, then he stroked his chin. "No," he said. "No, I ain't threatenin' him. I was just talkin' to him, that's all."

"Anymore trouble, and I'll lock you all up . . . in the same cell, and let you beat each other to death." He looked at Todd. "And I don't think anyone would want to be locked into a cell with this hombre."

"Hell, Marshal, you think you have a jail-cell strong enough to keep that big ox locked up?" the bartender asked.

The bartender's question had the effect of easing the tension and most of the patrons of the bar laughed. However, none of the men who worked for Metzger joined in the laughter.

TWELVE

Todd had just finished breakfast and was coming out of the cowboys' mess hall when a boy, no more than fifteen years old, came riding onto the ranch. The arrival of a stranger aroused the curiosity of the others, but Todd knew immediately what it was about.

"Are you delivering a telegram?" he asked, stepping out to meet him.

"Yes, sir," the boy replied. "Are you Dr. Todd?"

"I am."

The boy swung down from the saddle, then reached into a little bag he was carrying, slung around his shoulder. "This here telegram come in at six o'clock this mornin'," he said, pulling out an envelope and handing it to Todd. "It come all the way from New York."

Todd took the telegram. "Thank you for delivering it so promptly," he said. He

246

tipped the boy half a dollar.

"Gee, thanks, mister!" the boy said, smiling broadly at his windfall.

Although the others were curious as to what the telegram might be, none of them asked about it, because that wasn't their way. Instead, they just watched, their curiosity becoming even greater as Todd glanced at it, then walked straight to the big house.

"Hi, Doc," Roselyn greeted when she answered his knock at the door. "Are you here to see Papa?"

"Yes," Todd said, "if I'm not intruding."

"Not intruding at all. Come on in and have a seat, Papa's shaving. I'll tell him you are here."

As Todd waited, he examined the parlor. Against one wall sat a bookcase with a curved glass front, behind which were four shelves of books. A photograph sat on top of the bookcase depicting a much younger Ivan and Alice Vavak. They were holding a baby that Todd imagined must be Roselyn. A tattered Confederate flag was on the wall and, alongside it, the red and white ensign of Poland.

He was surprised, also, to see a picture of his own father standing alongside Vavak. He walked over to pick it up for a closer examination. Seeing it caused him to think of his father. He and his father had not had a particularly close relationship through the years, but there was never any animosity between them, either. Todd knew that his father loved him in his own way, but knew, also, that it was difficult for the senior Williams to express that love. At this moment, he felt a keen sense of sadness over the fact that his father was no longer alive.

"So what do you think, Dad? Would you approve of what I'm doing?" Todd asked under his breath.

"Mr. Williams was good man," Vavak said, startling Todd as he came into the room.

"Yes, he was," Todd said, examining Vavak through narrowed eyes. Had Vavak overheard him?

"I have known many men; in Europe, at sea, and in America. Mr. Williams is best man ever I know."

"I know he thought the same thing about you," Todd said, putting the photo back on top of the bookcase.

"Mr. Williams you knew?" Todd breathed a sigh of relief. If Vavak had to ask if he knew him, then he had not overheard Todd's comment.

"Yes," Todd said. "I knew him."

"Then you know he was good man."

"Yes," Todd agreed.

Todd thought of what Vavak had told him about his father buying up the remaining mortgages on the small ranchers in order to help them preserve their holdings. His father had never mentioned that to him, nor, as far as he knew, did he mention it to anyone. Such generous acts were entirely contrary to the cutthroat reputation his father had, though he recalled Ernie Virdin's comment to the effect that his father had allowed that reputation to continue because it gave him a business advantage.

"Roselyn said you wish to see me."

"Oh, yes," Todd said. "I want us to go back into town Monday, to go before the Board of the Water Management Commission."

"If they will only listen to a land owner, why go, just to be turned away again?" Roselyn asked, returning to the room just in time to hear Todd's proposal.

Todd smiled. "We will have a land owner," he said.

"Who will it be?" Vavak asked.

Todd looked at Vavak. "It is you, Mr. Vavak," he said.

"No, I cannot because —" Vavak started, but Todd cut him off with a wave of his hand.

"Do you remember yesterday, when we left, I asked if it mattered how much land someone owned?"

"I remember."

Todd held up the telegram. "As of now, Mr. Vavak, you own this house, all collateral buildings, and fifteen acres of land, all of which is adjacent to Duck Creek. That makes you, not only a land owner, but eligible to petition the decision made by the Water Management Commission."

By now, Alice had come in as well. "What?" she asked. "I don't understand. How can this be?"

"Yesterday, I sent a telegram to Mr. Virdin in New York, explaining the situation."

"Mr. Virdin? That would be Mr. Williams's private secretary?" Roselyn asked.

"Yes," Todd said. He held up the telegram. "I got the reply this morning. As of now, this house, all the outbuildings, and fifteen acres of land have been deeded over to Ivan Vavak." He looked over at Roselyn, who was shocked at hearing the words. "By the way, that fifteen acres includes Sky Meadow," he said.

"How did you know about Sky Meadow?" Roselyn asked in surprise.

Todd chuckled. "I've been here for a while now. It's not exactly a closely guarded secret."

"No, I guess not," Roselyn agreed. "And you say Mr. Williams's son did this?"

"Yes, ma'am, that is exactly what I'm telling you," Todd replied. "Mr. Todd Williams."

"I, I can't believe it," Roselyn said.

"Believe it," Todd said. Clearing his throat, he began to read:

"To the Honorable Jay Jensen, Commissioner, Southwest Texas Water Management Commission, stop. Be it known by this telegram, that the house and all adjacent outbuildings, as well as fifteen acres of contiguous land, said land being served by Duck Creek, has herewith been transferred to Mr. Ivan Vavak. Stop.

"Notarized deeds, and all necessary documentation will be sent by U.S. Mail soonest. Stop.

"Regards, Todd Williams."

"Is this for real?" Vavak asked.

"Yes, sir, it is as real as rain," Todd

replied. "Mr. Vavak, you are now a land owner."

Vavak turned to his wife, a broad smile spreading across his face.

"What do you think, Alice?" he asked.

"Oh, do you know what this means?" Alice replied in an awed voice.

"Yes. It means I can talk to Water Management Commission."

"It means much more than that, Ivan Vavak," Alice said. "It means we own this house. For the first time in our lives, we own our own house." Alice's eyes were glistening with tears.

"I don't understand," Roselyn said.

"What is there not to understand?" Todd asked.

"I don't understand why Mr. Todd Williams would do such a thing."

"It could be that you have Mr. Todd Williams all wrong," Todd suggested. "Perhaps there is much more to him than you suspect."

"Perhaps," Roselyn said. "On the other hand, he may realize that if he doesn't have someone who can represent his interest before the board, he may wind up losing everything."

Todd chuckled. "You are a hard woman to win over, Roselyn Vavak."

As the surrey rolled into town, Todd and Vavak looked over toward the Brown Dirt Cowboy Saloon. There were boards nailed across the gap in the front window, broken out Friday when Todd tossed Galen through the glass.

Vavak chuckled. "I think it would be more better if you throw young Metzger through window today. It would hurt to go through wood, I think."

Todd laughed. "Why, Mr. Vavak, who would have ever thought you could be so vindictive? Would you stop over there for a moment, please?" Todd pointed to the law office of Tom Murchison.

"Will we need lawyer?" Vavak asked.

"No, I just need to borrow something from him."

"Do you wish to be introduce?" Vavak asked.

"No, that's all right. I'll introduce myself."

Vavak waited outside, sitting in the surrey, as Todd went into the lawyer's office. Tom Murchison was a rather digni-fied-looking man with silver hair, blue eyes, and just the ghostly suggestion of the freckles that had covered his face in his youth. He was sitting at his desk, reading a telegram, and he looked up when Todd stepped inside.

"Yes, sir, what can I do for you?" Murchison asked, putting the telegram to one side.

Todd nodded toward the little paper Murchison put down. "Would that be a telegram from Mr. Ernie Virdin?" he asked.

"It would," Murchison answered. "You must be Dr. William Todd."

"Is there a sentence in the telegram that reads, 'Dr. Todd has something to reveal to you'?"

Murchison nodded. "As a matter of fact, there is such a sentence," he said. "And I must confess, I am curious as to what it might be."

"I am telling you this in complete confidence, Mr. Murchison. And I would like for it to remain confidential."

"Of course," Murchison replied, soberly. "Confidence is my stock in trade, Dr. Todd."

"My name is not William Todd. It is Todd Williams. Endicott Williams was my father."

"You are the heir . . . now the *owner* of Trailback?"

"Yes," Todd said easily.

"Does Vavak know who you are?"

"No. No one knows, except, now, you."

Murchison looked confused. "Why are you keeping your identity secret? I would think it would be to your advantage for everyone to know who you are. Especially considering the circumstances."

"When I first came out here I believed my reason for not telling anyone who I am to be a good one. Now, I'm not so sure my reason was valid, but under the current circumstances, I feel as if I am holding a tiger by the tail. I'm afraid that if I revealed my identity at this late date it would create even more problems. I have to work through a few things before I can do that. I hope you understand."

"I'm sure it has something to do with all the folderol over your bringing Herefords onto the range," Murchison said.

"Yes."

"I heard about the Water Management Commission shutting down Duck Creek. It seems to me like you are going to have to reveal yourself now in order to get a hearing."

"No, I think I have found a way around that," Todd said. "But I'll need to borrow a copy of the Texas Civil Code, if you don't mind."

"Sure, I'll be glad to lend it to you," Murchison said. "That book is pretty complicated, though. All law codes are. Do you know what you are looking for?"

"Yes, Mr. Virdin gave me the chapter and verse," Todd said.

Murchison got up from his desk, then walked over to his bookshelf to take down a large, red-bound book. He brought it back to Todd, but held onto it for a moment.

"You know, Mr. Williams, your father and I did business for many years, and satisfactorily, too, I think. I hope you know that you can count on me for any help you might need while you are out here." He handed the book to Todd.

"Yes, I do know that," Todd said. He held up the book. "And I just did. Thanks for the loan of the book."

When Vavak pulled up to the bank, there were several horses and a couple of carriages out front. He and Todd went in, Todd carrying the large, red book he had gotten from the lawyer's office. Todd knew that Vavak was curious about the book, but the ranch manager had not inquired about it. Todd found this taciturn nature of the Westerner to be one of their most intriguing qualities.

They went through the bank, then pushed the door open into the office of the Water Management Commission. The board meeting was in progress in the back room and Jensen, seeing Todd and Vavak through the open door, excused himself from the meeting. He closed the door behind him as he stepped into the outer office.

"Well, Mr. Vavak, I didn't expect to see you back today," Jensen said.

"I see the board is meeting," Vavak said.

"Yes, as I told you Friday, today is their regularly scheduled meeting." Jensen noticed Vavak's black eye. "Oh, I heard about your problem in the saloon," he said. "I'm sorry about that. I want you to know that I don't hold with such a thing."

"I think maybe others are hurt more bad than me," Vavak said.

Jensen looked at Todd, visibly measuring his size by running his eyes up and down Todd's large frame. "Yes, so I heard," he said. "Now, Mr. Vavak, what can I do for you?"

"I want to go in there, to go before board."

Jensen shook his head. "Now, Mr. Vavak, we discussed all this on Friday. Only land owners can petition the board of directors."

"I am land owner," Vavak said, showing Jensen the telegram.

Jensen read the telegram, then shook his head. "This is just a telegram, Mr. Vavak. It doesn't prove anything," he said. "I'd have to see the deed of transfer before I could accept your claim of land ownership."

"No, you don't," Todd said. He held up the book he had gotten from Tom Murchison. "This is a book of the Texas Civil Code, dated 1881." He opened the book, and began to read. "Under the heading of Rules of Civil Evidence, Article Nine, Authentication and Identification, section a, General Provision, it reads: 'The requirement of authentication or identification is satisfied by evidence sufficient to support the claim.' And, under section b, paragraph 7, Public Records or Reports, it states, 'Evidence that is recorded or filed in a public office may be authenticated by telegram, provided that telegram is notarized by a public telegrapher.' You will notice, Mr. Jensen, that this telegram," Todd said, pointing to the yellow paper Vavak was holding, "has been notarized by the telegrapher. I should also tell you that a copy of this same telegram was sent directly to Governor John Ireland. Mr. Williams wanted to make the Governor aware of the situation here. I don't know if you are aware of this, but Mr. Williams was a rather major contributor to Governor Ireland's campaign. I'm sure the Governor will take a personal interest in this case."

"The Governor has a personal interest in this case?" Jensen asked in a weak voice.

"Yes. Now, about this telegram. As you can see by the paragraph and section I just cited, it is as binding as a recorded deed."

The door to the back office opened, and Metzger stuck his head out. "What in the Sam Hill is going on out here, Jensen? It's time to get this meeting started." Seeing Vavak, Metzger sneered. "What are you doing here?"

"I have one more item to add to the agenda," Jensen said. "Mr. Vavak will be addressing the board."

"The hell he will," Metzger exploded. "You know the rules. Only land owners —"

"He *is* a land owner," Jensen said, cutting Metzger off in mid-sentence.

"What are you talking about? He manages Trailback, he doesn't own it."

"No, but he owns land, and the land he owns is contiguous to Duck Creek," Todd said. "That means he is a land owner, with a vested interest in what this board decides about Duck Creek."

"The board has already decided about Duck Creek," Metzger said.

By now, some of the other members of the board had drifted out into the outer office to see what was going on.

"Well, you are going to reconsider the case," Todd said.

"Who the hell are you to tell us what we are going to do?" Metzger asked angrily.

"I'm just a citizen, with a personal interest in seeing justice done," Todd said. He held up the civil code book. "According to the civil code of the state of Texas, Mr. Vavak, who is now a land owner, has a right to petition the board of directors of the Water Management Commission."

"I don't give a damn what —"

"Lon, the way I see it, we don't have any choice," Steve Warren said. "If he's a land owner —"

"*If* he's a land owner," Metzger interrupted. He pointed to Vavak. "Since when did you become a land owner?" he asked.

"He owns the house, all adjacent buildings, and fifteen acres along Duck Creek," Todd said.

"Fifteen acres? Don't make me laugh. You think fifteen acres makes him a land owner?"

"It's not what I think, Mr. Metzger, it's what the law of Texas thinks," Todd replied. "The law of Texas states that any land owner whose property is directly affected by a decision made by the Water Management Commission has the right to petition the Water Management Commission."

Metzger looked at Jensen. "What kind of nonsense is this?" he asked.

"I'm afraid he is right," Jensen said.

Metzger turned his attention back to Todd. "Are you his lawyer?"

"I'm a veterinarian," Todd said.

"Not a lawyer?"

"No."

"Then you've got no business here."

"As a veterinarian, working on Trailback, I am also Mr. Vavak's consultant with regard to all things concerning the health of his livestock. Since the unrestricted flow of water concerns the health of his livestock, I have a right to be here."

"You're the big son of a bitch who sneaked up behind my son, aren't you?"

"Sneaked up behind him?" Todd asked. Then, he remembered that he had come up behind the younger Metzger. He chuckled. "Yes," he said. "Now that I think about it, I suppose you can say that."

"You think that's funny, do you?" Metzger said, blustering.

"I thought it was sort of funny, watching him fly through the glass, yes," Todd said.

"Well, let me tell you something, Mister, you'd just better watch your step around me and mine."

"Lon," Carl Phillips said.

"What?"

Phillips handed a bound notebook to Metzger. "Here are the bylaws of the Water Management Commission."

"I'm familiar with the bylaws," Metzger said, obviously irritated at the interruption.

"You might be interested in this particular bylaw," Phillips said, pointing to something on the page.

Glaring at Phillips for interfering, Metzger began to read the paragraph that was pointed out to him. Then, as he read, a smile spread across his face. He looked up at Vavak.

"Vavak, how many cows are you running on your spread?"

"I don't know. I have not made count since —"

"No, I'm not talking about Trailback's cows," Metzger interrupted. "I'm talking about *your* cows, on *your* . . . fifteen acre . . . ranch," he added, setting the final words apart with a little sneer.

The others, hearing Metzger refer to the fifteen acres as a ranch, laughed.

"On your land, how many of your cows do you have?"

"I have no cattle."

Metzger looked over at Jensen, a triumphant expression on his face. He pointed to a paragraph on the document he was holding. "Jensen, this is from the bylaws and charter of the Water Management Commission, and I quote, 'Only bona fide land owners *whose livestock may be threatened* by any action taken by the Water Management Commission, may petition the board of directors.' Now, since, by his own admission, he has no livestock, he has no right to be here."

Jensen took the book from Metzger, and read the appropriate page. Clearing his throat, he looked up at Ivan Vavak.

"I'm sorry, Mr. Vavak. It would appear that Mr. Metzger is correct. The only way you can petition the board is if you have cattle affected."

"That's not what it says," Todd said.

"Would you care to read it for yourself?" Jensen asked, holding the book out toward Todd.

"No need for me to read it. Read it again. Read it aloud," Todd said.

As if making a point, Metzger began again, reading slowly and distinctly. "Only bona fide land owners whose livestock may be threat—"

"Stop!" Todd said.

Metzger looked up.

"Only bona fide land owners whose *livestock* may be threatened. It says nothing about cows."

"Cattle is livestock," Metzger pointed out angrily. "You bein' a veterinarian, should know that."

"So are horses, livestock," Todd replied. "And you being a rancher, should know that."

"Horses?"

"Doc, I have no —" Vavak started, but Todd held out his hand to interrupt him.

"Miss Roselyn Vavak owns a horse," Todd said. "Her horse's name is Pepper."

"Have you lost your mind?" Metzger spouted. "His daughter has a pet pony and you think that's all you need?"

"Yes, that's all we need," Todd replied. "There is no mention of how much livestock a land owner must own to qualify. Therefore, one animal, whose well-being is threatened by action taken by the Water Management Commission, is all the justification needed for an appeal to the board." Todd looked pointedly at Jensen. "And I'm sure that the governor would agree with that interpretation," he said.

"The, uh, governor," Jensen said. He used his forefinger to pull his collar away from his neck.

"Jensen, throw these idiots out!" Metzger demanded, making an impatient gesture with his arm. "Then come on back inside. We have some important matters to discuss."

"I can't do that," Jensen said.

"What?" Metzger exploded angrily. "What do you mean, you can't do that?"

"There is no other way to interpret the Civil Code," Jensen said.

"Surely you don't intend to let them attend the meeting?"

Jensen shook his head in defeat. "I'm afraid I intend to do just that."

Metzger fumed for a moment, then finally relented. "Alright, alright, come on in and make your case, if you think you can," he said. "I was just trying to save us all some time, that's all."

Returning to the boardroom, Jensen took his place at the head of a long table. Metzger, Warren, and Phillips sat on one side, while Peters, Johnson, and Simmons sat on the other. The expression on Metzger's face, which was one of unbridled hostility, was nearly matched by the expression on the faces of Steve Warren and Carl Phillips. Andrew Peters, Bill Johnson, and Brad Simmons appeared to be more curious than hostile.

"I can speak English, but not so good for something important like this," Vavak said. "So, I let my friend speak for me."

Vavak sat down, and Todd stood up. This was the first time most of the members of the board had actually seen Todd, though they certainly knew of this giant from the East and, by now, all had heard about the incident in the saloon.

"Gentlemen," Todd began, "let's get right to the heart of the matter. Lon Metzger didn't close the sluice gate on his ranch because of drought conditions. He didn't have two of his men hold Mr. Vavak, while his son gave him the black eye that you see now, because of drought conditions."

Todd watched the reaction to his mention of the beating Vavak had taken, and was pleased to see that Peters, Johnson, and Simmons appeared to be genuinely chagrined by the words. And even Steve Warren and Carl Phillips seemed uncomfortable by it.

"No, gentlemen," Todd continued. "This entire situation has been brought on by fear and ignorance. Fear of the unknown, and ignorance of the outcome.

"Trailback Ranch is introducing Hereford cattle onto the range. If we are successful —" he stopped and held up his finger to emphasize the point — "and there are so many variables that it is a big *if* . . . but if we are successful, Herefords will be the cattle of the future. Every cattle rancher in Texas stands to gain by switching over to Herefords. Every rancher, including you gentlemen. But someone must make that first step someone must . . . take that risk," he added, setting the last phrase apart to emphasize it, "and Trailback is taking that risk for everyone.

"Instead of fighting Trailback, every rancher in the county, indeed, every rancher in the state, should support the operation. So, let's not kid ourselves. Shutting down the water supply has nothing to do with drought, and everything to do with ignorance. I urge you to order the gates open so that . . ." Todd paused, then smiled broadly, "Miss Roselyn's horse, Pepper, will have an adequate supply of water."

As he hoped, Peters, Johnson, and Simmons laughed out loud, and even Steve Warren smiled.

When Todd sat down, Brad Simmons raised his hand. "I move that we order the gate opened."

"Simmons, I will remember that!" Metzger said, pointing his finger at Simmons.

"I second the motion," Bill Johnson said, looking defiantly at Metzger.

"The motion has been made and seconded, that the sluice gate be raised," Jensen said. "All in favor, say aye."

Simmons, Johnson, and Peters said aye. Metzger glared, angrily, at all three of them.

"I will remember that," Metzger said.

"All opposed?" Jensen asked.

Metzger, Warren, and Phillips said no.

Metzger smiled broadly. "Well, it was a good try, Vavak, but you lost," he said. He looked at Johnson, Peters, and Simmons. "And as for you three —"

"Wait a minute," Todd interrupted. "It was a tie. I believe, according to the procedures, it is now up to Mr. Jensen to break the tie."

Todd stared at Jensen. The Commissioner was obviously uncomfortable at being placed in this position, and, as he had earlier, he used a crooked index finger to pull his collar away from his neck.

"You are wasting your breath and our time," Metzger said, confidently. "Everyone knows where Mr. Jensen stands."

"I don't know where he stands," Todd said. "I would like to have his vote on record. How say you, Mr. Jensen? What message are we to send to Governor Ireland? Are we suffering a drought?"

Jensen licked his lips, and ran his hand through his hair.

"Go ahead, Jensen, cast your vote so we can get back to business here," Metzger ordered, almost dismissively.

"I, uh, vote to," Jensen paused, then took a deep breath, "open the sluice gate," he said.

"What?" Metzger thundered, jumping up from his chair so energetically that it tumbled over behind him. "Why, you backstabbing son of a bitch! I'll have your job for this!"

"Thank you, Mr. Jensen, and members of the board," Todd said.

THIRTEEN

Pecos, Texas, Monday, June 22nd:

At almost the same moment Todd and Vavak were making their pitch to the Board of Directors of the Texas Land and Water Commission, Marshal Marcus Tanner was getting off a train in Pecos, Texas. He stood on the depot platform for a moment as the engine vented steam and the wheel boxes popped and snapped as they cooled behind him.

The depot was a small wooden structure, with a sign that announced, proudly: PECOS, TEXAS, COUNTY SEAT OF REEVES COUNTY, POPULATION 643.

"Do you have any luggage to claim?" a baggage handler asked.

"No," Tanner answered. "I'll be returning on the next train."

"Very good, sir."

Leaving the depot, Tanner walked down Oak Street until he reached the sheriff's office. There, he pushed the door open and went inside. The room was typical of the many county and city law enforcement offices Tanner had been in over the course of his career. One wall was covered with Wanted posters and just beneath the posters was a table, on which sat the water bucket. A dipper hung from a nail above the water bucket. A pot-bellied, wood-burning stove stood in a box of sand to the right of the door, while Sheriff Cory Denton's desk sat across the room from it, on the left side. On the wall just behind Denton's desk, was a gun rack with two Winchesters, one Henry, and a double-barreled shotgun.

"Hello, Marcus," Denton said.

"Cory."

Denton was at his desk, paring an apple, and one long, thin peel hung, unbroken, from the apple all the way to the floor.

"What time did you leave Sierra Blanca?"

"Nine o'clock this morning."

"A hundred miles in four hours. We truly live in wondrous times." Denton went back to paring the apple.

Tanner watched him for a second, chuckled, then walked over to the water bucket. Slipping the dipper from the hook, he got a drink.

"Don't be shaking the floor now, you

might cause the peel to break," Denton said, not looking up from his apple. "I think this is going to be a new record."

"What are you going to do, Cory? Hang it up on your wall and charge people to see it?" Tanner drank the water, then returned the dipper to the hook, and wiped his mouth with the back of his hand.

"That's an idea," Denton replied. "You think folks would pay to see it?"

"Some folks is dumb enough to pay to see anything," Tanner replied. "Thanks for the telegram. Is he still here?"

"He is."

"Where've you got him? In the back?" Tanner nodded toward the back of the building, where the jail was.

"You think I'm crazy enough to try and arrest Lucien Shardeen by myself? He's over at the Hog Waller Saloon, gamblin', drinkin', carousin' with the women like he owns the place."

"How long has he been here?"

"Like I said in the telegram, he's been here three days," Denton said. "Well, four, now. You still wantin' him?"

"I'm still wantin' him," Tanner said.

"What are you going to do with him?"

"I'm going to take him over to Pecos County."

"Pecos County? Not El Paso?" Denton asked. Then he smiled. "Oh, I see. You not being a lawman in Pecos County, you'll be eligible for the reward."

"I'm not doing it for the reward."

"Maybe not. But there's no need to turn your back on it, either. I mean, if you're going to take him over there anyway."

"Yeah, well, first things first," Tanner said. "It's like the recipe for rabbit stew."

"How's that?"

"First, you have to catch the rabbit."

Denton laughed. "Shardeen being the rabbit, huh? You want some help in making the arrest?"

"I would like it, yes. You sure you want to take a hand in this?"

"Well, I didn't want to try and arrest him by myself, but I won't send you out to do it alone."

"I appreciate that, Cory," Tanner said. "And I appreciate you sending the wire to me, instead of to Fort Stockton."

"Yeah, well, the folks in Pecos County didn't treat you right, Marcus. They had no right to turn you out of office like they done," Denton said. "Hey, look at that," he added, spreading the apple peel out on his desk. "Now, ain't that a thing of beauty?" He put ·the freshly peeled

273

apple to one side.

"Damn, Cory, aren't you going to eat that apple?"

"I might get around to it later," Denton said. "It was the peelin' I was after."

Tanner laughed.

Denton stood up, then turned to the gun rack to look over his selection of weapons. He took down the Greener. "Sorry I only got one of these," he said, holding the double-barreled shotgun up.

"One shotgun and one pistol ought to be enough for one man," Tanner said.

"Ordinarily, I'd say so," Denton agreed. "But this here ain't no ordinary man we're goin' after. Did you hear what he done down in Corpus?"

"No."

"Killed a gambler," Denton said.

"So he's wanted down there, too?"

Denton broke the shotgun open, slid two shells into the breech, then snapped it shut.

"Well, actually, he's not. They say the gambler already had his gun out, pointin' it at Shardeen before Shardeen even started his draw, but Shardeen killed him anyway. From what I hear, it was the damnedest thing anyone ever saw. So they're sayin' it was a fair fight. Besides, I don't think anybody cried any tears over the gambler."

Tanner slipped his pistol from the holder, spun the cylinder to check the loads, then put his pistol back in the holster, making certain that the gun was loose.

"Alright," Tanner said. "Let's go get him."

At a table at the rear of the saloon, Lucien Shardeen sat with his back to the wall, playing a game of solitaire. Shardeen was a fairly small man with dark hair, dark, beady eyes, a narrow mouth, and a nose shaped somewhat like a hawk's beak. He was an ugly little man who, in an ordinary world, would not garner a second glance.

But this was not an ordinary world. This was West Texas, and a man's skill with a gun could overcome any physical shortcomings he might have. Sam Colt called his pistol the Equalizer, especially for people like Lucien Shardeen.

When Sheriff Denton came into the saloon, Shardeen paid him no attention. Denton had come in several times over the last few days and had not spoken to him. Shardeen found it funny that Denton wouldn't even talk to him, knowing that Shardeen was a wanted man. It could only mean one thing, that Denton was afraid. And that was good. Shardeen knew that as long as men were afraid of him, he would always have the edge.

Shardeen started to go back to his card game, then he noticed something that caught his attention, something different.

Sheriff Denton was carrying a shotgun.

None of the previous times that Denton had come into the saloon had he been carrying a shotgun. That alone would have raised his suspicions. But when he saw who had come in with Denton, he was on full alert. The man with Denton was Marcus Tanner!

Shardeen felt an old, familiar tingling in the middle of his back, in his arms and legs, and in the pit of his stomach. His nostrils opened wider, his eyes narrowed, and his muscles tensed. He always felt this way just before he killed. It was a condition he called, "the scent of sulfur."

"Well, well, well, if it isn't Marcus Tanner," Shardeen said. "Good to see you, Tanner. It's always nice to see old friends."

"I'm no friend of yours, Lucien Shardeen, and you know it," Tanner replied.

"Oh, yes, well, there was that little incident back in Pecos County a couple of years ago, wasn't there?"

Two years earlier Shardeen had been a prisoner in the Pecos County jail, awaiting trial for murder. Marcus Tanner was the county sheriff then, and had made the initial arrest. But before the trial could take place Shardeen escaped, killing Marcus's deputy.

"Deputy Anderson left behind a wife and two kids. He was a fine, Christian man," Tanner said.

"Is that a fact? Well, then he is with the Lord, isn't he?" Shardeen replied with an evil chuckle. "By the way, I heard you lost your job over that. You went from being a big, important county sheriff, to being nothing more than a town marshal in some little mud hole somewhere. Is that right?"

"I'm taking you back, Shardeen."

"Taking me back? Back to where?"

"Back to Pecos County."

"You think those folks are going to give you your job back, if you take me in?"

"I don't want the job back," Tanner said. "I'm happy where I am. It's just that I don't like to finish a job undone. And my job over there won't be finished until your sorry ass is hung."

The other patrons of the saloon had come to an uneasy acceptance of Shardeen's presence in the saloon over the last few days. They had even come around to enjoying, in some macabre way, the fact that they were drinking with a man as notorious as Lucien Shardeen. This was something they would be able to tell their grandchildren, years from now.

But it seemed obvious that the uneasy truce they had established with Shardeen was about to come to an end. Slowly, without calling attention to themselves, the other saloon patrons began moving away from the bar, to be out of the line of fire should shooting break out. But they were faced with a dilemma. No one wanted to be close enough to be hurt, but everyone wanted to be close enough to witness whatever was about to happen.

"You plannin' on helpin' this fella take me in, Denton?" Shardeen asked.

"I am."

"And here, me'n you've been getting along so well these last few days," Shardeen said. "I guess the reward got to you, huh? Just too much money for a greedy fella to pass up."

Denton pointed the shotgun at Shardeen, and pulled back both hammers. They made a loud, double click in the room.

"Unbuckle your gunbelt and come along

with us, nice and easy," Denton said.

Shardeen shook his head. "No," he said. "No, I don't think I want to do that."

The three men stared at each other for a long, still, moment. None of the participants, nor anyone else in the saloon moved or talked, thus creating an eerie tableau, a scene that could have been reproduced in *Harper's Weekly.*

Then, suddenly, Shardeen drew his pistol, drawing and firing so fast that it appeared to be no more than a twitch of his shoulder. Seeing Shardeen start his draw, Denton pulled the trigger on both barrels of his shotgun, but it was too late. By the time he reacted to what he was seeing, it was over. The double-aught charges from his shotgun tore large, jagged holes in the floor of the saloon, even as the heavy bullet from Shardeen's gun was slamming into his heart.

Nobody was more surprised than Marcus Tanner. He had not even bothered to draw his pistol believing that, because Denton had the drop on Shardeen with a double-barreled shotgun, the situation was well in hand. He realized, too late, that he was wrong, because even as his pistol was clearing leather, Shardeen's second shot crashed into his forehead. Tanner went down, dead before his body hit the floor.

"You all saw it!" Shardeen shouted, still pumped up from the excitement of the incident. He pointed to the two bodies. "They drew on me first."

"Of course they did. They was lawmen," someone said. "They was here to arrest you."

"Arrest me, or kill me?" Shardeen said. "Did anyone see a warrant?"

"If you ask me, it was self-defense," one of the men said.

"Are you crazy, Henry? They was tryin' to arrest him."

"It was self-defense, Jim, pure and simple," Henry said, staring pointedly at Jim.

Jim got the message. "Oh, uh, yes," he said. "Yes, now that I think about it, it *was* self-defense."

The others in the saloon, catching on quickly to Henry's lead, began agreeing that it surely was self-defense.

"But here's the thing, Mr. Shardeen," Henry said. "I don't see no way the Texas Rangers ain't goin' to hear about what just happened. Now, far as I'm concerned, and ever'one else for that matter, I mean, you've heard 'em —" he took in the others with a wave of his hand — "they all say you didn't have no choice except to do what you done. But, if the Texas Rangers come here, why, it's just goin' to wind up makin' trouble for you. So, uh." Henry cleared his throat. "It might, uh, be better if you was to leave now."

"You trying to run me off?" Shardeen asked.

"No, no, uh, I wasn't doin' nothin' of the sort," Henry said, frightened that he may have angered Shardeen.

Shardeen laughed. "Don't worry about it, Henry," he said. "I know you've just got my best interest at heart. You do have my best interest at heart, don't you?"

"Oh, yes, sir! Absolutely!" Henry said in a relieved voice.

"I thought you did. But the truth is, I can't leave," Shardeen said.

"You can't leave?"

"I don't have any money."

"Oh, well, uh, I think we might be able to help out a little on that," Henry said. He took off his hat. "I bet if I passed my hat around, we could maybe scrape up enough to get you out of here. Don't you fellas think so?" he asked the others.

"Absolutely," someone replied.

"Anything for a friend," Jim said.

"Good, good," Shardeen said. "I knew I

could count on my . . . friends. Collect the money. Oh, I'd say about two hundred dollars ought to be enough."

"Two hundred dollars?" Henry gasped. "Why, Mr. Shardeen, I doubt if there is two hundred dollars in this room with all of us combined, even if we emptied the cash register."

"That seems like a simple enough problem to solve," Shardeen replied. "Go outside and collect from the townspeople. I'm sure they would be happy to help out. Two hundred dollars," he said.

"Mr. Shardeen . . ."

"Three hundred dollars," Shardeen said. "You want to make it four hundred?"

"Three . . . three hundred dollars. Yes, sir," Henry said. "Three hundred dollars."

FOURTEEN

Snores rent the air as ten cowboys slept. At this hour of the morning, only Crites was awake, and he was in the cookhouse, rolling out biscuits.

A rooster crowed.

Someone groaned.

The rooster crowed again.

"One of these mornings I'm going to shoot that rooster right in his furry little ass," Harold mumbled.

Don laughed. "Chickens don't have fur."

"Feathers, then," Harold said. "As long as I shoot the son of a bitch."

"You been promisin' to do that for more'n a year now," Timmy said. "How come you ain't done it?"

"How come none of you ain't done it?" Harold replied. "He wakes you up, too."

"Well, hell, Harold, don't nobody want to rob you of your fun in doin' it," John said, and the others laughed.

283

John lit a candle, and a soft, golden bubble of light spilled out into the room. The cowboys rolled out of their bunks, rubbed their eyes, ran their hands through their hair, and started reaching for their clothes.

Dewayne farted.

"Damn, Dewayne, you couldn't wait 'til you got outside to do that?" Don scolded. "You'll stink the place up."

"You taken a good whiff lately?" Dewayne replied. "Iffen you ask me, a few farts can only improve the smell."

Harold went outside to relieve himself. Then he walked down to check the creek.

"Damn!" he said. Turning, he ran back to the bunkhouse. "Hey, fellas," he said. "The creek is still dry."

"What? How can that be? I thought it was supposed to be flowing again by this morning. Hey, Doc, you went into town with Mr. Vavak yesterday. Didn't the water commission say the water would be back by today?"

"That's what they said, yes," Todd answered.

"Yeah? Well, it ain't here," Harold said.

When Vavak and Todd went into Sierra Blanca to check on why the water wasn't flowing they went by horseback. That was because Todd said that he was getting a little more accustomed to the saddle and thought he was up for the ride. About a mile before they reached the outskirts of Sierra Blanca, they could see the train coming from the east. By the time they reached town, the train was standing in the station blowing smoke and venting steam. When they passed by the depot they were surprised to see that a very large crowd was gathered on the platform.

"Wonder what that's all about?" Todd asked.

"Someone dead, I think," Vavak said, pointing to the black, glass-sided hearse that was backed up to the train.

"Must be someone important to draw this many people."

"Marshal Tanner," Vavak said.

"What? How do you know?"

Vavak pointed to a woman, dressed in black, and wearing a black veil. She was weeping quietly as a coffin was being taken from the baggage car and put onto the hearse. There were two women with her, trying to comfort her.

"That is Mrs. Tanner," he said.

Todd had only seen Tanner one time, and that was when he had come into the saloon to break up the fight. The marshal had seemed like a good man then, taking an even-handed approach to the situation.

They rode over to the depot and dismounted, intending to ask what happened. They didn't have to ask. The story of the shootout with Lucien Shardeen was on everyone's lips.

"They say both Sheriff Denton and Marshal Tanner had their guns out and pointin' at Shardeen, but he drawed down on 'em and kilt 'em both."

"No such thing," another corrected. "Marshal Tanner didn't even have his gun out."

"No matter, they said what Shardeen done was pure unbelievable."

Vavak walked over to extend his personal condolences to the widow, and Todd went with him, even though he didn't know her.

"Mrs. Tanner, it is truly sorry I am," Vavak said, taking her hand in his.

"Thank you, Mr. Vavak," the grieving widow said.

"If you need something, tell me, and I will do."

"I appreciate that," Mrs. Tanner said. "I can't think of anything right now."

Awkwardly, Todd extended his own condolences, then leaving the depot and the morbidly curious crowd, they rode on down to the bank. Dismounting in front of the red brick building, they went inside, and straight back to Jensen's office.

Jensen looked up from his desk as they came through the door, then he stood. "Did you hear about Marshal Tanner?" he asked.

"Yes, his body just arrived on the train," Todd said.

Jensen shook his head. "It is a terrible thing," he said. "Marshal Tanner was a good, upstanding citizen of the community."

"Yes," Vavak said. "Mr. Jensen —"

"Before you go on," Jensen said, holding up his hand to interrupt Vavak, "I want you to know that didn't have a thing to do with it."

"Then you know why we are here?" Todd asked.

"I expect it is because Duck Creek is dry."

"As the bone," Vavak said.

"Well, I can explain that. Metzger went to the judge in El Paso and got a court injunction. The judge ruled that the gate will not be opened until Metzger's appeal has been heard."

"How long will it take for his appeal to

be acted upon?" Todd asked.

Jensen shook his head. "Who knows?" he asked. "We have cases that have been pending court action for more than two years."

"Two years? Without water, in two weeks dead all the cattle," Vavak said emphatically.

"My suggestion is that you file an immediate appeal to have the injunction lifted," Jensen said. "You can list me as in support of your suit."

"Thank you, Mr. Jensen, we'll do that," Todd said.

The next stop was the law office of Tom Murchison.

"Good afternoon, gentlemen," Murchison said, greeting them as they came in. "I suppose you've heard about Marshal Tanner."

"Yes."

"I am not a man of violence," Murchison said. "But believe me, if I had a gunman's skill, I would hunt down Mr. Lucien Shardeen and bring him to justice."

"From what they were saying over at the depot, it would take someone of considerable skill to do it," Todd said.

"Yes. Someone like Cold Blood Collier, I expect."

"I've heard of him," Todd said. He recalled Harold saying he would like to see the two gunmen fight each other. "But, wouldn't that be jumping from the frying pan into the fire? I mean, isn't this Cold Blood Collier also a killer?"

"Not the same kind of killer," Murchison said. "Oh, he is every bit as deadly, but as far as I know, he never killed anyone who wasn't trying to kill him. Anyway, it is all academic. I think Collier is dead."

"Yes, I think he is dead too," Vavak said.

"It's a shame, though. We could sure use someone like him now." Murchison picked up a sheet of paper from his desk. "I'm sure you didn't come here to talk about Lucien Shardeen, though. I imagine you are here for this." He handed the paper to Vavak.

"What is this?" Vavak asked.

"It is an appeal to Judge Crane to lift his injunction against opening the floodgate."

"Yes, that is why we are here," Todd said. "How did you know?"

"When I heard what happened, I figured you would want to counter," Murchison replied. "At any rate, I was going to suggest it. So, to expedite matters, I got it ready. If you'll sign it, Mr. Vavak, I'll get it in the mail, and it will be in the county court at El Paso by mid-morning tomorrow."

"Yes, I will sign," Vavak said, taking the pen Murchison offered him. "Do you think the judge will change his mind?"

"I'm sure he will, once he sees all the pertinent facts," Murchison replied. "Metzger knows this, as well. In fact, I wouldn't be surprised if he didn't withdraw his own request for an injunction within a few days. He knows it has no merit."

"Then, why did he do it?" Vavak asked.

"It was just a nuisance suit," Murchison said.

"Nuisance suit?" Vavak asked.

"Just to cause trouble and delay," Todd put in. "My father had to put up with them all the time."

"Your father?" Murchison said. "Have you . . ."

He was about to ask if Todd had told Vavak who he was, but, with a vigorous shake of his head, Todd let Murchison know that he had not. His mention of his father had been a slip of the tongue.

"My father was in business," Todd said quickly.

Vavak signed the paper, then returned

290

the pen to the inkwell.

"I'll get this in today's mail," Murchison said, folding the paper and putting it in an envelope. "All we can do now is wait."

"Wait, and watch cattle die," Vavak said.

When Todd and Vavak returned to the ranch late that afternoon, they brought with them the news that Marcus Tanner had been killed by Lucien Shardeen.

"Tanner always did have more guts than sense," John said. "But he was a good man."

They also told about the injunction.

"What does that mean, Doc?" Harold asked.

"It means the judge has overturned the Water Commission's decision," Todd explained.

"What the hell?" Don exclaimed. "How can a judge do that? I mean, isn't what the commission says the law?"

"The commission's ruling has the effect of law, yes," Todd said. "But, unfortunately, so does the injunction, and right now the injunction prevails."

"It ain't right that the commission says one thing, and some judge comes along and says somethin' else," Don said.

"What do we do now?" Harold asked.

"Well, since it has moved into the courts, the only thing we can do is to attempt to counter the injunction and we've already done that. We filed today."

"How long will something like that take?" John asked.

"If the judge in El Paso recognizes the urgency of our situation, he could withdraw his injunction tomorrow," Todd replied.

"What if he don't do that?"

"Then the appeal will have to go to a higher court."

"And how long would that take?"

Todd shook his head. "I can't answer," he said. "Several days at the soonest, or it could go on for weeks, maybe even months."

"Hell, Doc, the way things are going, all the cows could be long dead before we get water again," John said.

"That's true," Todd agreed.

"It ain't right."

After supper that evening, Crites was just finishing cleaning up in the kitchen when he heard gunshots outside. Moving quickly to the door, he saw that it was only Harold and Don, and Harold was shooting at bottles. Crites stepped onto the back porch to toss away the dishpan of water.

"Hey, Mr. Crites!" Harold called up to the porch. "Look at this."

Harold put his pistol in his holster, bent his knees slightly, held his arms out by his side, then drew his pistol and fired. The draw was very quick, and the shot was accurate, smashing the bottle into pieces.

With a wide, proud grin on his face, Harold turned back to look at Crites.

"What do you think about that?"

"Not bad," Crites replied.

"Not bad? Not bad?" Don said. "Is that all you've got to say about it? I'd like to see Lucien Shardeen match that. Why, I bet Harold is as fast as he is."

"He may be."

"Wait, you say I may be as fast as Shardeen, but all you can say is not bad?" Harold challenged.

"You don't understand," Crites asked, his tone condescending.

Harold was confused. "What is it I don't understand?"

"You don't understand what it takes to be a good gunfighter. Shardeen isn't good because he is fast or accurate. He is good because he can kill a man without compunction."

"What does compunction mean?"

Harold asked.

"Let me explain it this way. If you saw a roach crawling across the bunkhouse floor, could you step on and kill it?"

"Hell yes, I could. I do it all the time."

"What do you think about, when you step on it?"

"Why, I don't think about anything," Harold said.

"All right, that means you can kill a roach without compunction," Crites said. "Do you think you could kill a man as easily as you can kill a roach?"

"Well, I . . ." Harold started, then he paused. "I suppose I could if I had to," he concluded.

Crites shook his head. "You're too late," he said. "You stopped to think about it. If it was real, you would be dead. Taking a man's life isn't like killing a roach, Harold. It's an awesome thing, and at that last moment, just before it's time to pull the trigger, most decent men will hesitate, just like you did when I asked you the question."

"Yeah, well, everyone would," Harold insisted.

"No, not everyone," Crites disputed. "The difference between a decent man and a gunman is that a gunman can kill a man as easily as you can step on a cockroach. Lucien Shardeen is such a man."

"What would I have to do to get to be like that?" Harold asked.

"You would have to sell your soul to the Devil," Crites answered. "And I don't think that is something you want to do."

Crites went back into the kitchen, leaving Harold and Don staring at the back door.

"What do you suppose that was all about?" Don asked. "That business about selling your soul to the devil?"

"I don't know," Harold answered. He pulled the cylinder from his pistol and poked out all the empty shell casings, then began reloading. "And what's more, I'm not sure I want to know."

Sierra Blanca, Thursday, June 25th:

The funeral cortege moved slowly down Union Street, headed toward the cemetery that was just north of town. The hearse, its black lacquer and brass fittings highly polished and flashing brilliantly in the sun, led the way, pulled by a team of matching black horses. Marcus Tanner's coffin could be seen through the glass.

Almost the entire town had turned out

for the funeral, for Tanner was not only well known, he was well-liked. In addition to the townspeople, many of the ranchers and cowboys had come into town to pay their last respects, and as the hearse turned into the cemetery, it was followed by hundreds of people, some on horseback, some in carriages, surreys, buckboards, and wagons, but most on foot.

The preacher was tall and thin. He was clean-shaven, but he had a full head of hair that was so white that it had a halo-like glow in the sun. It stood out in brilliant contrast to his dark suit.

Although the Reverend G. Allen Landers had performed funerals in Sierra Blanca before, Marshal Tanner's was, by far, the most notable. As a result, the crowd of people gathered around the open grave was larger than any group Landers had ever spoken to, and he couldn't pass the opportunity to spread the word of the Lord. He preached a thirty-minute sermon, admonishing all in the crowd to repent now, and reminding them that repentance was too late for poor Marshal Marcus Tanner.

"Some say he was a God-fearing man, and I won't question that," the Reverend Landers said. He held up a long, bony

296

finger. "But I never saw him in church, so I tell you this. He had every reason to fear God, because two days ago, in the blink of an eye, our beloved marshal was dispatched from this mortal coil and sent to stand before the judgment seat of The Almighty. Now, while it pains me to say this in front of his grieving widow, I have no doubt but that Marshal Marcus Tanner is in hell today, wishing he had turned to the Lord when he had the chance."

Mrs. Tanner's weeping had been quiet until then. But, with the Reverend Landers's pronouncement that her husband was in hell, her quiet sobs turned to loud wails.

"That ignorant bastard," Todd heard Crites say under his breath.

Landers ended the sermon, then nodded toward four men who took the ends of the two ropes, one at the head of the coffin and one at the foot, then lowered it into the grave. When the coffin reached the bottom of the hole, Landers picked up a handful of dirt and let it fall as he committed the body.

"Earth to earth, ashes to ashes, dust to dust."

With the conclusion of the funeral, the crowd began walking back to town. Vavak,

Alice, Roselyn, and Todd returned to the surrey.

"Mr. Vavak, wait a moment, would you?" someone called. Looking around, Todd saw Steve Warren and Carl Phillips coming toward them.

"Yes?" Vavak asked.

Warren and Phillips looked at each other. Both had their hats off, and Phillips was nervously turning his in his hand. "Uh, look, we want you to know that we didn't have anything to do with getting that injunction," Phillips said.

"We voted to shut the gate because we thought maybe it would get your attention and you wouldn't bring in the Herefords," Warren added. "But we don't go along with what Metzger's doing now."

"In fact, we told him we disagreed, as soon as we heard what he done," Phillips said.

"Thank you," Vavak said.

Looking across the cemetery, Todd saw Lon and Galen Metzger climbing into a buckboard. The father and son were looking, with barely concealed hostility, at the meeting that was taking place between Warren, Phillips, and Vavak.

"I, that is, we, still wish you would reconsider this crazy idea of bringing in

Herefords," Phillips said. "I fear you are going to bring economic ruin to us all."

"On the contrary," Todd said. "As I explained at the board meeting the other day, this is the dawn of a new age for cattle ranchers. The Hereford is going to be a greater money producer than anything that has ever happened to the industry."

"I hope you are right," Phillips said. "Anyway, Mr. Vavak, like I say, we just wanted you to know that we aren't allied with Metzger anymore. Whatever he does from now on is his doing, and his alone."

Vavak nodded at them and, after a moment of awkward silence, the two men touched the brim of their hats and nodded slightly toward Alice and Roselyn, then they left.

"That was decent of them to come tell you that," Alice said, as the four climbed into the surrey.

"It would be more decent if they did not vote to close gate the first time," Vavak said.

"Perhaps so. Still, it was nice of them."

"Roselyn!" a female voice called.

"Oh, Papa, wait," Roselyn said. "It's Cindy."

Cindy Murchison hurried over to the surrey. "I thought if your invitation to visit is still open, I might come out tomorrow and stay until Sunday afternoon."

"Of course it is still open," Roselyn said. "I'll come into town to get you tomorrow. We'll have a wonderful time."

While the two girls were talking, Todd was looking over at the men who had come from Trailback to attend the funeral. Most had mounted and started back already, but Ken Crites wasn't with them. The cook had gone over to talk to Mrs. Tanner and now he was leaning down over her chair, holding her hand. Mrs. Tanner was looking up at him, nodding, as if listening intently. Crites lingered a moment longer, and then Todd saw a strange thing. Mrs. Tanner lifted Crites's hand to her lips and kissed it.

"I wonder what . . ." Todd started to say, but when he looked around, he saw that everyone was paying attention to Cindy Murchison.

"Did you say something?" Vavak asked.

Todd watched Crites walk across the cemetery, then climb onto his horse and urge it into a quick trot to catch up with the others. "No," he said. "It was nothing."

On the Road from Sierra Blanca,
Friday, June 26th:

When Roselyn arrived to pick up Cindy,

she was greeted with good news.

"Father has already received a telegram from the judge up at El Paso," Cindy said. "The judge has rescinded his order!"

"He has?" Roselyn asked. "Oh, Papa will be so pleased! How soon will the gate be opened?"

"It will be opened today, I'm certain of it," Cindy said. "The telegram said the judge was sending a special deputy to serve the order."

"That's wonderful news," Roselyn said. "And we're going to have a wonderful weekend. I've got the surrey parked out front. Let's hurry back, I want to tell Papa."

Roselyn was driving the surrey. Cindy Murchison was on the seat beside her, and Cindy's bag was behind them. As they made the hour-long trip to Trailback, their visit had already begun.

"Tell me about him," Cindy said.

"Tell you about who?"

"Who? You know who, silly," Cindy said. "Dr. Todd."

"Oh, him."

"Oh, him," Cindy repeated, mocking Roselyn. "He's just about the most handsome man I've ever seen, that's all. What do you mean, 'oh him'?"

"You think he's handsome? I suppose he is, I've never noticed."

"Roselyn Marie Vavak, what a fibber you are," Cindy said.

"Well, alright, I've noticed a little."

"What about the Independence Day Dance next week? Are you going?"

"Of course I'm going," Roselyn said. "That's just the biggest social event in Sierra Blanca."

Cindy laughed. "It is also the only social event in Sierra Blanca."

Roselyn joined her in laughter. "Well, I suppose you are right about that."

"Will you be dancing with Dr. Todd?"

"I will if he asks me," Roselyn said, not mentioning the fact that she had already broached the subject with Todd.

"Tell me about the tenderfoot."

"Well, it turns out his feet aren't that tender. But his backside is."

"What do you mean his backside is?"

Roselyn told about the problems Todd had riding a horse when he first arrived. "However, I am happy to report that he is finally coming around. He actually rode a horse all the way into town day before yesterday. But I'll bet if I gave him a spank on his rear, he'd jump a mile."

"Well, now, is that something you are likely to do? Give him a spank on the rump?" Cindy teased.

"I might," Roselyn said, smiling. "I might just sneak up on him someday and —" she made a spanking motion with her hand — "*bam!* Hit him right on the rump."

Cindy laughed out loud. "Roselyn, you are awful," she said. "Simply awful."

"I know. I'm just teasing. Actually, he's really a very nice person . . . and strong? You have no idea how strong he is." She told the story of Todd lifting the tree from Timmy.

"Well, that figures, considering what they are telling about him in town," Cindy said.

"What is that?"

"You know. I'm talking about how he cleaned out the Brown Dirt Cowboy, practically single-handedly."

"Oh, that. I knew something had happened down town, because Papa came home with a black eye, and that's not something I'd ever seen before. But he wouldn't talk about it and neither would Harold or Doc. So I gave up trying to find out."

"I can tell you what they are saying in town."

"Do tell," Roselyn said.

Cindy told the story as she had heard it. And, because she had gotten it second hand, there were already several embellishments, some so outlandish that Roselyn was sure they couldn't be true. But, it made a good story, and it kept the two girls entertained for some distance. It also kept them distracted, so that they didn't notice when four men approached them from behind a rock outcropping in front of them. The four were Galen Metzger and three of his cowhands: Lou Shannon, Slim Posey, and Jack Spence.

When the men suddenly appeared, Roselyn hauled back on the reins, and, with a small shout of alarm, managed to bring the team to a halt. Galen reached out to grab the halter of one of the horses, steadying it.

"Hello, ladies," he said.

"Galen Metzger, what are you doing out here?" she asked.

"What do you mean what am I doing out here?" Metzger replied. "This is my ranch. I live here. What are you doing here?"

"It's obvious, isn't it? I'm on my way home."

Galen looked at the men who were with him. "Did you hear Miss Vavak? She is on her way home." He looked back at Roselyn. "And I'll just bet you weren't even going to stop by the house for a friendly visit, were you?"

"We aren't friends," Roselyn retorted.

"Oh, now, that really pains me. Especially since I was once your beau."

The men laughed.

"What?" Roselyn asked, shocked by his words. "You were never my beau, Galen Metzger. And you never could be."

"If I'm not your beau, who is? Have you set your cap for that tenderfoot doctor?"

"Who is or isn't my beau is of no concern of yours."

"Does that mean I can't put my name on your dance card at the Independence Day Dance next week?"

"If you even approach me, I will turn my back," Roselyn said.

"Now I'm truly distressed that you don't like me. I think if you would get to know me well, I mean *really well*," he added crudely, "you would really like me."

"I think you are disgusting. And what on earth happened to you? Your nose is flat, you've got scars and bruises all over you. You look as if you had a run-in with a grizzly bear."

Roselyn knew what happened to him

because of the story Cindy had just told, but she asked him because she knew it would irritate him. And, right now, she wanted nothing more in the world than to irritate Galen Metzger.

The mocking smile left Galen's face to be replaced with an expression of annoyance. "Never you mind what happened to me," Galen replied.

Now it was Roselyn's time to smile. She had irritated him, just as she hoped.

"Go away, Mr. Metzger," she said. "Go away and leave us alone."

Galen stared at her for a moment, then he sighed. "You treat me like this and all I've ever done is try to be nice to you."

"You have a strange definition of nice."

"I'm allowing you to pass through private property, aren't I? That's nice."

"What do you mean you are allowing me to pass through private property? I'm on the road," Roselyn replied.

"Yeah, but this road cuts right through our land. That makes it private property."

"Excuse me, but it doesn't," Cindy said. It was the first time she had spoken since the surrey was stopped.

"What's that?" Galen asked.

"I said, this road is not private property," Cindy repeated. "You may own the land on

306

both sides of the road, but you do not and cannot own the road. This road has been established by tradition and use as an unrestricted throughway which makes the highway public by right of eminent domain."

Galen looked at Cindy. "Just because your pa is a lawyer, don't make you one," Galen said.

"Actually, she is a lawyer," Roselyn said. "Or at least, she is reading for the law."

"Yeah? Well, she better go back to her books if she is going to come up with fool-ishness like this."

"It's not foolishness," Cindy replied. "According to the law of the state of Texas, you can't stop anyone from coming through here."

"Who says I can't stop you? How are you going to go anywhere with a dead horse?"

Galen pulled his pistol and pointed it at the head of one of the horses, pulling the hammer back as he did so.

"No!" Roselyn screamed. "Galen, please, don't shoot the horse!"

"Oh, it's Galen now, is it? While ago it was Mr. Metzger, now it is Galen."

"Please don't shoot the poor animal," Roselyn said.

Galen chuckled, then eased the hammer

back down. "I was just funnin' with you," he said. "If you want to use the road, why you just go ahead and use it. In fact, why don't you get on down the road now?" Suddenly, Galen began firing into the air.

The horses, already skittish by the confrontation, reacted instantly to the gunshots, and leaped forward into a gallop.

Cindy screamed, but, even over her scream and the sound of pounding hooves and rapidly rolling wheels, Roselyn could hear the loud, raucous laughter of the four men behind her. She fought to regain control of the team, and as she did so Galen and the others galloped up beside her, shouting and firing their guns into the air, making it even more difficult for her.

"Hang on, Cindy!" Roselyn called to her.

Roselyn was as good a driver as she was a rider, and that was fortunate, for had a driver of less skill been at the reins, the surrey surely would have overturned. Galen and his men continued to ride alongside her for about half a mile, harassing her with shouts and gunshots. Finally, mercifully, Galen held up his hand, stopping those who were with him. It took Roselyn at least another half-mile before she was able to slow the frenetic pace of the team. She brought the team to a slow walk, and she spoke soothingly to them until she was certain they had regained their composure.

With the team under control, Roselyn looked over at Cindy, who had such a grip on the seat that her knuckles were white.

"Are you all right?" Roselyn asked.

Cindy didn't respond.

"They're gone and the team is under control," Roselyn said. "We're in no danger now."

Cindy let out a long breath before she spoke. "That is the most terrified I have ever been," she said. Her voice was shaking with fear. "Why would Galen Metzger do such a thing?"

"I'm afraid it has to do with a feud the Metzgers are having with us right now."

Cindy nodded. "Yes, I know about the new cattle and the closed flood gate."

"I'm sorry you got dragged into this," she said. "I could've gotten you killed."

"Nonsense," Cindy replied. "You saved our lives. If anyone but you had been driving just now, I don't think we would have made it."

"Cindy," Roselyn said. "When we get home, say nothing to Papa about this. And when you go back home, don't tell your father either."

"Why not? Those crazy men could've killed us," Cindy said. "Something should be done about them.

"But they didn't kill us. And if we tell Papa, and he goes over to Metzger to complain," Roselyn sighed. "Well, the way things are between Metzger and Papa right now, there's no telling what might happen. Just promise me that you won't say a word about it."

"I promise."

"Now, smooth out your hair and dress," Roselyn said. "We mustn't arouse any suspicions when we get home."

Cindy and Roselyn groomed themselves, and each other, until they were certain they were presentable, then they continued their trip. Within a few minutes, the incident was almost forgotten, and they were laughing and talking again, planning the weekend ahead.

Todd was standing at the window of the cookhouse, drinking a cup of coffee, when he saw the surrey with Roselyn and Cindy roll into the front yard of the big house.

"Here they are," he said.

"I hope they like the cake I baked them,"

Crites said from behind him.

"Well, if looks and smell are any indication, they are going to like it," Todd said. He reached his finger toward the icing.

"You want to keep that finger?" Crites asked.

Todd held the finger up and looked at it, then he held both hands up and wiggled all ten fingers.

"Yes, I'd like to," he said. "It's part of a matched set."

Crites laughed, then gave Todd a bowl and a spoon. The bowl was the one in which the icing had been made.

"What is this for?"

"You can sop the bowl," Crites said.

"Sop the bowl?"

"You know, use the spoon to get the rest of the icing. Didn't your mama ever let you sop the bowl when she made a cake?"

"I don't remember much of my mother," Todd said. "She died when I was very young."

"I'm sorry to hear that."

Todd took some of the icing residue up with the spoon, then licked it. "Oh, this is good," he said. "This is very good." He scraped up another spoonful.

"Thanks."

"Mr. Crites, the other day at the marshal's funeral, you went over to talk to Mrs. Tanner."

"Yes."

"What was that all about?"

"Didn't you hear what that fool preacher said? About her husband being in hell?"

"Yes, I heard it. I thought it was in very poor taste."

"It was more than poor taste. It was heresy."

"Heresy. Now there's a word you don't hear all that often," Todd said.

"It's a word that should be used more. As far as I'm concerned, half the clergy I've ever known are heretics."

"What did you say to her?"

"What I said to Mrs. Tanner is between her and me," Crites said.

"Yes, of course, and it should be. I'm sorry, I was just curious, that's all. Whatever you said, it appeared to be the right thing. I saw her reaction to your words."

Crites nodded, but didn't answer.

"You are an intriguing man, Mr. Crites."

FIFTEEN

Sierra Blanca, Saturday, June 27th, 6:00 P.M.:

On Saturday, Harold got permission to use the buckboard so he, Don, and Timmy could go into town. The buckboard was a concession to Timmy, who, as a result of his broken leg, was still in a cast.

Harold parked in front of the Brown Dirt Cowboy, then hurried around to help Timmy down. Once on the ground, Timmy used his crutches and was able to move inside under his own power.

The three cowboys took a table under a Currier and Ives print of a train, barreling through the night, with stars and moon overhead, spark-filled smoke spewing from the stack, and every window of every car unrealistically illuminated. As soon as they found a table they were joined by Belle Sinclair and two other girls. Belle came straight to Harold and he reached out to put his arm around her.

"Belle's my girl," Harold informed the others. "So keep your hands off her."

"Ah, she's too skinny for me anyway," Don said. "I like my women with a little meat on their bones." He pinched the well-rounded derriere of the woman nearest him.

"Honey, I've got enough meat on my bones to feed a young boy like you for a week," the woman said, laughing. "My name's Clara. What's yours?"

"I'm Don. And this here is Timmy. Timmy's got a broke leg."

"Well, Timmy, Lil is real good with folks that's laid up," Clara said. "I mean, she's got just a real gentle nature about her."

Lil, the third woman of the trio, smiled and moved around to drape her arm around Timmy. Lil was the oldest of the three, and the dissipation of several years "on the line" showed in her face. But, there was a gentleness in her eyes, and, although rather worn looking, she wasn't unattractive.

"We was just about to get something to eat," Harold said. "Would you ladies like to join us?"

"You want us to eat with you?" Belle asked.

"Sure, even soiled doves have to eat, don't they?"

"I reckon so," Belle replied. "It's just

that no man has ever asked me to eat with him. They're always interested in something else."

Harold chuckled. "Well, now, I may be interested in something else, too. But, right now, I'm more interested in something to eat."

"I'll go back to the kitchen and tell the cook to fix something for us," Belle said. "What do you want?"

"I tell you what I'd like," Timmy said. "I'd like me a Hereford steak."

"Yeah," Don said. "But we're going to have to wait a bit for that."

"What's a Hereford steak?" Clara asked.

"It's about the best thing you've ever put in your mouth, that's what it is," Don said.

"Well, we don't have that, but we've got ham. How about some ham and eggs?" Belle asked.

"Ham and eggs will be fine," Harold said.

Fifteen minutes later they were eating, when Galen Metzger, Lou Shannon, Slim Posey, and Jack Spence walked in.

"Harold," Don said quietly. "There's Galen Metzger."

Harold turned in his seat to look at the four men from Metzger's Ranch.

"Hey, Galen, before I left Trailback this

afternoon, I seen that water is flowin' in Duck Creek again. I reckon that means hell's froze over, since you said that was the only way you'd open that gate," Harold said.

Don, Timmy, and the three women laughed.

"Go back to your whores, cowboy," Galen said, dismissively.

Harold laughed, then turned back to the table to resume their conversation. Galen, Shannon, Posey, and Spence walked up to the bar and ordered drinks. Then, Galen turned around to look back toward Harold's table.

"On second thought," Galen said, "why don't you just send those whores over here to us? I don't think any of you are man enough to know what to do with them."

Harold ignored the comment.

"I'm talking to you Shedd. Shedd-head," Galen added, laughing. He looked at his friends. "Have you ever noticed how much Shedd's name sounds like shit? Shit-head, Shedd-head, it's the same thing."

"Bartender," Shannon said, laughing at his boss's joke, "get the smell of shit out of a man's drinkin' bar."

Harold continued to ignore them.

"Hey, shit-head, what does it take to put

a burr under your saddle?" Galen asked. "Are you that big of a coward that you are afraid to even talk?"

The smile left Harold's face, but only the others at the table saw it, because he still didn't turn around.

"Honey, don't let them goad you," Belle said, quietly, soothingly. "They're nothing but trash."

"Shit-head, answer your superior when he talks to you," Galen demanded.

Whereas the other remarks had been bantering, this one had an ominous ring to it, and it brought all the conversation in the saloon to a complete halt. Harold shook his head, sighed, then stood up and turned to face Galen.

"Slim, me'n you were friends for a long time," Harold said. "It pains me to see you licking the boots of a son of a bitch like Galen Metzger."

"Sometimes that's just the way things break," Posey said.

"No sense in jawin' with Posey," Galen said. "I'm the one you got to worry about."

"You've got a big mouth, Galen Metzger. Did you know that?"

"Have I?"

"Yeah. And I might just have to shut it for you."

"You'd better be careful there, Harold. You don't have the giant with you today," Posey said.

"I don't need anyone to handle the likes of the son of a bitch you've throwed in with," Harold said. He raised his fists in front of him.

Galen shook his head. "Uh-uh. That's no good. If we do it this way, we're just going to be at loggerheads every time we run in to each other. If we're going to fight, we may as well make it permanent."

Harold lowered his fists. "Permanent?" he asked. "What do you mean?"

"I'll show you what I mean!" Galen said, starting for his gun.

"Harold, he's drawing on you!" Timmy shouted.

Timmy's shout wasn't necessary. Harold answered the challenge by drawing his own pistol. He drew faster than he had ever done before, and, even as he brought the gun up, he was thumbing the hammer back.

Galen's pistol was only halfway out of the holster by the time Harold had brought his weapon to bear. When Galen saw how badly he was beaten, he let the gun slip back into his holster, then held his hands out in front of him.

"No!" he shouted. "No, for God's sake, don't shoot!"

Slowly, Harold let the hammer back down. "Get out of here," he said, making a waving motion with his pistol. "All of you, get out."

"We ain't finished our drinks yet," Posey said.

Harold turned his pistol toward the bar and began shooting, shooting four times so quickly that it sounded almost like one sustained roar. The women screamed, Galen, Posey, and the other two men with him shouted in alarm, and dived for the floor. Those who were watching what was going on marveled as they saw each of the four shot glasses explode in a shower of glass and whiskey. Harold's four shots had leveled every one of the glasses.

Harold turned back toward Galen, Posey, Shannon, and Spence. All four were slowly getting back to their feet. A cloud of gun smoke from the four discharges drifted slowly over the room.

"Your drinks are finished," Harold said. "Now get out."

Galen glared at Harold for a long moment, then he looked at the others. "Let's go," he said.

The four started toward the door, but

just before they left, Galen turned toward Harold and pointed at him.

"This isn't over," he said.

"I don't expect it is," Harold said.

There was absolute silence in the saloon until they heard the hoof beats of Galen and the others riding away.

"Whoowee!" Don said. "I ain't never seen shootin' like that!"

"It's a good thing he stopped when he did," Timmy said. "You would've killed him sure."

Harold smiled wanly, then sat back down and put his hands under the table so the others couldn't see them shaking. He knew now what Crites had been talking about when he said that Harold would hesitate before he killed. It wasn't seeing Galen's interrupted draw that stopped him. Even if Galen had gotten his gun out as quickly as Harold, that moment of hesitation would have still been there. But this was not information he intended to share with anyone else.

Everyone in the saloon wanted to congratulate Harold, and for the next hour drinks kept appearing at the table, not just in front of him, but for Timmy and Don, as well. By the time it was dark, Harold was pleasantly drunk, well fed, and still had enough money to go upstairs with Belle.

For the entire ride back to his ranch, Galen Metzger stewed over his run-in with Harold. He had been humiliated.

"Who would've thought a no-count cowboy could draw a gun that fast?" he said.

"I could'a told you that," Posey said. "Harold's been practicing with them guns for as long as I've know'd him."

Galen glared at Posey. "Don't you think that's something I should've known?"

"Hell, Galen, I didn't know you was goin' to draw on him," Posey said. "If I'd'a know'd, I would'a told you."

They rode by the sluice gate on the way back to the ranch house and Galen stopped. "Wait a minute," he said.

The others stopped with him as Galen dismounted and went over to the capstan. He began turning it.

"What are you doin', Galen?" Shannon asked.

"What does it look like I'm doing?" Galen answered with a growl. "I'm closing the gate."

"I thought the law said it had to be left open," Posey said.

"Right now, in this place, I *am* the law," Galen said resolutely.

Sierra Blanca, Sunday morning, June 28th:

Harold was awakened the next morning by the ringing of church bells. For just a moment, he didn't know where he was, then, he realized that he was in Belle Sinclair's room over the saloon. Not only was he in her room, he was in her bed, for she was asleep beside him.

Turning toward her, he saw that the cover was askew so that one breast was exposed. Harold had seen women's breasts before, in fact he had seen Belle's last night, and other soiled doves before her. But, last night, as before, was a moment of sexual intimacy, and under such circumstances he had never really taken the time to closely scrutinize a breast.

He took that time now, and, turning onto his side, he crooked his arm, dug his elbow into the bed, rested his head on the palm of his hand, and looked. He did more than look, he studied it. He was intrigued by the curve of the milky-white flesh of the globe of the breast, then the pink nipple, protruding from a little circle of pink, that pink circle textured with little dimples.

"How long are you goin' to look at my tittie?" Belle asked without opening her eyes.

"I, uh, wasn't," Harold answered, startled by the question. He thought she was sound asleep.

"Well, if you wasn't lookin', then I just went to a lot of trouble to uncover it so's you could see it, didn't I?" Belle teased, opening her eyes now and smiling at him.

"You mean . . . you mean you done that on purpose?" Harold asked.

"I done it on purpose," Belle said. "I wanted to get you interested again."

Harold shook his head. "Won't do you no good to get me interested again," he said. "I done spent all the money I had."

Belle tossed the cover aside, displaying her entire nude body to him.

"Honey, this one won't cost you nothin'," she said. "This one is free."

Belle reached for him, and, with a smile, he went to her.

John was the first one to notice that the water had stopped again. Although the water had run free all day the day before, the streambed was dry once more.

Cindy had gone back home that morning when Vavak, Alice, and Roselyn went into town to go to church. When the Vavaks returned to Trailback, John greeted them with the unpleasant news that the water had stopped again.

"Near as I can figure, he must'a shut the gate again," John said.

"Ivan, you should tell Mr. Jensen," Alice said.

Vavak shook his head. "It will not do good to tell Jensen. Jensen did not do this. Metzger did."

"He is defying the law, because there is no law," Todd said.

"There's no law in Sierra Blanca. But there is a sheriff in El Paso," Alice said. "Tomorrow, you should send a telegram to Judge Crane, telling him what happened."

"Yes," Vavak said. "It is what I will do."

"You folks go on in," John offered. "I'll put the surrey away and take care of the team."

When Harold, Don, and Timmy got back from town that afternoon, they were greeted with the news that Metzger had shut the gate again.

"If we don't do something about that son of a bitch we're never going to have any peace," Harold said.

324

"What, exactly, would you do?" Todd asked.

"I don't know," Harold replied. "But something needs to be done. I mean, you went to the judge and got a legal order to open the gate, but what good did it do? It's closed now."

"That's true," Todd said.

"Well, like I said, somethin' ought to be done about it."

Trailback Bunkhouse, Monday, June 29th:

Harold was shaken awake. When he opened his eyes, he saw that John was looking down at him. The room resonated with snoring and the deep breathing of sleeping men. John put his fingers to his lips, cautioning Harold to be quiet.

Looking around, Harold saw that Don was putting on his clothes.

"What is it?" Harold asked, quietly. "What's going on?"

"You still want to do something about the gate?" John whispered.

"Yeah."

"Then get dressed," John said.

"Where are we going?"

"Today, Mr. Vavak plans to send a telegram to the judge, telling him that the gate is closed. That'll take a day, another day for the judge to think about it, and prob'ly another day before he sends anyone down here to do anything about it." John held up a stick of dynamite. "I don't think there's any need to wait that long."

With a broad smile, Harold sat up and reached for his own clothes. "Now you're talking," he said. "What about the others?" He took the sleeping men in with a wave of his hand.

"If this goes right, we don't need any others," John said. "And if it goes wrong, there's no sense in getting any of the others involved."

"I reckon you're right," Harold agreed.

Five minutes later Harold, Don, and John were in the barn, saddling their horses. Once saddled, Harold started to mount, but John held his hand out.

"No, don't mount yet. We'll lead them out real slow," John said. "I don't want to take no chances on wakin' anyone else up."

The three men walked the horses nearly half a mile from the main house before John said it would be all right for them to mount.

It took them half an hour to reach the sluice gate. John held up his hand to stop the other two, then they dismounted and ground hobbled their horses. John had shown Harold only one stick of dynamite back in the bunkhouse, but now he opened the flap to his saddle bag and took out several sticks.

Just a slice was missing from a nearly full moon and it was reflecting off the water, providing the three men with an excellent view of the stream and the three sluice gates. They moved to within about 20 yards of the stream, then stopped behind a rock outcropping for a closer examination of the area.

"Looks like they don't have anyone watching it," Don said. "Hell, we could just walk right down there and open the gate."

"Yeah," John said. "And they'll have it closed again by morning. I aim to fix it so they can't close it again without buildin' a new one."

"Let's do it," Harold said.

The three men moved cautiously on down to the gate. There, Harold gave each of the other two men a stick of dynamite.

"Get the other two gates," he said. "Put it right here, between the gate and the pulley," he showed them, by wedging the stick in between the lifting mechanism and the gate itself. "That way you'll get the whole thing. Don't light 'em until we are all ready, and we'll light them together."

"Why we doin' the other two? They ain't even shut," Don said.

"To keep Metzger from being able to use them to rebuild this one," John said. "The son of a bitch is lower than a snake, but he ain't dumb."

"Yeah, good idea," Harold agreed.

Harold and Don moved to the other two gates, put the dynamite into position, then waited for John's order.

"Ready?" John called.

"Ready," answered Don first, and then Harold.

"Light the fuses, then get the hell away!" John shouted.

Harold struck the match, cupped his hand around the flame to keep it from blowing out, then held it to the fuse. The end of the fuse glowed, then caught and began spitting off sparks.

Harold turned away from it and ran back toward the rock outcropping, arriving at about the same time as John and Don. Don stuck his fingers in his ears as the three waited.

Harold's charge went first, a flash of light, followed a second later by the heavy thump of the explosion. Then came the gate Don blew, and almost immediately thereafter, John's gate. Pieces of debris rained down from the sky, followed by the sound of rushing water as Duck Creek began to flow again.

"Yahoo!" Harold shouted. "Damn that was good."

"Have you got any dynamite left?" Don asked.

"One stick."

"Let's take out the line shack, too," Don suggested.

"Yeah," Harold said. "Let's let them know we were here."

John smiled. "Good idea," he said.

Leaving the gates, the three men rode to the nearest line shack, which was about a mile away.

"Make sure there's nobody in there before we do it," Harold said.

"If there's anyone in there, it's their tough luck," Don said.

"You don't mean that, Don," Harold said.

"Yeah, think about it," John said. "If there is anyone in there, they're cowboys, just like us. Metzger is the one who's causing all the trouble."

"Yeah, you're right," Don said. "I was just blowin', that's all."

The three dismounted in front of the

line shack, a small building, made of un-painted, whipsawed lumber.

"I don't see no horses," Don said. "It looks deserted to me."

"Maybe we'd better check it out," John said, drawing his pistol and starting toward it.

The door wasn't locked, and John pushed it open. "Anyone in here?" he called. When he didn't get an answer, he called again. "Anyone in here?"

Harold lit a match and stepped inside. The wavering light of the match disclosed a candle on a table, and Harold lit the candle. The flame on the candle wick steadied, and Harold held it aloft so they could examine the room.

The room consisted of two bunks, a table, two chairs, a cabinet, and a pot-bellied stove. Harold knew the layout well, for he had wintered in line shacks before. The stove was both for heat and cooking, and the cabinet normally held the meager supply of dishes, cooking utensils, and food, mostly coffee, dry beans, and rice. The bunks were empty.

"It don't look like anyone's here," Harold said.

"Any coffee in the possibles cabinet?" John asked.

Harold opened the door. "Nothin' in here but a couple of dishes and a skillet."

"Too bad there wasn't no coffee," John said. "Alright, give me the candle. You two boys get on back out of the way."

Harold and Don retreated back to their horses. Harold took the reins of his horse and John's and held them, talking soothingly to the animals because he knew the explosion would make them nervous.

Harold saw John use the candle to light the dynamite, then he tossed both candle and dynamite into the shack. Turning, he ran from the shack, out to where Harold and Don were waiting.

Once more there was the heavy, stomach-jarring thump of an explosion as the dynamite detonated. The roof was lifted up, the walls fell out, and pieces of lumber rained back down from the smoke cloud, generated by the explosion.

"Let's get back home," John said. "We've done a good night's work here."

Metzger Ranch, Monday,
  June 29th, 8:00 A.M.:

Lon Metzger was having breakfast on the patio when Galen came outside, still rubbing the sleep from his eyes.

"Breakfast, Señor Galen?" the maid asked.

"No, just coffee," Galen said.

"Did you get drunk again last night?" Metzger asked.

"I had a few drinks," Galen replied.

"I wish you wouldn't do that," Metzger said.

"Are you going to tell me you never got drunk when you were my age?"

"I'm not trying to make a teetotaler out of you, son," Metzger said. "But I think you should be aware of the fact that you have certain responsibilities. You are helping me run the largest ranch in the valley and . . ."

"It isn't the largest," Galen interrupted. "Trailback is."

"I know Trailback is larger," Metzger replied, irritably. "But I don't expect that condition to last forever."

At that moment Babcock walked up onto the patio. He took his hat off and held it in front of his belt buckle, waiting until his presence was acknowledged.

"What is it, Babcock?" Metzger asked, his voice showing his irritation at being interrupted at breakfast by one of the hired hands. Metzger didn't offer breakfast to his foreman. He didn't even offer coffee.

"Good morning, Mr. Metzger," Babcock said. "Uh, Mr. Metzger, we got trouble."

Metzger was drinking coffee, and he set the cup down, then tapped at his lips with a table linen. "What sort of trouble?" he asked.

"Well, Lou and Roy went out to check on the sluice gate this morning. The water's flowing again."

"Why are you telling me?" Metzger asked. "Obviously, Vavak or one of his men sneaked over in the middle of the night and opened the gate. Just close the damn thing, and don't bother me with such petty details."

Babcock shook his head. "It ain't that easy," he said.

"What do you mean it isn't that easy? Take a little initiative, man. You are the foreman, after all. Now get back out there and close the gate."

"We can't close the gate, 'cause there ain't no gate to close. It got blowed up last night."

"What?"

"Someone took dynamite to it," Babcock said. "It's blowed all to pieces."

"All right, get some men out there, clean up the pieces and move one of the other gates over there. I want the water shut off again."

Again, Babcock shook his head. "Can't do that either. They blowed up the other two gates, and also the line shack."

"Damn!" Metzger said, slamming his fist on the table so hard that it knocked over his and Galen's coffee cups. "That son of a bitch doesn't know when he is licked."

"Pop, why don't I take a few men over there and teach them a lesson?" Galen asked.

"What kind of lesson are you going to teach them, Galen?" Metzger asked. "You let the tenderfoot throw you through a window, and that saddle tramp of a cowboy run you out of the saloon with your tail tucked between your legs."

"Pop, the tenderfoot came up behind me," Galen said. "I never even saw him."

"You want to fight him, do you?"

"I think I could handle him in a fair fight," Galen said.

"You think so, huh?" Metzger pointed to a large, live oak tree. "I tell you what you do for me, Galen. Walk out there and knock that tree down with your bare hands. If you can do that, then you should be able to handle the tenderfoot all right."

Babcock chuckled and Galen glared at him. Babcock coughed, and looked away.

"And as for the saddle tramp, from what I heard, he could've killed you if he wanted to." Metzger shook his head.

"I was just foolin' with him," Galen said. "I didn't have any idea the son of a bitch was really going to draw. I mean, if I had known that . . ." Galen let the words trail off, sounding weak even to his own ears.

Metzger's voice softened. "Son, I've built . . . that is, we've built quite a nice spread here. I want it to go to you when I die. If you go out and get yourself killed by some foolishness, then it's all for nothing."

"So, we're just going to let them get away with blowing up our sluice gates and the line shack? We're going to do nothing?" Galen protested.

"I didn't say we weren't going to do anything. We're going to do something, we're just going to choose our fight, that's all. Hell, let 'em have the water. By tomorrow or the next day the judge would've sent deputies down here to open the gates anyway. It's time to move on to the next phase."

"What's that?"

"I know a man who knows a man who makes a living by hiring himself out to settle disputes. I think it might be time for me to get in touch with him."

Vavak was driving the surrey, Alice was by his side, and Roselyn and Todd were in the back seat. Entering town from the south, they crossed the railroad, then proceeded north on Ranch Road. They passed under a large banner that spanned the street and danced in the breeze as it welcomed arrivals to Sierra Blanca. The banner was connected to Dunnigan's Butcher Shop on one side of the street, and Belding's General Store on the other.

The banner read: "Happy 109th Birthday, America!" In addition to the welcoming banner, every post and pillar in town was decorated with red, white, and blue bunting. Kids, laughing and shouting, were running about, setting off firecrackers.

On the little shelf behind the back seat of the surrey were boxes of fried chicken, as well as a couple of cakes that Alice had prepared for the big potluck picnic the town would have for dinner.

Fried chicken and chocolate cake weren't the only contributions Trailback was making to the town's potluck picnic. Ken Crites had come into town the previous day to take delivery of a side of beef, shipped from Kansas City by refrigerated railcar. Early this morning he had built a fire of mesquite and spent the entire day barbequing, turning the beef slowly over a mesquite fire and filling the town with the delicious aroma of roasting meat. It was Hereford beef, furnished by Trailback Ranch in order to show others just what Trailback was trying to do.

It was Todd's idea to barbeque a side of Hereford beef for the entire town. It was the first step in "selling the idea of Herefords" to the town and the other ranchers. The difficulties Trailback had already encountered proved to Todd that a selling job needed to be done, otherwise they would be in a constant battle with their neighbors.

On the positive side, Duck Creek had been running in an unrestricted flow for the last five days. Todd hoped that was a sign that Metzger was finally coming around, or at least, had given up his position of belligerency.

As they passed under the banner, they could see that a long table had been set up at the far end of the street in front of the bank. Even before Vavak and the others arrived, the table was filled with viands of all kinds: glistening hams, baked chickens, baskets of fried chicken, bowls of corn, peas, beans, carrots, potatoes, and dozens of cakes, pies, and cobblers. Kegs of beer and pitchers of lemonade completed the offering.

"I can smell Mr. Crites," Vavak said. "It is good."

Alice laughed. "Dear, you don't smell Mr. Crites. You smell his cooking," she corrected.

"Yes. Is good," Vavak said.

"I don't think anyone would argue with you on that," Todd said. He sniffed. "It *does* smell good."

The Independence Day picnic was a potluck dinner open, not only to the townpeople, but to the ranchers and farmers throughout the whole valley. The picnic was to be followed by a dance, and because no single building in Sierra Blanca was big enough to hold such an event, carpenters had constructed a wooden dance floor at the far end of the street. A band was hired for the occasion, coming all the way from San Antonio and arriving by train earlier in the day. Now, as the band warmed up, their music could be heard all over town, adding to the excitement that was already in the air.

Though most of the other cowboys from

Trailback were already in town, Harold, John, and Don came in with the surrey, riding alongside them, rather than going ahead. This had been John's suggestion and Harold thought it was a pretty good idea.

The bombing of the three sluice gates and the line shack had, so far, brought no response from the Metzgers. Neither Vavak, nor anyone else on Trailback knew about the middle of the night raid that John, Harold, and Don had conducted.

To Harold, the fact that they had heard nothing in response, meant only that the Metzgers were waiting for the opportunity to respond. It was just a matter of what the response would be. It was for that reason that the three men decided to ride as body-guards for Vavak and his family as they went into town for the Independence Day celebration.

SIXTEEN

On a train, 75 miles east of Sierra Blanca:

Ernie Virdin opened the box lunch he had bought at the last depot stop and examined the contents. It contained a ham sandwich, a handful of Saratoga chips, which some people were now calling potato chips, and an apple.

"Happy Independence Day," he said to himself, as he bit into the sandwich.

Virdin had not informed Todd that he was coming to Sierra Blanca, Texas to see him. He would not have come at all, had a crisis not arisen. The crisis was brought about by Pierpont Braxton of Braxton, Powers, Jacobs, and Field. Braxton was still angry over the fact that his personal plans for the disposition of Endicott Williams's estate had been thwarted, so he devised another way of accomplishing that same evil goal. It was to counter that plan that Virdin was making an unexpected journey to Sierra Blanca.

Braxton, Powers, Jacobs, and Field had

filed an Amicus Curiae Brief in which they claimed that many innocent people were in danger of being hurt because the estate of the late Endicott Williams was in danger of imminent collapse. The suit further alleged that this situation was brought about because the estate was left to a son who was taking no interest in the business, and who had departed the state of New York for place or places unknown. His mysterious departure, according to the lawsuit, left the various businesses of the estate without effective management.

As Virdin ate the tasteless sandwich, he read the brief again.

We have tried, but to no avail, to contact Mr. Todd James Williams. As he has a reputation of reckless behavior, it is entirely possible that he has, by some dangerous activity, met with an untimely end.

The livelihoods of several people are dependant upon, either directly, or indirectly, the efficient operation of the various businesses of the Williams estate. Accordingly, we feel it is incumbent upon us to act as friend of the court and to point out the fact that the afore mentioned people will surely be adversely affected by the mismanagement and ultimate collapse of the estate.

It is our recommendation that the court attempt to find Mr. Williams, to ascertain whether he is alive and if he is actively involved with the day-to-day business operation of the estate. If Mr. Williams cannot be found of sound mind and body, then, as the last legal representative of Endicott Williams during his lifetime, we shall petition the court to turn over operation of all businesses of the estate to the firm of Braxton, Powers, Jacobs, and Field.

It was signed by Pierpont Braxton.
Virdin also had a court order which demanded a response to the lawsuit. He reread the court order.

To satisfy this complaint a signed affidavit stating that Mr. Todd James Williams understands the gravity of the lawsuit, and is behaving in a way that negates the concerns brought up by the lawsuit, must be placed in the hands of this court within a period of 30 days. The affidavit must be accompanied by a notarized document, providing proof that Todd James Williams is alive and that the signature on the document is his.

This was much too important a document to entrust to the mail. Therefore Virdin had taken it upon himself to personally deliver it to Todd, to get his notarized signature, then personally carry it back to the court in New York.

Sierra Blanca:

The barbequed beef was clearly the hit of the day. All who ate it congratulated Crites, extolling it as the best thing they had ever tasted. Crites was quick to point out that it wasn't *how* the meat was cooked that made it so good, it was *what* the meat was. It had the effect Todd wanted, for he and Vavak were deluged with questions about introducing Herefords. Some of the ranchers, including Steve Warren of Lariat and Carl Phillips of the Flying P, suggested that they would be interested to see how the Trailback experiment worked out.

"If it goes well for you, I might try this myself, next year," Warren said.

"If you do it, I will," Phillips said.

With the two large ranchers agreeing to convert to Hereford cattle, the small ranchers had no choice but to come along as well.

Now, only the Metzger Land and Cattle Company was still holding out. But their hold-out was quite significant, because they were such a large ranch.

By dusk, the excitement that had been growing for the entire day in Sierra Blanca was full blown. Dinner was eaten, the long table was cleared, and the band set up to provide music for dancing. Children gathered around the floor in curiosity, some of them eating a second piece of pie or cake, and getting nearly as much on their faces as in their mouths. Others gathered around to watch, as well, those who were too old, too uncoordinated, or simply unable to get a partner.

The band did a few numbers just to warm up the crowd, "Buffalo Gals," "The Gandy Dancers Ball," and "Little Joe the Wrangler" being the most popular. Men and women streamed along the boardwalks toward the dance floor, the women in colorful ginghams, the men in clean, blue denims and brightly decorated vests.

Todd stood out from most of the men, not only because of his size, but also because of what he was wearing. He had taken a hotel room as soon as they arrived in town, and used it to change from the denims he was wearing into his current garb, which was a tan suit with a dark silk vest covering a white shirt.

"Whoowee, Doc, I'll say this for you. You do know how to turn out," Harold teased, when Todd came back to the dance floor.

Todd smiled "I haven't worn this suit since I left New York. You don't think people will think it's a little sissified, do you?"

Harold laughed. "If they do, who is going to dare say it to your face? Oh my," Harold suddenly said. "Look over there. Look at Miss Vavak."

Todd looked toward Roselyn. Like Todd, Roselyn had brought something to wear to the dance, using Cindy's house as a place to change. She was now wearing a bright blue dress, trimmed in white faille. A wide white sash was around her waist, and it accented her figure beautifully. Todd took in a sharp breath of admiration when he saw her.

Roselyn returned Todd's look with her own appraising stare. She knew that if anyone else in the county had attempted to dress as Todd was dressed, they would have been considered vain and a dandy. But Todd could bring it off because he was handsome enough to do justice to the clothes and big enough to falsify any charge of dandyism.

As Roselyn examined Todd, she felt a slow building heat in her body, and she wondered what it would be like to be kissed by him. Embarrassed by what she was thinking, she felt a flushing in her cheeks and she put the thought away as quickly as she could, absolutely certain that someone could read it in her face.

To one side of the dance floor a large punchbowl and several glass cups were set on a table, and Roselyn watched as one of the cowboys walked over to the punchbowl to, unobtrusively, pour in whiskey from a bottle he had concealed beneath his vest. A moment later another cowboy did the same thing, and Roselyn smiled as she thought of the growing potency of the punch.

The music was playing, but as yet no one was dancing. Then the music stopped, and the caller lifted a megaphone.

"Choose up your squares!" the caller shouted.

The cowboys started toward the young women who, giggling and turning their faces away shyly, accepted their invitations. In a moment there were three squares formed and waiting. Todd and Roselyn were in the square nearest the band, and as she looked across the square she saw

Cindy. The two women smiled at each other.

The music began, with the fiddles loud and clear, the guitars carrying the rhythm, the accordion providing the counterpoint, and the dobro singing over everything. The caller began to shout, and he stomped his feet and danced around on the platform in compliance with his own calls. He was the center of fascinated attention from those who weren't dancing, as the caller bowed and whirled just as if he had a girl and was in one of the squares himself. The dancers moved and swirled to the caller's commands.

Around the dance floor sat those who were without partners, looking on wistfully; those who were too old, holding back those who were too young. At the punchbowl table, cowboys continued to add their own ingredients, and though many drank from the punchbowl, the contents of the punchbowl never seemed to diminish.

About two hours into the dance, with everyone having fun, Galen Metzger and three of his cowboys arrived on the scene. They went directly to the punchbowl, pushing their way past the cowboys who had gathered there.

Several noticed their arrival, and they watched with interest and some anxiety, as Galen and the others drank the spiked punch. Although not everyone knew about the dynamited sluice gates, everyone did know about the trouble that had sprung up between Trailback and the Metzger Land and Cattle Company.

After several minutes, during which time Galen did nothing but down one cup of punch after another, it became obvious to everyone that something was brewing. And though Galen had not spoken to anyone, everyone was aware of his presence, because all had moved away until Galen and the men who had come with him found themselves on one side of the floor, all by themselves.

After a while, Galen came over to Roselyn.

"I wonder if I could have the honor of this dance?" Galen asked with forced politeness.

"Galen Metzger, after everything you have done to my family, you have the audacity to ask me for a dance?" Roselyn replied. "Thank you, sir, but the answer is no. I wouldn't dance with you if you were the only man here."

Galen glared at her for a long moment,

then he returned to the punchbowl where he continued to brood until a break in the music allowed the band a short rest. Normally, this would have been the time for the dancers to visit the punchbowl but no one wanted to be near Galen and his men.

"Your jilted admirer seems a bit upset," Todd said.

"You're talking about Galen?"

Todd chuckled. "Well, I hope I'm talking about Galen. Why? Have you jilted any other admirers that I don't know about?"

"Hundreds," Roselyn replied with a smile. Then, the smile left as she glanced toward Galen. "What is he doing here, anyway?" she asked.

"Why, I guess he's celebrating the Fourth of July. It *is* a free country." Todd chuckled. "Come to think of it, being a free country is why we celebrate."

"You laugh, but Galen Metzger means trouble. I can tell it."

"Oh, I don't think anything will come of his being here," Todd said. "Of course, he and his cronies did take over the punch-bowl, but from what I've seen go in that punch tonight, I don't know who would want to drink it anyway."

Roselyn laughed. "You're right about

that," she said. She fanned herself. "Tell me, Doc, don't you think it's a little hot in here?"

"*In* here? What do you mean, in here? We aren't inside," Todd replied.

"Just how obtuse are you, Dr. William Todd?" Roselyn asked. "Can't you tell when a girl is asking you to take her for a walk?"

"Oh!" Todd said. "Oh, I'm sorry, I guess I *am* being a little dense. Miss Roselyn Vavak, might I have the pleasure of your company for a stroll around town?" He offered her his arm.

"You may, indeed, sir," she replied with a smile, putting her hand through his arm.

Leaving the dance floor, they stepped up onto the boardwalk, then walked, arm in arm, south down Ranch Road, all the way to the tracks at the far end of town.

Behind them, the lights around the dance floor glittered brightly. The rest of the town was dark, or nearly so. Here and there a candle or lantern gleamed. Overhead the moon was just over half full, but shining brightly enough to paint the surrounding countryside in shades of silver and black. The sky was filled with stars, some so bright that it looked as if you could almost pluck them from the sky, then, between the very bright ones were thousands of stars of lesser magnitude, then lesser still, until the entire night sky seemed to glow dimly with a soft blue light from those stars that couldn't quite be seen. That made the night sky just a little lighter than the Quitman Mountains so that the range stood out in bold, black relief on the distant horizon.

"Have you ever seen anything so beautiful?" Roselyn asked.

"No," Todd replied. "I haven't."

There was something in the tone of Todd's voice that caused Roselyn to look back at him and when she did, she saw that he was staring at her.

"I mean the sky," she said, self-consciously.

"I mean you," Todd answered. He put his hands on her shoulders then leaned down toward her. She turned her face up, offering him her mouth, and they kissed. Todd held the kiss for a long time, feeling first Roselyn's surrender to it, then her embrace of it as she wrapped her arms around his neck and pressed herself against him. Behind them the fireworks started, and a rocket hissed up into the sky then burst, to add its own golden twinkles to the myriad stars that shined down upon the lovers' kiss.

Finally the kiss ended, and Todd and Roselyn stood there, staring into each other's eyes for a long time. In the distance could be heard the whistle of an approaching train.

"Well, that was a surprise," Roselyn said.

"I hope it wasn't an unpleasant surprise."

Roselyn smiled. "No," she said. "No, it wasn't at all unpleasant."

"Good. Maybe we can do it again sometime," Todd suggested. He bent toward her again, but this time she stopped him by placing her hands, gently, on his chest.

"Maybe . . . later," she said, smiling up at him.

"All right," Todd agreed. "Later."

From the other end of Ranch Road they could hear the high skirling of a fiddle.

"Sounds like they are getting ready to start again," Roselyn said. "We should get back."

"My arm, madam," Todd said, offering her his arm again.

"Thank you, sir," Roselyn said with a little curtsey. Then, laughing, she took it and they started back.

The train whistle blew again, the sound, though still high and lonesome, indicating that the train was a little closer.

When Todd and Roselyn were halfway back to the dance floor, Galen Metzger and the three men who had come to town with him suddenly stepped out of the darkness of the space between the photographer's shop and the apothecary. Galen was brandishing an axe handle. He held it in his right hand and tapped it softly into the palm of his left hand.

"Well now, what do we have here? You two didn't sneak off and do something you shouldn't be doing, did you?" Galen asked, sarcastically.

"Galen, what do you want?" Roselyn asked.

"Oh, my, you did do something you shouldn't have done, didn't you? Should I be shocked? No," Galen said, shaking his head. "I've always known you were a whore."

"Mister, with a mouth like that, someone just might hand you your tongue one of these days," Todd said.

"You perhaps?" Galen challenged.

"Perhaps," Todd agreed.

"Last time, you sneaked up behind me. I want to see how well you can do while I'm facing you."

"With an axe handle?" Roselyn asked.

Galen chuckled. "Maybe I had better explain that," he said. "When I told my Pop what I had in mind, he said your beau, here, was like a tree. So, what better way to take down a tree, than with an axe?" Now he put the axe in both hands, holding it as if it were a baseball bat.

"Get out of here, Roselyn," Todd ordered.

"No, I'm not going to leave you with —"

"Get out of here!" Todd said more sternly.

Roselyn hesitated just a second, then she started running back toward the lights at the end of the street.

Galen swung at Todd, and Todd danced back out of the way.

Galen swung again, this time managing to hit Todd a glancing blow on the shoulder. Todd felt the pain shoot down his arm, but he was sure it was a bruise and not a break.

Galen got overconfident then. With a triumphant yell, he raised the axe handle straight up over his head, intending to bring it smashing down onto Todd. But Todd stepped into him, not away from him, and Galen had no leverage. He tried to back up but Todd grabbed the axe handle, jerked it from Galen's hand,

and tossed it away.

"No!" Galen shouted in sudden panic, realizing he had just lost the advantage.

Todd could have hit Galen then, but instead, he put his hand on Galen's chest and pushed him away, hard. Galen fell back onto the porch of the photographer's shop.

"Get him!" Galen shouted, and the three others, who, until now, had just been watching, raised axe handles of their own. They had had them all along but Todd hadn't noticed them because he had been occupied with Galen.

Todd took a few cautious steps back, staring at the three men, all of whom were smiling evilly as they approached him.

With Todd backing away, Galen was able to scramble back to his feet.

"What are you going to do now, big man?" he taunted. "I've got three friends."

"And Doc has seven friends," an unexpected voice suddenly said.

Galen turned to see Harold coming down the street toward them, just now materializing from the darkness.

"What do you mean he has seven friends?" Galen asked. "I just see you."

"I mean me," Harold said. He drew his gun and cocked it. "And the six bullets in this gun," he added. "That makes a total of seven. Well, there's eight of us, if you count Doc, here." Harold chuckled. "And I think you have to count him."

Galen glared at Harold for a long moment then back at Todd. By now, several others were coming down the street as well, all brought to the scene by Roselyn's call for help.

"Let's go," Galen said to his men. They walked back into the darkness between the two buildings from which they had come earlier. But, just before they disappeared into the gloom, Galen turned and pointed at Todd. "This isn't over," he said. "Not by a long shot is this over."

"Whatever you say, Mr. Metzger," Todd said calmly.

Galen and the others had left their horses behind the buildings in the dark, so they were able to mount them rather quickly and ride away. The sound of their departure, however, was masked by the whistle, escaping steam, clanging bell, and rattle of joints and couplers from the train that was arriving at the station.

"Come on," someone said. "Let's not let a sidewinder like Galen Metzger spoil all our fun. We've got more dancin' to do."

"Yahoo!" someone shouted, and several

others laughed.

With the danger passed and the excitement over, everyone returned to the dance.

On board the arriving train:

"This is Sierra Blanca?" Virdin asked as he stepped down from the car.

"Sierra Blanca, yes, sir," the conductor replied.

"My, it's quite small, isn't it?"

"Oh, it's about average, I'd say," the conductor answered. He looked at his watch. "Board!" he called.

One person, a drummer carrying his samples kit, boarded.

"Enjoy your stay in beautiful Sierra Blanca," the conductor said with a little chuckle. Holding his lantern out, he moved it up and down two times, in a straight, vertical line, signaling the engineer that he may proceed, then he stepped back onto the train.

The engineer answered with two long whistles, then there was a rush of steam and a rattle of couplings as the train started forward. Virdin watched it pull out of the station, leaving him standing on the depot platform, all alone. He continued to watch, almost wistfully, as the train drew away. He had been on a train for six days and nights, and watching this one leave gave him somewhat of an empty feeling. It was as if his last connection with civilization had just been severed.

No one was here to meet him. Of course, he hadn't expected to be met by Todd, or even by Mr. Murchison, the local lawyer, because he hadn't informed either of them of his impending arrival. But he thought there would be someone here: a station manager, a baggage handler, perhaps. Surely, there was someone whose duty it was to meet the train and provide assistance to the arriving passengers.

But there was no one, and as the train grew smaller and smaller in the distance, Virdin began to feel very lost and very alone. Then, as the noise of the train receded, he realized that he was hearing music. Curious, he walked to the edge of the depot platform and saw lights and people at the far end of the street. Perhaps, there, he could get some information on how to locate Todd Williams.

Trailback Ranch, July 4th, 9:08 P.M.:

Timmy Baker laughed. "You know what I'm thinkin'? I'm thinkin' you're bluffin'

358

me," he said. "You don't have an ace in the hole."

Dewayne Blackwell stroked his chin in an effort to project a poker face. "Well now, Timmy, m'boy. You might be right, and then again, you might be wrong," he said. "But it's going to cost you three matchsticks to find out."

The two men, the only two left on the ranch, were sitting at a table in the bunkhouse, playing poker with a deck of well-worn cards. They were playing for matchsticks, and the pile in front of each was about even.

"Three matchsticks, huh? Well, you can't scare me off. I call."

Timmy slid his matchsticks forward.

"Now, what have you got?"

Dewayne turned over his hole card. It was a four of spades.

"I guess you win, pardner," Dewayne said, ruefully. "You're right. I was trying to run a bluff on you."

"Ha!" Timmy laughed. "I knew it! Dewayne, you couldn't bluff your way out of a paper bag. Just be glad this ain't real money we're playin' for."

"Ahh, iffen it was real money, I wouldn't of tried to bluff you," Dewayne said. He stood up and stretched. "I wonder if Mr.

Crites has any coffee in the kitchen?"

"I wouldn't go in Mr. Crites's kitchen, if I was you," Timmy warned. "You know how he is about folks messin' around where they don't belong."

"Yeah, but he isn't here right now. He went into town to cook that beef, remember?"

"Hey, you reckon he'll bring us back some of it?" Timmy asked. "I wouldn't mind me havin' some right now. Damn, that was good."

"He said he would," Dewayne replied. "And long as I've known Mr. Crites, I've always known him to be a man of his word."

"Listen, Dewayne, I appreciate you staying out here with me." Timmy patted himself on his broken leg. "I don't think I would've had much fun tryin' to dance on this."

"I didn't mind staying," Dewayne said. "There's just too much folderol at all these big to-dos for me."

The front door to the bunkhouse opened.

"Is the party over already?" Timmy asked with a broad smile. He and Dewayne looked toward the front door.

The smile left Timmy's face, to be

replaced with a look of curiosity.

"Who are you? Is there something I can help you with, Mister?" Timmy asked.

The bunkhouse echoed with the sound of two shots. Timmy and Dewayne went down, both men, shot through the heart.

Sierra Blanca, July 4th, 9:12 P.M.:

During the break the punchbowl had been refilled with a somewhat more potable liquid and, as it was between dances, Todd escorted Roselyn over to the refreshment table. He was just filling a cup for her when he looked up and saw Ernie Virdin.

"Mr. Virdin!" Todd said in surprise. "What on earth are you doing here?"

"I'm sorry to appear so unexpectedly, Mr. Williams," Virdin said. "But a problem has come up. A problem that requires your urgent attention. Mr. Braxton, your father's old lawyer, has filed a lawsuit. He is trying to take the estate away from you. Everything, the shipping company, the copper mines in Arizona, the cotton plantation in Georgia, he is even trying to take Trailback away from you."

"What does he mean take Trailback away from you?" Roselyn asked, confused by what she had just heard? "Wait, did he just call you Mr. Williams?"

Todd looked at Roselyn, with a sheepish expression on his face.

"My God. You aren't William Todd. You are Todd Williams, aren't you?"

"Oh, Mr. Williams, I apologize, I should have been more discreet," Virdin said. "I just . . . well, this lawsuit had me so upset that . . ." he let the sentence trail off.

"It's all right, Mr. Virdin," Todd said, holding his hand out toward him to still his protest. He looked at Roselyn. The expression on her face was a cross between shock and anger. "Roselyn, I'm sorry I haven't told you before now," he said.

"William Todd is Todd Williams. How dumb was I not to figure that out. You could've at least shown a little more imagination. Just when were you going to tell us who you were, Mr. Williams?" Roselyn asked in an icy voice. "As you were getting on the train heading back to New York?"

"When the time was right," Todd replied.

"I'm sure we country bumpkins provided you with a lot of entertainment. You'll have a lot of stories to share with your society friends, won't you?"

"No, it isn't like that," Todd said.

"Then, what *were* you doing? Spying on us?"

"What? No, that's not it. That's not it at all."

Tears sprang to Roselyn's eyes.

"Roselyn, I'm sorry if . . ."

"I'm going to find mother and father and ask them to take me home now," Roselyn said, interrupting Todd's apology. She started to walk away, but after a few steps she turned back toward him. "Or *is* it our home?" she asked. "Was the paper transferring the house and grounds to my parents as phony as everything else about you?"

"The title is real," Todd said. "The house and grounds belong to your parents."

"And that was what? An attempt to ease your conscience?"

"Please, try to understand," Todd said. "I didn't mean anything untoward by all this. I just wanted to try and sell the idea of Hereford cattle on its own merits, and not because I am who I am. I know now that it was a dumb idea. But it all sort of got out of hand, somehow."

"Goodbye, Mr. Williams," Roselyn said.

Todd sighed. "I'll walk you to —"

"Don't bother," Roselyn said, coldly. She

363

turned and walked away quickly, leaving Todd to stare awkwardly at her retreating form.

"I'm so sorry, Todd. I just didn't think," Virdin said.

"It's not your fault, Ernie," Todd replied. "I should've told them long ago. Now, what is the problem? Do I need to come back to New York with you?"

"No, I don't think so," Virdin said. "All I need is your notarized signature on some papers I have brought with me. I'm sure that will stop any proceedings against you. But, I thought it better to handle this personally, rather than by mail."

"You're probably right," Todd said. Seeing the chagrined expression on Virdin's face, Todd smiled. "Don't let it bother you," he said. "I told you, it isn't your fault."

"I do hope you can get everything straightened out," Virdin said.

"Whatever is meant to happen, will happen," Todd said. "Do you have a place to stay?"

"No, I just got off the train," Virdin said.

"Well, come on, we'll get you a room at the hotel. I suspect it's best for me to stay there as well, at least for tonight."

SEVENTEEN

Sierra Blanca, Sunday, July 5th, 9:27 A.M.:

Even though it was Sunday morning, Todd and Virdin went to Tom Murchison's house, catching him just before he left for church. Todd had the lawyer draw up and notarize a paper, stating that Todd James Williams was alive, and was actively participating in the business of Trailback Ranch. Todd also signed the papers Virdin brought for him to sign, then walked with him back to the train depot. The ten o'clock eastbound was already standing in the station when they arrived.

"Todd, I'm really sorry about barging in the way I did last night," Virdin said. "I know now that I should've used a bit more prudence when I approached you."

"Don't worry about it, Ernie," Todd said. "Sooner or later I was going to have to tell everyone who I was, anyway. I guess now was as good a time as any."

"But the young lady seemed terribly upset."

"Well, she will either get over it, or she won't," Todd said. "And I have absolutely no control over that."

Virdin chuckled. "It has been my observation that men seldom have any control over anything a woman does."

"All aboard!" the conductor called.

Todd laughed. "You may have a point there. And I hope it is of great consolation to you to know that you did the right thing by bringing these papers to me. I would hate to trust something this important to the mail."

"Don't worry about a thing," Virdin said as he stepped up onto the train. "These papers will take care of everything."

The train began to move.

"You're a good man, Ernie, and a very good friend," Todd called to him.

"I appreciate your confidence," Virdin replied, just before he stepped into the car.

Todd stood on the platform and watched through the windows as Virdin moved through the car to take his seat near the back. The train began moving then, and, with a final wave, Todd turned away. When he did so, he was surprised to see the Trailback surrey sitting at the end of the depot platform. Harold was sitting in the driver's seat, waiting patiently.

"Harold?" Todd asked, coming toward him. "What are you doing here?"

"I came for you, Doc, uh, Mr. Williams."

"I'm still a veterinarian," Todd said. "Doc is fine. Or Todd."

"Yes, sir. Uh, well, somethin' terrible has happened out at the ranch," Harold said. "Mr. Vavak thought you ought to know."

"What has happened?"

"When we got back to the bunkhouse last night, we found Timmy and Dewayne."

"Found them? What do you mean, you found them?"

"They was dead, Doc. Both of 'em. Shot right through the heart."

"What?" Todd gasped. "How? I mean, who would do such a thing?"

"Why hell, Doc, that ain't no big mystery," Harold said. "It was the Metzgers that done it."

Trailback Ranch, Monday, July 6th, 10:00 A.M.:

Timmy Baker and Dewayne Blackwell were being buried at Trailback. Although Timmy was from Philadelphia, he had no remaining family, and when Vavak asked the other cowboys what they thought, they all agreed that Timmy and Dewayne would probably appreciate being buried on the ranch where they worked and had friends.

All the cowboys had put on their finest clothes for the funeral, and were now standing alongside the two open graves, heads bowed, hats in their hands. They were told that Mr. Crites was going to "say a few words" over Timmy and Dewayne, and they were waiting for him to join them. Roselyn and Alice were there as well, wearing funeral black dresses. Ivan Vavak was wearing a suit, as was Todd.

"What do you reckon is keepin' Crites?" Harold asked under his breath.

"Maybe he's tryin' to come up with the right words to say," Don replied.

"Yeah, I guess that's it."

Crites was still in his room at the back end of the bunkhouse, standing by his bed, looking down into the open trunk. Leaning over the trunk, he took out the stole and Book of Common Prayer and put them both on his bed. Then he took out his pistol and holster, and set them on the bed, as well. After that, he reached down to remove the false bottom of the trunk and there, in the well beneath the false bottom, were a cleric's collar, a priest's white surplice, and black cassock.

Crites paused for a moment, recalling a question he had once asked of Bishop Polk. Bishop Leonidas Polk, later to be Confederate General Polk, was killed by Sherman's artillery just prior to the Battle of Kennesaw Mountain. When Crites asked the question, though, Crites was a seminary student and Polk was the Episcopal Bishop of the state of Louisiana.

"Bishop Polk," Crites had asked. "Suppose an imposter, one who is not ordained and has not been installed into the priesthood, should give communion. If he has not the authority to do such a thing, then do the communicants suffer from his sin?"

"No," Bishop Polk had answered. "For those who receive the sacraments in the belief that the celebrant is a true minister are blessed for their faith. Even though the person conducting the Eucharist, or administering any other sacrament, might be a heretic, the innocent are held blameless in the eyes of God."

Crites took a deep breath, then bowed his head for a quick prayer.

"Lord, I know that I conduct this sacrament at the peril of my own soul. I pray only that Timmy and Dewayne, and those who may take comfort from my words, do not fall from your grace for my sins. Amen."

★ ★ ★

Todd was the first one to see Crites as he approached the gravesite. He gasped at the site of the cook in full ecclesiastical vestments. The others saw him almost immediately thereafter.

"Whoa!" Harold said under his breath. "What is Mister Crites doing in that garb?"

"Is Crites a priest?" Todd asked.

"Yes, Mr. Williams," Alice Vavak said. "As you can see, you were not the only one with a secret identity."

Todd looked over at the Vavak family. Alice and Ivan Vavak were completely nonplussed, but Roselyn was as surprised by this revelation as was everyone else.

Crites looked everyone in the eyes, not in challenge or defiance, but in self-assurance. It took but a moment for the cowboys to accept what they were seeing, then they bowed their heads as Crites began to read.

"Man, that is born of a woman, hath but a short time to live, and is full of misery. He cometh up and is cut down, like a flower; he fleeth as it were a shadow, and never continueth in one stay.

"In the midst of life we are in death; of whom may we seek for succor, but of thee, O Lord, who for our sins art justly displeased?

"Yet, O Lord God most holy, O Lord most mighty, O holy and most merciful Savior, deliver us not into the bitter pains of eternal death.

"Thou knowest, Lord, the secrets of our hearts; shut not thy merciful ears to our prayer; but spare us, Lord most holy, O God most mighty, O holy and merciful Savior, thou most worthy Judge eternal, suffer us not, at our last hour, for any pains of death to fall from thee."

Crites picked up a handful of dirt, and dropped some of it onto each of the two pine coffins.

"For as much as it hath pleased Almighty God in his wise providence to take out of this world the souls of our deceased brothers, Timmy and Dewayne, we therefore commit their bodies to the ground; earth to earth, ashes to ashes, dust to dust; looking for the general Resurrection in the last day, and the life of the world to come, through our Lord Jesus Christ; at whose second coming in glorious majesty to judge the world, the earth and the sea shall give up their dead; and the corruptible bodies of those who sleep in him shall be changed, and made like unto his own glorious body according to the mighty working whereby he is able to subdue all things unto himself.

"The grace of our Lord Jesus Christ, and the love of God, and the fellowship of the Holy Ghost, be with us all evermore. Amen."

"Amen," the others said.

Before anyone could speak to him, Crites turned and walked back toward the bunkhouse.

"Boys, let's get Timmy and Dewayne covered," John said, and they all grabbed shovels and began closing the graves.

The Vavaks started back toward the big house.

"Roselyn?" Todd called.

Roselyn stopped, but she didn't turn around.

"Roselyn, please let me explain."

Roselyn turned toward him then. Her eyes were red with tears.

"Not now, Doc," she said. "This isn't a

good time. Later, perhaps."

"Then, you haven't closed your mind and your heart? You aren't angry?"

"Angry? Perhaps a little. And hurt. But mostly I'm confused."

"The last thing I ever wanted, or want, to do is hurt you," Todd said. "Or your family. You've got to believe that."

Roselyn held up her hand. "Give me some time," she said. "I need to think this through."

"All right," Todd agreed. "Take all the time you need. Just know that . . ." he paused, took a deep breath, then let it out in a resigned sigh. "Just know that I love you," he said.

"Ohhh," Roselyn said, the word sliding out almost as a sibilant sigh. She shook her head. "Oh, that's not fair. That's not fair at all."

"It's true."

Roselyn held her hand up, palm toward him as if warding him off. Biting her lower lip, she shook her head no, then turned and ran back toward the big house, catching up with her parents who had gone on before her.

Todd stood rooted in place, watching Roselyn and her parents until they disappeared into the house. Then, buoyed by what he thought might be a glimmer of hope, he turned and walked back to the bunkhouse.

He was alone in the bunkhouse because all the others were outside, still closing Timmy and Dewayne's graves. He sat on the edge of his bunk and just stared morosely at the floor.

At the other end of the bunkhouse, the door to Crites's room opened and he came out, no longer in clerical garb.

"I heard the news last night," Crites said. "So, you own this spread, do you?"

Todd nodded.

"I always figured there was something beneath your surface."

"What about you?" Todd asked. "Turns out you spread a lot more sail than you've been showing. Who would have ever guessed you were an Episcopal priest? And yet, somehow, I must say I'm not all that surprised."

"I was a priest," Crites answered. "I am no longer worthy to call myself that."

"And yet, you just conducted a funeral."

"I did," Crites said. "But anyone can conduct a funeral. You don't have to be a priest to do that."

Todd nodded. "True," he said. "However, you chose to vest for the occasion.

Why did you do that?"

Crites shook his head. "I'm not sure why," he replied. "Maybe it was because your secret identity was revealed last night. Maybe this was just the time to do it."

"Or, maybe you thought that by revealing yourself at this time, it might take some of the pressure off me," Todd suggested.

Crites smiled. "I think you are giving me more credit for subtlety than I deserve," he said.

"I'm not so sure about that," Todd said. "I've always known there was something about you, your language, your knowledge, your demeanor. I knew you were more than just a cook."

"Just a cook?" Crites replied. "Son, don't ever refer to a cook as 'just a cook.' Tell me one thing more important than food. In my mind, there is no more noble a profession than that of feeding people."

"You're right, of course. And I didn't mean it in any demeaning way," Todd said.

"I should hope not."

"I am curious, though."

"About what?"

"Why did you leave the ministry?"

"I cannot serve the Lord, and Satan, too," Crites said.

"I don't understand."

"Have you ever heard of William Clark Quantrill?" Crites asked.

"Yes, of course. Everyone has heard of him."

"What have you heard about him?"

"That he was a Southern guerrilla during the war, that he and his men murdered and terrorized innocent civilians."

"You have heard correctly."

"But what does that have to do with . . ." Todd started, then he stopped in mid-sentence. "You? You were with Quantrill?"

"I was."

"That's what you meant about serving the Lord and Satan?"

"Quantrill *was* Satan," Crites said. "And I served him faithfully for four years."

"But that was a long time ago," Todd said. "And that was war."

Crites shook his head. "Don't you understand, son? Time means nothing as far as your soul is concerned. The soul is eternal, and mine has been consigned to hell."

Trailback Ranch, Tuesday, July 7th, 4:13 A.M.:

Don saw it first, an unusual glow coming through the windows and projecting onto the bunkhouse. Curious as to what it might be, he raised up to look outside. That was when he saw flames leaping up from the roof of the barn.

"Fire!" he shouted at the top of his voice. "The barn is on fire!"

Don's shout awakened the others in the bunkhouse and within moments all the cowboys were outside, looking at the barn. They could hear the panicked horses from inside.

"The horses!" John said. "We've got to get the horses out!"

John opened the gate to the corral and ran inside, followed by the others. Todd, who insisted on continuing to sleep with the cowboys in the bunkhouse, went in as well.

Most of the horses were out in the corral, but there were six horses that stayed in the barn all the time. Roselyn's horse, Pepper, Vavak's personal mount, the two horses that pulled the surrey, and the two that pulled the buckboard had individual stalls within the barn.

As the men ran inside, they could see burning bits of hay falling through the cracks of the loft almost as if raining fire. The horses were in an absolute state of panic.

"Take your shirts off!" Todd shouted. "Take your shirts off and throw them over the animals' heads. They will be calmer if they can't see the fire!"

John, Don, Harold, and Crites did as Todd instructed. Removing his own shirt, Todd started for Pepper.

"I'll take him, Todd," Roselyn said. "You get papa's horse."

Todd turned around, surprised to see that Roselyn was here.

"Roselyn, you shouldn't be in here," Todd said.

"But I am, and there's no need to waste time talking."

"All right, here," Todd said. He wrapped his shirt around Pepper's head. "Get him out of here, and away from the barn. Don't try to come back in."

"All right," Roselyn answered. "Come, Pepper," she said. "Come on, baby."

Pepper was calmed somewhat, by hearing Roselyn's voice, and Roselyn was able to lead him out of the barn.

Vavak's horse was at the far end of the barn, so Todd ran down there, passed the others, who were now leading their horses out, blindfolded as Todd had instructed.

Todd opened the stall door for Vavak's horse, but the animal was now out of control with fear. He reared up as Todd approached him. Todd waited until he came back down, then he grabbed him by the ear and held on tight.

Suddenly an entire corner of the loft collapsed, and what had been only smoke and raining bits of burning hay, was now a flaming wall of fire. And Todd had no shirt to put over the horse's head.

Looking around in desperation, Todd saw a saddle blanket. Grabbing it, he draped it over the horse's head, then led the horse out of its stall.

Then, with a roaring crash, almost half the loft caved in, right in front of him. They sent huge flames licking up all the way around him, blocking both front and rear exits. Todd and the horse were trapped inside the burning barn.

"Oh!" Roselyn said, putting her hand to her mouth when she saw the explosive intensification of the fire inside the barn.

"The loft must've fallen in," John said.

"Oh, my God! That means Todd is trapped inside!" Roselyn said. She started toward the barn, but Vavak reached out and grabbed her.

"No, daughter!" he shouted. "Nothing now you can do."

"Papa, please, someone has to do something!" Roselyn pleaded. "He will burn to death in there. Mr. Crites!"

Crites shook his head. "I'm sorry, Roselyn. There's nothing anyone can do. If anyone tried to go in there now, they'd just be committing suicide."

"You can pray," Roselyn said. "You can at least do that."

"I am doing that, child," Crites answered. "I think we are all doing that."

They stood in horrified silence, watching the barn burn. The roof caved in, and the fire got even bigger. Roselyn began sobbing quietly.

"He was a hell of a good man," Harold said.

The fire roared and snapped.

Suddenly, with a loud, crashing sound, Todd burst through the side wall of the barn, crashing through the timbers by the strength of his own effort. Once he was through the hole in the wall, he turned back and, grabbing one of the one-by-eight timbers, pulled on it until it broke. That made a big enough hole for the horse, and Todd stepped back through the hole, then reappeared a moment later with the animal. He led it several feet away from the barn, then let it go. The horse whinnied, shook its head, then trotted off to join the other recently freed horses on the far side of the corral.

With a little cry of joy, Roselyn ran to him and threw her arms around him. She hugged and kissed him.

"Son of a bitch!" Harold shouted, then laughed. "Yahoo! Son of a bitch! I ain't never seen nothin' like that. Damn. You come right through that wall like it was nothin'! Mrs. Vavak, Miss Vavak, excuse my language, but, son of a bitch! That was really somethin'!"

"Harold, I don't think I could have expressed it more eloquently myself," Roselyn said, smiling broadly. "It really was something!" She hugged him again, squeezing him hard, and this time he winced.

"Damn, Doc, don't tell me a little ole' girl could hurt you?"

Todd rubbed his shoulder, and everyone could see then, that it was black and blue. It was the same shoulder that Galen had struck with the axe handle, two days earlier, and now he had used it to crash through the side of the barn.

"Oh!" Roselyn said. "I did hurt you!"

Todd smiled down at her. "After that greeting, nothing you could do to me would hurt," he said.

"Yes, well, you aren't entirely forgiven," Roselyn said, but she ameliorated her remark with her own smile. "I am working on it, though."

"That's very good to hear," Todd said.

Suddenly there was a whistling sound, then the sound of a bullet striking flesh.

"*Uhnn!*" Don said. He grabbed his shoulder, and by the light of the burning barn, everyone could see blood streaming through his fingers.

"Down!" Crites shouted. "Everyone down! There, behind the watering trough!"

Todd led Roselyn to the watering trough, while Vavak took Alice. Don and John joined them but Harold and Crites ran toward the bunkhouse.

There was a second shot, then a third, and Todd saw dirt kick up near the two men who were running toward the bunkhouse. Both of them made it safely inside. Very quickly thereafter, shots started coming from the bunkhouse, and they could hear the sound of galloping hooves as their attackers rode away into the night.

Harold and Crites came back outside then, Harold carrying a pistol and Crites carrying a rifle.

"They're gone," Crites said.

Todd looked at Don's shoulder. "It's not a bad wound," he said. "No more than a deep crease. A little alcohol to clean it, and a bandage to keep the dirt out, and you'll be all right."

"Thanks, Doc."

John looked back at the barn, which, though still burning, was now almost entirely consumed.

"Well," John said. "If there was any question about how that fire got started, I think what just happened pretty well answers it."

"This far they went," Vavak said. "To burn my barn, attack my family, this, I did not think even Metzger would do."

Harold looked at John. "Maybe we should tell him what we done, John," Harold said.

"Tell me?" Vavak asked. "What you should tell me you did?"

John cleared his throat before he spoke. "Mr. Vavak, me and two others went over to Metzger's place last week and blew all of his sluice gates," he said. "That's how come we've had water all week, not 'cause he opened them up."

"That was not good thing to do, John," Vavak said.

"I know," John replied. "And I reckon if

383

you want to fire me, then I got it comin'. Only, I'm the one that done it. I talked the others into it, so, if you please, don't take it out on them."

"It was not good thing," Vavak said again. He looked at the barn. "Because you did that, they do this. Now my barn, I do not have. And tonight, my wife, my daughter, they could be killed. Don is shot. What you did was not good thing."

"I know, and I'm sorry," John said. "I'll just get my things from the bunkhouse and . . ."

"No," Vavak said. He shook his head. "What you did was not good here," he put his hand to his head. "But it was good here." He put his hand to his heart. "For doing what your heart says do, I cannot fire a man. Think, next time, before you do, is all I ask."

"I promise, Mr. Vavak. I won't go off half-cocked again."

Metzger Ranch, Tuesday, July 7th, 5:51 A.M.:

The sun was just coming up by the time Galen, Roy Croft, Lou Shannon, Slim Posey, and Jack Spence returned to the Metzger Ranch.

"Whoowee!" Galen said excitedly. "By

384

god we showed them a thing or two, didn't we boys?"

Posey was weaving in his saddle, and his face was pasty white. It wasn't until then that the others noticed he was bleeding.

"Posey," Galen said. "Posey, what's wrong with you?"

Posey was holding his hand over his stomach and he pulled the hand away from his wound. The palm of his hand was filled with blood, and it spilled down onto his saddle and down his pants leg, though, as his saddle and trousers were already soaked with blood, it was hard to discern new from old.

"Sorry, Galen, I got hit back there when all the shootin' started," Posey said. He weaved back and forth a couple of times, then fell from his saddle.

"Pa!" Galen shouted.

Metzger came out onto the patio then, and saw Posey's blood-soaked body lying very still.

"What the hell happened?" Metzger asked, kneeling beside his foreman. He put his hand on Posey's neck, felt for a pulse, then looked up. "He's dead."

"Damn, they killed him," Galen said.

"Who killed him?"

"Those sons of bitches over at Trailback," Galen said. "We rode over there early this morning, just to teach them a lesson for dynamiting our gates." Despite the fact that Posey lay dead on the ground in front of him, Galen laughed. "We burned their barn, pa! All the way to the ground."

"And they started shooting?"

"Yeah," Galen said. "Yeah, they just opened up on us, so, we started shooting back."

The others looked at each other knowingly, but none of them corrected Galen's comment.

"That's when they killed Posey."

"They didn't kill him, sonny. You did," a sibilant voice said.

"What do you mean, I killed him?" Galen asked.

Lucien Shardeen crossed his arms across his chest and leaned back against one of the columns that fronted the patio.

"You had no business going over there," Shardeen said. "Your pa hired me, so it's my business now. And I don't like other people butting into my business."

"Yeah, well, I was just . . ."

"You just don't do anything anymore unless I tell you to do it," Shardeen said.

"Now, you wait a damn minute here,"

Galen said angrily. "You work for me, I don't work for you."

Shardeen uncrossed his arms. "Sonny, I never did work for you," he said. "I worked for your pa, but now I don't work for him anymore." Shardeen started toward the barn.

"No, wait!" Metzger said. He glared at his son. "Galen, Shardeen is right. You've got no business messing in his business. And you won't do anything unless he tells you to do it."

Galen stood there for a moment, seething, as he clenched and unclenched his fists. It wasn't right, Galen thought. Without his guns, Galen could make quick work of Shardeen, who was nothing but a sawed-off little pissant. But, he knew there would never be a time when Shardeen would be without his guns.

"Do you understand what I just told you?" Metzger asked his son.

"Yeah," Galen said, biting off his words. "Yeah, I understand it."

"And you won't go off on your own anymore? You won't do anything like that unless Shardeen tells you it's all right?"

Galen sighed. "Yes."

"Yes, what?"

"Yeah, I won't do anything unless

Shardeen tells me it's all right," Galen said, nearly choking on the words.

"Shardeen?" Metzger said. "You'll stay?"

Shardeen didn't make a verbal response, but he answered in the affirmative by making an almost imperceptible nod of his head.

The other hands were so fixated on the drama of Posey's death, and the fact that they were witnessing Galen being dressed down by his father, and humbled by Shardeen, that not one of them saw Wade Babcock riding away. If they had seen him, they might have wondered why he had a complete pack roll behind his saddle.

EIGHTEEN

Todd, Vavak, Roselyn, Crites, and the others were standing around the still-smoldering ruins of the barn when a lone rider came up behind them. Turning, they were surprised to see that it was Lon Metzger's foreman, Wade Babcock.

Harold drew his pistol.

"Hold it right there!" Harold called menacingly.

"No, no, don't shoot me," Babcock said, holding his hands out in front of him. "I ain't comin' to cause any trouble."

"Then why did Metzger send you over here?" Harold asked.

"He didn't," Babcock answered. "He don't even know I'm here." Babcock looked at the blackened timbers of what had been the barn. "I'm sorry about this, Mr. Vavak," he said. "I didn't know nothin' about it, and if I had'a know'd they was goin' to come over here and do this, I would've stopped 'em if I could."

389

"Why you have come here?" Vavak asked.

Babcock looked over toward the watering trough. "Do you mind if I water my horse?" he asked.

"The horse is not my enemy," Vavak said. "Give him water."

"Thanks."

Babcock swung down from the saddle and led his horse to the trough. The horse dipped his mouth down into the water and began drinking deeply.

"I ain't plannin' on goin' back to Metzger's ranch," Babcock said as the horse continued to drink. "I mean, I believe in being loyal to the man that pays me, but if you ask me, Mr. Metzger's gone too far now."

"We provoked it some," John said.

"You're talking about dynamiting the sluice gates and the line shack?" Babcock asked.

"Yeah," John said.

"Well, I reckon so, but Galen had no right shuttin' down the gate again, not after the law said it had to be opened," Babcock said. "But, when I say he's gone too far, I'm not talkin' just about burnin' your barn. I'm talking about the fella he hired."

"What fella is that?" Vavak asked.

Babcock hesitated before answering, looking everyone in the face, playing the moment for maximum drama.

"I'm talking about Lucien Shardeen," he said.

"Lucien Shardeen? The gunfighter?" Don asked with a gasp.

"Yeah."

"Has this fella, Shardeen, already arrived?" John asked.

"Yeah, he's here."

"You've seen him?"

"I've seen him."

"What's he look like?" Harold asked. "What's he like?"

"He's an evil-lookin' son of a bitch," Babcock said, then realizing there were two women present, he touched the brim of his hat and nodded his head, slightly. "Sorry Mrs. Vavak, Miss Vavak, excuse the language. But, there really is a scent of sulfur around this fella. He's a little man, with evil eyes. Just lookin' at him can set a man on edge."

"Why would Mr. Metzger hire such a man?" Alice asked.

"Ma'am, I reckon it's 'cause he's done lost the support of all the other ranchers in the valley. When this all begun, it was everyone else against Trailback. But now, everyone else has come over to your side, and Metzger's the one who is all alone."

"It is good other ranchers are on our side," Vavak said. "But it is not good that Metzger has hired a killer."

"Did Shardeen kill Timmy and Dewayne?" Crites asked.

Babcock nodded. "If you want my opinion, I'd say it was him," he said. "But I'm not sure. He works alone."

"There was more than one person here last night," Harold said.

"Shardeen didn't have anything to do with burnin' your barn. The ones that done that was Galen, Roy Croft, Lou Shannon, Jack Spence, and Slim Posey," Babcock said. "And Posey got hisself killed."

"What? What are you talking about?" Harold asked. "We shot back at 'em, but we didn't kill nobody."

"Yeah, you did," Babcock said. "Posey caught a bullet in the gut while he was here. He rode all the way back, but he died on the patio, right in front Mr. Metzger's house."

Harold pinched the bridge of his nose and shook his head. He was silent for a long moment, then he took a deep breath.

"I hate it that me'n Posey wound up on the opposite sides. Me'n him was good friends 'fore all this started happenin'," Harold said. "We've worked together, hunted together, we even wintered together once. He knew so many stories that, havin' him around was like havin' a book. He was a good man."

"Yeah, Slim was a pretty good man, all right," Babcock agreed. "Before Galen led him wrong," he added.

"My God, I just realized. I'm the one that killed him," Harold said. He got ashen-faced, then walked away a few feet.

"Harold, they were shooting at us," John said. "You didn't have any choice."

Harold took a deep breath. "I suppose you're right," he said. "But that don't make it no easier."

"Alice," Vavak said. "You and Roselyn, pack your bags."

"Pack our things? What for?" Roselyn asked.

"I think it will be more better if you are not here for now."

"Where would you have us go, Ivan?" Alice asked.

"I think to Mr. Murchison's house you can go. He is good friend."

"We can't impose on Mr. Murchison like

that," Alice complained. "We have no right to get him involved."

"I think you should do it, Mrs. Vavak," Todd said. "At least until we see what is going to happen."

"Harold, you will drive them to town and look out for them?"

"Yes, sir, Mr. Vavak," Harold said. "I'll get them there all right. You can count on me."

"Then, back to the ranch you come. We will meet and see what to do."

"Uh, Mr. Vavak, the surrey and the buckboard both got burned up in the barn," John said.

"Take the wagon," Vavak said.

"Yes, sir. I'll hook it up for you, Harold," John said.

"I'll help you," Don offered.

Alice and Roselyn started toward the house to get ready, while John and Don headed toward the corral to get the team harnessed and connected to the wagon.

"Mr. Vavak," Babcock said, swinging back into the saddle. "I'll be goin' now. I wish you folks the best of luck in all this. And I'm sorry for the part I had in it when it all begun."

"It takes good man to apologize," Vavak said. "You are good man. Thank you," Vavak replied.

"I appreciate you sayin' that. You folks be careful of this fella Shardeen. He is a mean one."

As they watched Babcock ride away, Vavak shook his head. "Who would think we have so much trouble just for changing cows?"

"This is all my fault," Todd said. "None of this would have happened if I hadn't gotten such a wild idea. I made a big mistake here."

"Herefords are cows for future?"

"Yes, they are definitely cows for the future," Todd said.

"Then a mistake, you did not make. Trailback is a big important ranch. Who better than Trailback to go to the future?"

"Maybe so," Todd said. "But I sure didn't know it was going to cause this much trouble."

When Crites went into the bunkhouse he saw Harold sitting on his bed. Harold was holding his pistol in his lap, and staring down at it, morosely. Crites picked up one of the two chairs that sat by the corner table, and carried it down to the other end, close to Harold's bunk. Putting the chair down, he took a seat just across from

Harold, and looked at the young cowboy, without saying a word.

The moment of silence stretched on, until finally Harold spoke. "I just can't get it out of my mind that I killed Slim."

"Harold, do you know that in some places, condemned prisoners are executed by a firing squad?"

"What?" Harold asked.

"Firing squads," Crites repeated. "In some places legally condemned prisoners are put to death by firing squads."

"Yeah, I guess I've heard that. Excuse me, Mr. Crites, but what does that have to do with —"

Crites held up his hand, indicating he had more to say.

"Here is an interesting fact about firing squads. One rifle is always loaded with a blank shell, and that blank cartridge has a heavy wad so it will give a recoil. That way nobody on the firing squad will ever know for sure whether they actually shot the prisoner. There is always the possibility, you see, that they might have had the rifle with the blank. It keeps them from dwelling on it."

"Yeah, well, what good does that do me? I wasn't firing blanks," Harold said.

"No, you weren't, but consider this.

Although both of us were shooting, only one of us hit him," Crites said. "Babcock said he caught a bullet in the gut, remember? One bullet. So if only one of us hit him, what makes you think it was you? I was shooting, too."

"Come on, Mr. Crites. I mean, you've seen me shoot. I always hit what I'm shooting at. And you don't even carry a gun."

"True," Crites said. "But, it was night and you were using a pistol, whereas I was using a rifle. Given the fact that a rifle is inherently more accurate than a pistol, don't you think there is at least a possibility that it could have been my bullet that killed him?"

"Yeah," Harold said, brightening a little. "Yeah, that's right. You *were* shooting a rifle, weren't you? I guess it could've been your bullet. But . . . how do you feel about that? I mean, you bein' a preacher and all. How do you feel about maybe it was your bullet that killed Slim?"

Crites smiled at Harold. "It could've been your bullet," he said.

"I thought you just said . . ." Harold started, then he smiled back at Crites. "Oh. I see what you mean. Yeah, it could've been either one of us who did it, or either one of us who didn't do it."

Crites didn't answer directly. Instead, he just reached out and gave Harold's shoulder a little squeeze.

The door to the bunkhouse opened.

"Hey, Harold," Don called out. "The wagon's hooked up and the ladies is ready to go."

"All right, thanks, I'll be right there," Harold replied. He reached out to shake Crites's hand. "Thanks, Mr. Crites. I've never known anyone as smart as you are. You always seem to know the right thing to say. It was nice knowing you."

On the road to Sierra Blanca, Tuesday, July 7th, 10:47 A.M.:

Vavak had put a couple of chairs in the back of the wagon in order to make the trip into town more comfortable for Alice and Roselyn. Although the wagon had insets for bows, over which canvas could be spread, neither the bows nor the canvas were attached, so the two women were sitting in the open. Such an arrangement had its advantages and disadvantages. They didn't stifle in the trapped air of a small, covered space, but they were exposed to the broiling sun.

During the long, leisurely trip into town,

Roselyn and her mother were talking about Todd, and the fact that he had told her, just yesterday afternoon, that he was in love with her.

"How do you feel about him?" Alice asked.

"I . . . I don't know," Roselyn replied. "On the one hand it seems too early for me to know how I feel about him. But on the other hand, when he was trapped in that burning barn, I thought my world had just collapsed. I can't tell you how happy I was to see him come out."

Alice chuckled. "You don't have to tell me, my dear. You showed me. If fact, you showed everyone, the way you ran to him."

Roselyn laughed with her mother. "Yes, I guess I did, didn't I? Well, as I said, I was really happy to see him come out."

"I don't mean to be buttin' into the conversation you ladies is havin', but ole' Doc didn't just come out," Harold said. "I mean, *bam!*" Harold said, slamming his fist into his hand. "He busted out. He come right through the wall, like a bull. I don't believe I've ever seen a stronger man."

"He is strong," Roselyn agreed. "It's almost frightening just how strong he is."

"You got no call to ever be frightened of someone like Doc," Harold said. "He is a pure gentleman, that one is. I mean, they invented the word gentleman, just for someone like him."

"It doesn't bother you that he came down here and lived with us, right there in the bunkhouse with you and the others, without telling you who he really was?" Roselyn asked.

Harold shook his head. "No, ma'am, that don't bother me none," he said. "Fact is, it makes me think all the more of him. I mean, here he is, rich as a king, but he comes down here and what does he do? He lives in the bunkhouse with the ordinary cowboys. And he didn't just live with us, he actually become us. You can ask Mr. Crites about that. Doc helped out around the chuck wagon in ways that real cowboys would just never do."

"I guess that's true, isn't it?" Roselyn said. "I really had no call to be upset with him the way I was. I hope he isn't angry with me because of it."

Harold chuckled. "Didn't look to me like he was none too angry with you. When he come bustin' through that wall, the first thing he done was head right toward you."

"Mr. Shedd," Alice suddenly said. Her voice was strangely constricted. "Mr. Shedd, there are two men coming up behind us. They are moving very fast."

Harold turned in his seat and saw two men in the road behind them. As Alice had pointed out, they were riding fast, and they were quickly overtaking the wagon.

"Whoa," Harold said, pulling back on the reins. When the team stopped, he set the brakes on the wagon.

"Why are you stopping? Don't you think we ought to try and run away from them?" Alice asked.

"Ain't no use in that," Harold replied. "In the first place, we don't know what they want. And in the second place, we're in a freight wagon and they're well mounted. We couldn't outrun them if we tried."

In a matter of seconds the riders were close enough that they could recognize one of them.

"It's Galen Metzger," Roselyn said.

"I wonder who the man with him is," Alice asked.

"I don't know, Mama. I've never seen him before," Roselyn answered.

They watched until the riders were near enough for a closer scrutiny. The man with Galen was rather small, without any apparent distinguishing feature.

The riders reined up alongside the wagon.

"What are you doing here, Miss Vavak?" Galen asked, his voice cold and unfriendly.

"We're going into town, if you must know," Roselyn answered.

Galen shook his head. "Uh-uh, not this way you aren't," he said. "Like I told you the last time you came through here, this is private property." He looked at Harold. "Shedd, turn this wagon around, and take these women back to their ranch."

"I don't take orders from you, Galen," Harold replied. "Mr. Vavak sent me along to look out for these ladies and if they're wantin' to go on into town, then I aim see to it that they get there."

"Oh?" Galen said. "And how are you going to do that? With that fast draw and fancy shooting of yours?"

Harold stood up in the box, then turned to face Galen and the other rider. He let his arm hang loosely, ready, by his side.

"I'd rather not use my gun," Harold said. "But I reckon if it comes right down to it, I'm prepared to do it."

The little man who had ridden up with Galen had not looked away from Harold for the whole time they were there. His eyes were dull, gray, and, with just a hint of red, deep down in the center of them, that made it look as if they were reflecting the burning fires of hell.

The intensity of the little man's stare made Harold nervous, and he began flexing his gun-hand, opening and closing his fingers. He tried to stop, but knew if he did stop, his hand might start shaking, and he didn't want to show that.

Galen turned to the little man.

"This gentleman is Harold Shedd," he said. "Harold fancies himself quite the virtuoso when it comes to handling guns. As a matter of fact, Mr. Shedd put on a little demonstration for us at the Brown Dirt Cowboy Saloon recently. He shot four whiskey glasses off the bar."

"Whiskey glasses?" the little man asked. The words slid out, as if they were oiled.

"Oh yes. He was very good, four shots, four glasses. He didn't miss once. It was very impressive."

"Whiskey glasses," the little man said again. This time there was a dismissive sneer to his voice.

"Oh, where are my manners?" Galen said. "Ladies, allow me to introduce my friend."

"I'd just as soon forgo the honor, if you don't mind," Roselyn said.

"But surely, you would want to meet this gentleman. He's actually quite famous, in his own way."

"I know who he is," Harold said.

"You do?" Galen replied. He smiled, but the smile was more mocking than friendly. "And, who do you think he is?"

"He is Lucien Shardeen."

The little man did not respond, but Galen clapped his hands, slowly and mordantly. "Indeed it is Lucien Shardeen," he said. "Congratulations, you have just won yourself a cigar."

"What do you want, Shardeen?"

"Oh, didn't I mention what he wanted? Shardeen wants . . . well, Mr. Shardeen, perhaps you had better tell him what you want."

"I want to kill the man who is so good at shooting whiskey glasses," Shardeen said. He said it as calmly and as devoid of emotion as if he had just asked for a drink of water.

Because of the lack of emotion and the flatness of tone of his voice when he said he wanted to kill Harold, it took a second before Roselyn realized what she had just heard.

"What?" Roselyn gasped. "No! You don't mean that!"

"What do you say, whiskey-glass killer?"

"Harold, no!" Roselyn said. "Let's turn

the wagon around. We'll go back home."

"I reckon it's too late for that, Miss Vavak. This fella's not going to let me pass this cup. You'n Mrs. Vavak had best just get back out of the way," Harold said. Harold's voice was more resigned than frightened.

"No, wait, Mr. Shardeen, we'll go back," Roselyn pleaded.

Shardeen did not respond.

"Galen, please, call him off," Roselyn said.

Galen rubbed his hands together as if washing them. "You see how it is," Galen said. "I don't have anything to do with what is going on between them."

"Go ahead, whiskey-glass killer. Let me see just how good you are," Shardeen said.

Harold started for his gun and, to his surprise, he had it out in a split second. He felt a sense of excitement and relief when he realized that he had clearly beaten Shardeen to the draw. He managed to bring his pistol to bear and thumb the hammer back before Shardeen's pistol had even come up to level position.

Harold had beaten Shardeen badly. He was sure that Shardeen, as had Galen when Harold had beaten him to the draw, would back down now. No man would continue his draw under these circumstances.

Harold relaxed just a little.

Shardeen continued his draw and when he brought his pistol to bear, he pulled the trigger.

Harold was surprised by the sudden, and unexpected outcome. He felt the heavy shock of the bullet going into his chest. Then pain began radiating out from the point of entry for the bullet, like ripples spreading out from a stone that had been cast into a pool. Only these ripples were ripples of fire.

The pain was excruciating. Harold was feeling more pain than he had ever experienced in his entire life, and it was over his entire body. He dropped his pistol and slapped his hand over the chest wound.

"Harold!" Roselyn screamed.

"Oh, God in Heaven!" Alice shouted.

To Harold, there was an unreality to the cries of the women. They sounded as if they were calling up to him from the bottom of a well. It began to grow dark in the periphery of his vision but Shardeen was very clearly in focus, and Harold studied the ugly little man, even noticing that a hair was growing from a mole on his cheek. The expression on Shardeen's face had not changed, and, suddenly, Harold recalled something Crites had told him. *The difference between an ordinary man and a gunman is that a gunman can kill without compunction.*

Harold could feel the blood spilling through his fingers. The blood seemed hot to him, as hot as scalding coffee. He looked over at Roselyn and Alice. He was very sorry they were having to watch him die, and he wanted desperately to smile reassuringly for them. He tried, but he couldn't make his face move.

Harold felt himself falling. He could make no effort to stop, or even do anything to break the fall. He fell backward, tumbling over the front edge of the wagon. He hit on the tongue of the wagon, then bounced off onto the ground.

The pain in his chest and in his body stopped, and he felt a numbness beginning to creep in. He knew that he needed to get up but he couldn't make himself move.

He was tired. He was so very, very tired.

"Oh my God!" Roselyn said. She didn't know if she was saying a prayer, or mouthing an oath. "Oh my God!" she repeated.

Roselyn climbed down from the wagon,

then crawled underneath to get to Harold. One of Harold's eyes was shut, the other was half open. The young cowboy wasn't breathing.

"You killed him!" she said. "You bastard you! You killed him!"

"Roselyn, go back and tell your father what just happened here," Galen ordered. "And remind him that he is the one who started it, him and his foolish notion of bringing Herefords into the Sierra Blanca Valley. This was all your father's fault. Every bit of it."

"Please, help me get Harold in the wagon," Roselyn asked.

Galen looked for a moment as if he might get down and help, then he shook his head.

"No. Let him lie there," he said. "He'll never know the difference."

Galen jerked his horse around, and Shardeen, who hadn't spoken a word since the shooting, turned to follow him. They left the road, then headed at a gallop, across the open range, heading in the direction of the Metzger Ranch house.

"Mama," Roselyn said. "We can't just leave poor Harold here. We've got to get him back home. Will you help me put him into the wagon?"

"Yes, dear, of course I will," Alice said, climbing down to help her daughter.

It was right after lunch and Don had just stepped out of the cookhouse when he saw the wagon returning. He was a little puzzled by seeing it because he knew that Harold hadn't had time to go all the way into town and back. At first he thought they might have forgotten something, then he saw that the wagon was being driven by Roselyn.

Where was Harold?

As he was wondering about Harold, he saw that there was blood on Roselyn's dress.

"Oh my God," Don said. He turned and ran back into the cookhouse.

Because he had sent Alice and Roselyn away, Vavak was having lunch with the cowboys and he, John, and Todd were sitting at the table. Crites, his work in the kitchen done for the moment, was sitting at the table with them. John had just said something funny, and the others were laughing when Don went back inside.

"Mr. Vavak, maybe you better come outside," Don said. "The wagon's comin' back, and Miss Vavak is drivin'. She's, uh, she's . . ." he paused in mid-sentence.

"She's what?" Todd asked.

"She's covered in blood," Don said.

With that, everyone at the table got up quickly, so quickly that two of the chairs fell over with a bang. They ran to the door, Todd getting there first, and all hurried outside.

The wagon was just then rolling through the front gate and, as Don had said, Roselyn's dress was covered with blood. Alice, who had been in the back, moved up to the front seat as the wagon arrived, and she, too, was covered in blood.

"Are you hurt?" Vavak asked, hurrying out to meet the wagon as Roselyn stopped it, then set the brake. "What happened?"

"No, Papa, we're not hurt, we're not hurt," Roselyn said, reassuringly. Then, looking down she saw, as if realizing for the first time, that she and her mother were covered in blood.

"But, the blood?"

"It's Harold's blood. Papa, they killed poor Harold."

"What? Where is he?"

"He's in the back of the wagon," she said with a nod of her head. "Mama and I put him there." She looked down at herself again. "That's how we got all bloody."

"Help me down, Ivan," Alice said. "I'm very tired."

Vavak moved around the wagon quickly to help his wife down. Todd offered the same assistance to Roselyn and she accepted it without hesitation. Don, John, and Crites looked into the back of the wagon at Harold's body.

"How did this happen?" Todd asked.

"We were met on the road by Galen Metzger."

"You mean Galen killed Harold?" John asked.

Roselyn shook her head. "No, not Galen. It was the other man, the gun fighter."

"Shardeen?" Don asked.

"Yes, Shardeen."

"Poor Harold. He thought he was so fast. He should've known he wasn't faster than Lucien Shardeen," Don said.

"Oh, but he *was* faster," Roselyn said.

"What? What do you mean?"

"Harold beat Shardeen to the draw, but then he just held his gun and didn't shoot. I think he thought that Shardeen, seeing he was beaten, would stop."

"But Shardeen didn't stop, did he?" Crites said.

Roselyn shook her head.

"No. Shardeen drew his gun and shot Harold down without . . ." she paused, looking for a word.

"Without compunction?" Don suggested, looking at Crites.

"Yes," Roselyn said, surprised at getting the word from Don. "He killed poor Harold without an ounce of compunction."

While the others walked away from the wagon with Roselyn and her mother, Crites remained behind, looking down at Harold's body.

It was nice knowing you, Harold had said to Crites, just before he left. Not it *is* nice knowing you, but, it *was* nice knowing you. It was almost as if he knew something was about to happen.

Crites glanced at the others, and seeing that he wasn't being observed, turned back to Harold. He made the sign of the cross over the young cowboy's body, then gave the Commendatory Prayer.

"Oh, Almighty God, with whom do live the spirits of just men made perfect, after they are delivered from their earthly prisons: I humbly commend the soul of this thy servant, my brother Harold, into thy hands, as into the hands of a faithful Creator and most merciful Savior; most humbly beseeching thee, that it may be precious in thy sight."

NINETEEN

Todd stopped at the top of the little hill and looked down toward Metzger's house. It was funny, he thought, how a man as evil as Metzger could have such a beautiful place. The Spanish-style house was large and U-shaped, with brown stucco walls and a red-tile roof. The "U" of the house wrapped around a stone patio, with an arched colonnade fronting the patio on three sides. The patio was surrounded by red, yellow, and orange flowers.

Todd had left Trailback Ranch early this morning, riding out without telling anyone where he was going, or what he was going to do. He kept his departure secret because he was afraid that someone might insist on coming with him and he didn't want to put anyone else in danger.

Back in Princeton one afternoon, during a boring lecture on Renaissance Art, Todd started reading about Hereford cattle. It was there that the idea of introducing Herefords onto Trailback Ranch was born. Now, four men were dead. How long ago and far away that Renaissance Art class seemed.

There was absolutely no connection between that world and this. In that world he had played football, sailed his yacht, attended parties, dined in fine restaurants, visited museums, libraries, and art galleries. What an important part of his life all that seemed then. How trivial it all was now.

If only he could undo all the harm his mistake had caused . . . if only he could go back in time. But of course, he couldn't. He could not change the past, but he was determined to change the future. He made the decision yesterday, right after Harold was buried next to Timmy and Dewayne, that not one more person would die because of something he had started.

Sighing, he took a stick from the otherwise empty rifle boot on his saddle. Earlier, he had tied a piece of bed sheet to the stick and now he unrolled it, then held it up, as a white flag. He started riding, slowly, down the gently sloping hill, toward the house.

Either Lon Metzger had seen Todd

approaching, or someone had reported Todd's arrival to him, because the rancher was standing out on the patio in front of his house by the time Todd arrived.

Metzger wasn't alone. His son, Galen, was with him, as was a small, evil-looking man. Todd didn't have to be told that this was Lucien Shardeen. Babcock had told them that there was a "hint of sulfur" about this man. That description of Shardeen, coming from a weathered cowboy, was as accurate as it was un-expectedly poetic.

Todd contrasted the expressions on the faces of the three men as they stood there. Lon Metzger's expression was one of curiosity. Galen's expression was of ill-concealed hate. Shardeen actually looked bored.

"Thank you for agreeing to see me," Todd said.

"I didn't agree to see you," Metzger replied. "You are here on your own."

"Well, that's true," Todd replied. He smiled, trying to lighten the moment. "But, seeing as you didn't shoot me as I rode down here, I figured that was at least a tacit agreement to see me."

"Tacit?" Metzger replied.

"Inferred. Implied," Todd said, trying to

find the word Metzger could understand.

"All right, all right, you're here," Metzger said, casting Todd's definitions aside with an irritable wave of his hand. "What can I do for you, Dr. Todd?"

"Well, for a start, I think it is time that I told you my real name. I'm not William Todd, I'm Todd Williams. Todd James Williams."

"Williams? Isn't that . . ." Metzger started, then he paused and screwed his face up in recognition. "Wait a minute, are you trying to tell me you are Endicott Williams's son?"

"Not trying to tell you, I am telling you. Endicott Williams was my father."

"So that means you own Trailback."

"It does."

"I don't believe you."

"It's easy enough to prove," Todd said. "Mr. Murchison knows who I am. So does Mr. Vavak."

"I see," Metzger said. He stroked his chin as he studied Todd for a long moment, then he pointed an accusing finger at him. "This is all your doing, isn't it? You're the one who came out here with this damn fool idea of raisin' Herefords."

"Yes," Todd admitted. "I'm sorry to say, it was my idea."

"Yeah, well you . . . wait. Did you say you are *sorry* to say?"

"I did," Todd said. "I wish I had never conceived the idea. And now, I'm here to tell you that I'm calling the whole thing off."

"What do you mean?"

"I am not going to replace my herd with Herefords."

"You could've saved everyone a lot of trouble, Williams, if you had come to this decision several days ago."

"I know," Todd said. "The decision to switch to Herefords is good business sense. In fact, I still think it would be good business sense for everyone in the Sierra Blanca Valley. But, I had no idea of the trouble it would cause, the damage it would do, or the lives it would cost. I don't want anyone else to get hurt, either from Trailback or from your ranch. It simply isn't worth it. You win, Mr. Metzger."

"Well, now," Metzger said, surprised by the sudden, and totally unexpected capitulation. "Well, now, that's very smart of you."

"I understand that some of our boys destroyed the sluice gates and one of your line shacks. I fully intend to pay to have them rebuilt," Todd said.

"Yeah? Well, you should." Metzger held up his finger to emphasize a point. "But, don't think I'm going to pay to have your barn rebuilt."

"That's actually Mr. Vavak's barn now," Todd said. "I gave him the house and all the outbuildings. And don't worry, you won't be asked to pay for its reconstruction. I will pay for that, as well."

"Your boys killed one of our men," Galen said, speaking for the first time. "And he was a good man, too. What are you going to do about that?"

"I'm afraid I can't do anything about that," Todd said. "I'd give anything if I could bring Mr. Posey back, along with Timmy Baker, Dewayne Blackwell, and Harold Shedd."

"You know, if you'd killed one of our horses, you'd be expected to pay for it," Galen said. "I figure a good hand is worth more than a good horse. I reckon you could make it up some by paying us for Posey, the way you'd pay us for a horse. Seems more'n fair to me."

Todd looked at Galen with ill-concealed disgust. "Galen Metzger, you are one sorry excuse for a human being," he said. "I would give everything I have if it would bring Slim Posey and the others back, but

I won't pay you one cent for compensation. And you are one sick son of a bitch to even suggest it."

Galen glared at Todd, but didn't answer him. Todd looked back at Metzger. "What do you say, Mr. Metzger? Do we have a truce? If I call everything off, will you do so as well?"

Metzger studied Todd through narrowed eyes. "You won't try this again anytime soon?"

"It's going to happen," Todd said. "But I won't do it first."

Metzger nodded. "All right," he said. "We have a truce."

"Good," Todd said. He looked directly at Shardeen. "Now, send this dried up little piece of dog shit back to whatever hole he crawled out of."

No one had ever spoken to Shardeen like that, and, for the first time since Todd arrived, Shardeen's face registered an expression. He actually looked shocked at Todd's words. Then the shock gave way to anger.

"You are a foolish man, Williams," Shardeen said.

"And you are an evil one," Todd replied. He turned his attention back to Metzger. "I'll go back over to Trailback and inform

Mr. Vavak that we will not be bringing in the Herefords."

"You do that," Metzger said.

Nodding once, Todd turned his horse and rode away.

Trailback Ranch, Thursday, July 9th, 8:30 A.M.:

Shortly after breakfast, Roselyn decided it was time to have her talk with Todd. She knew he was feeling guilty about everything that happened and she wanted to tell him that it wasn't his fault. What had happened over the last several weeks was the product of one man's evilness, not the result of a business decision.

She also wanted to talk to him about what he told her the other day, just after Timmy and Dewayne's funeral. Did he mean it when he told her that he loved her? Or had he just said that to ease the pain of the moment?

She had thought Todd might be with her father, poking through the remains of the barn to see what could be salvaged, but he wasn't there. She checked in the cookhouse to see if he was lingering over breakfast, but he wasn't there either.

Roselyn made it a point never to go into the bunkhouse uninvited. She regarded the bunkhouse as the private home of the cowboys who worked on the ranch. So, rather than go inside, she asked John if he would check for her.

"If he is in there, would you ask him to meet me over by the live oak tree?" she asked.

"Yes, ma'am," John promised.

Roselyn walked over to the live oak tree to wait. This was where they had the picnic when Mr. Crites barbequed a side of Hereford beef for the first time. What a happy time that was. It wasn't really all that long ago, but so much had happened since then that it seemed like it was ages ago.

John came back out of the bunkhouse, shaking his head.

"He's not in there, Miss Vavak."

Puzzled by the fact that she had been unable to find him, Roselyn screwed her face up in concern. "He's not in there?"

"No, ma'am."

"Well, where could he be? I've looked everywhere. You don't think he's left the ranch, do you?"

"I'll tell you what. There's only one horse he's comfortable with riding, we could go check the corral," John suggested.

Roselyn chuckled. "You're talking about Rhoda, aren't you? Todd might be quite a strong man, but he does require a gentle horse. Good idea, I'll come with you."

When they reached the corral, Roselyn looked over the fence at the remuda.

"What you lookin' for?" Don asked.

"I'm looking for Rhoda," Roselyn said. "Have you seen her?"

"You mean the horse Doc always rides?"

"Yes."

"Yes, ma'am, I seen Rhoda. Doc rode off on her early this morning, before breakfast, even," Don said.

"He did? Well, did he say where he was going?" Roselyn asked.

Don shook his head. "He's the one owns this here place, ain't he?"

"Yes."

"Didn't seem to me like it was my place to ask."

"Oh, John, he was awfully upset about what happened to Harold. You don't think he went over to Metzger's to do anything foolish, do you?"

"You mean give Galen Metzger another beatin'?" Don asked. "I sure hope that's what he went over there for."

"No, that could be very dangerous," Roselyn said.

"I don't see how it could be dangerous. He's already whupped Galen twice," Don said. "I reckon Doc could handle Galen, and all his cowboys put together."

"He can't handle a bullet, can he?" Roselyn asked.

The smile left Don's face, and he shook his head. "No ma'am," he said. "I don't guess I thought about that."

"John, would you —"

"Yes, ma'am, I'll go look for him," John said, answering the question before it was fully asked.

Metzger's Ranch:

Lon Metzger had gone back into his house and was standing near a window, drinking coffee and looking outside, when Galen came in. It had been nearly fifteen minutes since Todd left.

"Pop," Galen said. "We can't let him go. You know that."

Metzger took a swallow of his coffee, but said nothing.

"You know what he's doin', don't you? He's just buyin' himself a little time until he gets done exactly what he wanted to do in the first place."

Metzger still said nothing.

"Let me go take care of him."

"What do you mean, take care of him?"

Metzger asked. "He's already beaten you twice. Just what the hell makes you think you can take care of him?"

"I was playing games then, Pop. I'm not playing games anymore. When I say take care of him, I mean take care of him for good. I plan to kill the son of a bitch."

"No," Metzger said.

"Pop, it's going to have to be done and you know it. I don't care what he told us, I don't trust the son of a bitch any further than I can throw him, and you know how far that would be."

"I didn't say it didn't have to be done," Metzger replied. He sighed. "As a matter of fact, I've been thinking the same thing. If we don't take care of him now, we'll have to do it later. Right now, we've got him, Vavak, and everyone else over there on the run. Seems to me like this is the best time to do it."

Galen smiled broadly. "I knew you would see it my way," he said. "I'll take care of this job personally."

"No," Metzger said.

"Pop, I thought you just said —"

"Send Shardeen."

"Shardeen? I don't need Shardeen to kill that big son of a bitch. Hell, I doubt he even knows which end of a gun the bullets come out of."

"Are you that damn stupid?" Metzger asked.

The sharp response stung Galen, and he bristled. "What do you mean?"

"Think about it, son. You haven't killed anyone. I haven't killed anyone. The two cowboys who were killed the other night, and this fella, Harold, were all killed by Shardeen. This much killin' is sure to bring the law down to start sniffing around. When they start sniffing, we'll throw them a bone."

The frown on Galen's face changed to a conspiratorial smile. "Shardeen," he said.

"Shardeen," Metzger said. "Send him."

"Yes, sir. I'll tell him right now."

On the road between Metzger's Ranch and Trailback, July 9th, 9:30 A.M.:

"Doc," John said, shaking Todd. "Doc, wake up."

Opening his eyes, Todd saw John looking down at him with concern etched in his face. *What is John doing here? What am I doing here? For that matter, where* was *here?*

"Doc?" John said again. "Are you alright?"

"Yes, I —" Todd started, then, moving,

he felt a pain in his side. "I mean, no, I, don't know if I'm alright. What happened?"

"That's what I was askin' you, Doc," John said. "You mean you don't know what happened?"

"No. The last thing I remember, I was coming back home. Then the next thing I knew, you were shaking me."

"Well, you been shot, is what happened," John said.

Todd put his hand down to his side, felt the wound, then brought his hand back up and looked at the blood. "Yeah," he said. "So it would appear."

"You don't know who done it?"

"No. I never saw a thing."

"Well, it don't take much to figure it out," John said. "Can you get on your horse if I help you? I don't mind tellin' you, you're too damn big for me to put you up there by myself."

"Where is my horse?"

"She's standin' right here," John said.

"Help me up."

Trailback, Thursday, July 9th, 12:30 P.M.:

Todd was in bed, not in the bunkhouse, but in the guest room of the big house. Roselyn, Vavak, Alice and Crites were gathered around the bed. A bandage was wrapped all the way around Todd's waist, the wound having been treated and cleaned by Crites.

"The bullet went all the way through," Crites said. "And I don't think it hit any of the vitals, otherwise, he would already be dead."

"But he looks so . . . so still," Roselyn said in a small, worried voice.

"Yes," Crites said. "Well, I gave him some chloroform. More than likely, he'll sleep for the rest of the afternoon."

"He's going to be all right, isn't he, Mr. Crites?" Roselyn asked anxiously.

"I've seen weaker men survive worse wounds," Crites answered. "He's strong and in good health. I think he'll come through this all right."

"Oh, thank God," Roselyn said.

Crites walked to the bedroom door, then looked back on the three who were still standing there, staring anxiously down at Todd's sleeping figure.

"I'll just leave him in your good hands," Crites said.

"Thank you, Mr. Crites," Vavak said. "We appreciate all you have done."

"It's been my pleasure knowing you folks," Crites replied.

"Are you sure he's dead?" Metzger asked. "I rode out to where you said you shot him, and I didn't find a body. I didn't even find the sign of a body."

"When I shoot someone, they die," Shardeen said, smug with self-confidence.

"Then where is he?" Galen asked.

The three men were in the parlor of Metzger's house. Earlier in the day, Shardeen had come back with the report that the job was done. Todd Williams was dead, and he wanted his money. But when Metzger rode out to check, he found no body.

"How do I know where he is?" Shardeen asked. "Maybe someone from Trailback come to get him. Whatever happened to him is not my concern. This job is finished, and I want my money."

Metzger held up his finger. "As soon as I get verification that he is dead, I will pay you."

Shardeen shook his head. "I want the money now."

"I don't keep that much money here at the ranch," Metzger replied. "I don't trust the cowboys. I'll have to go into town for it, then I can —"

"Mr. Metzger?" Lou Shannon said, stopping at the door of the parlor, just short of coming into the room.

"What do you want, Shannon?" Metzger asked. "Can't you see I'm busy here?"

Shannon was now foreman of the ranch, having taken over for Babcock after Babcock left.

"Yes, sir. You want me to just send him away?"

"Send him away? Send who away?"

"The cook from Trailback."

"The cook from Trailback?" Galen asked. "What the hell is the cook doing over here? Yes, send him away. We don't have time for some cook."

"Wait," Metzger said, holding up a finger. "He might know something about Williams. Let's see what he has to say."

The three men followed Shannon out onto the patio. There, a bandy-legged man with gray hair and a weathered face stood leaning, almost casually, against one of the columns. His horse was drinking water from a trough.

"It's customary to ask before you start taking a man's water," Metzger said.

"Like you asked before you shut down Duck Creek?" Crites replied.

Metzger's eyes narrowed at Crites's

words. "That's a pretty smart-mouthed reply," he said. "You'd better watch yourself, Cook."

"Oh, did I offend you?" Crites asked.

"What are you doing here, anyway?" Metzger asked.

"Well, as you can see, I'm wearing a pistol," Crites replied.

"Yeah, I see," Metzger said.

"So, you might say I'm here as a soldier."

"A soldier?" Metzger said. Both he and Galen laughed out loud. "Well, boys, I guess we really have won the war now. Vavak has gone to the bottom of the barrel. The flour barrel," he added laughing hard at his own joke.

"I'm glad to see that the four of you are armed," Crites said easily.

"Oh? And why is that?" Metzger asked, patronizingly. Another laugh was just beneath the surface.

"Because I am going to kill all four of you," Crites said in a matter-of-fact voice. "Of course, I was going to kill all four of you, whether you were wearing guns or not, but this way, it might ease my conscience just a bit to know that I didn't kill unarmed men."

The laughter that was just beneath the

surface burst forth again. "You're what? You're going to kill all four of us? What about Lucien Shardeen? Do you plan to kill him, too?"

"Him first," Crites said.

Metzger started to laugh again.

"Metzger, shut up, you fool!" Shardeen said. Shardeen was a man who lived his life on the edge, and there was something about this bandy-legged little cook that was eating at him. The cook wasn't frightened. Shardeen had learned long ago that his adversary's fear of him was his strongest ally. So, why wasn't this man afraid?

"Who are you?" Shardeen asked.

"Who is he? He's Ken Crites, the cook from Trailback. He's just an old fool who —"

"I said, shut the hell up!" Shardeen shouted, his voice breaking from the controlled hiss he had worked so hard to develop.

Shardeen waited for the old familiar tingling in the middle of his back, in his arms and legs, and in the pit of his stomach. He waited for the condition he called "the scent of sulfur." But it didn't come. Instead, he felt the hair standing up on the back of his neck, a weakness in his knees, and an unsteadiness in his bowels. Who was this man? What was there about him that was bothering him so?

"I said, who are you, Mister?"

"Well, I've been flying under false colors for the last several years," Crites said. "In fact, I've gone by the name Ken Crites for so long that that seems more like my name than my real name. But my real name is Cole Collier."

"Collier?" Shardeen replied. It took but a moment to process the information. "Cold Blood!"

Shardeen started his draw, but it was too late.

My God! He already has his gun out! Where did that come from? How did he get . . .

Shardeen couldn't finish formulating the question, not even in his mind, for Cole's gun was as quick as thought. He fired one bullet into Shardeen's forehead, and the little man went down, dead before he hit the stone paving of the patio.

The Metzgers, father and son, and their foreman did not even comprehend the danger until it was too late. They were just beginning to reach for their guns when Cole turned his pistol toward them and began executing them, one by one.

TWENTY

Sky Meadow, One Year Later:

Vavak and Alice stopped the surrey in front of Todd and Roselyn's new house. The house had been built high atop Bread Loaf Hill, on the little grassy meadow that Roselyn had named Sky Meadow. When it was her secret place it could only be reached by a very narrow trail. The trail had been widened to become a road, sufficient to allow a wagon to pass. This was necessary in order to bring in the materials needed to build the house.

The front of the house had a large window that overlooked Sierra Blanca Valley, the valley filled now with the short-horned Hereford cattle. Once the Metzgers were gone, the transition from Longhorns to Herefords had gone quickly and smoothly. But Trailback wasn't alone in changing over to the new breed; every ranch in the valley was now running Herefords instead of Longhorns.

The ranch that had once been the

Metzger Land and Cattle Company was no more. Because there were no surviving relatives to inherit the ranch, it had gone to the State of Texas, where it was sold, in parcels, for tax. The other ranchers in the valley had divided it up among themselves, but there was one new ranch owner in the valley. The new owner was Don Walton.

Vavak and Alice opened the door to the house, also called Sky Meadow, and Alice called out.

"Anybody home?"

"We're back here with the baby," Roselyn answered. "Come on back."

Vavak and Alice walked to the back of the house where they saw Roselyn and Todd, standing over the baby's crib. The baby, smiling, had wrapped his hand around Todd's finger.

"You two are going to spoil that child," Alice scolded.

"Well, what are babies good for, if not to be spoiled?" Roselyn replied.

"Look how strong he is," Todd said. "Kenneth Cole Williams, you are going to be the best football player Princeton ever had."

"What do you mean, Princeton?" Roselyn asked. "Cole is not going back East to go to school. He will go to a Texas school."

"None of the colleges in Texas play foot-ball," Todd complained.

"Honey, he won't even enroll until 1904. I'm sure they'll be playing football out here by then."

"If not, we'll get it started, won't we, Cole?" Todd said to the baby. Raising up, he turned to Vavak. "How did the trip into town go?"

"Very good," Vavak said. "The packing house in Chicago, all our cows they will buy, and at three times the price for Long-horns."

"See what a smart man my husband is?" Roselyn said, proudly.

"I'd trade it all if I could bring Timmy, Dewayne, and Harold back. And Mr. Crites, uh, that is, Mr. Collier," he cor-rected. "He would still be here if all this hadn't happened." He looked at Vavak. "I've never asked you this, but you knew all along who he was, didn't you?"

"Yes," Vavak said. "On the road I find him, after the shoot out in Puxico. More dead than alive he was."

"Ivan brought him here, we nursed him back to health, and he stayed with us," Alice said. "And nobody could ever ask for a more loyal friend."

"I wonder where he is now," Todd said.

"I know where he is," Vavak said.

"Where is that?"

"He is in place where devil cannot find his soul."